THE WORLDS OF
ROBERT F. YOUNG

SIXTEEN STORIES OF SCIENCE FICTION AND FANTASY BY **Robert F. Young**

WILDSIDE PRESS

THE WORLDS OF
ROBERT F. YOUNG

SIXTEEN STORIES OF SCIENCE FICTION AND FANTASY BY **Robert F. Young**

WILDSIDE PRESS

ALL RIGHTS RESERVED, INCLUDING THE RIGHT OF REPRODUCTION IN WHOLE OR IN PART IN ANY FORM, COPYRIGHT © 1956, 1957, 1959, 1960, 1961, 1962, 1965 BY ROBERT F. YOUNG.
COPYRIGHT © 1957 BY ROYAL PUBLICATIONS, INC.; COPYRIGHT © 1955 BY THE QUINN PUBLISHING CO., INC.; COPYRIGHT © 1956 BY GALAXY PUBLISHING CORPORATION.

The Girl Who Made Time Stop: Reprinted from *The Saturday Evening Post*, April 22, 1961.

Added Inducement: Reprinted from *The Magazine of Fantasy and Science Fiction*, March 1957.

Hopsoil: Reprinted from *The Magazine of Fantasy and Science Fiction*, January 1961.

Flying Pan: Reprinted from *The Magazine of Fantasy and Science Fiction*, November 1956.

Emily and the Bards Sublime: Reprinted from *The Magazine of Fantasy and Science Fiction*, July 1956.

The Dandelion Girl: Reprinted from *The Saturday Evening Post*, April 1, 1961.

The Stars Are Calling, Mr. Keats: Reprinted from *Amazing Stories*, June 1959.

Goddess in Granite: Reprinted from *The Magazine of Fantasy and Science Fiction*, September 1957.

Promised Planet: Reprinted from *If*, December 1955.

Romance in a Twenty-First-Century Used-Car Lot: Reprinted from *The Magazine of Fantasy and Science Fiction*, November 1960.

The Courts of Jamshyd: Reprinted from *Infinity*.

Production Problem: Reprinted from *The Magazine of Fantasy and Science Fiction*, June 1959.

Little Red Schoolhouse: Reprinted from *Galaxy*, March 1956.

Written in the Stars: Reprinted from *Venture Science Fiction*, September 1957.

A Drink of Darkness: Reprinted from *Fantastic, Stories of Imagination*, July 1962.

Your Ghost Will Walk . . . Reprinted from *The Magazine of Fantasy and Science Fiction*, July 1957.

CONTENTS

INTRODUCTION BY AVRAM DAVIDSON	7
THE GIRL WHO MADE TIME STOP	9
ADDED INDUCEMENT	26
HOPSOIL	34
FLYING PAN	42
EMILY AND THE BARDS SUBLIME	53
THE DANDELION GIRL	67
THE STARS ARE CALLING, MR. KEATS	83
GODDESS IN GRANITE	100
PROMISED PLANET	128
ROMANCE IN A TWENTY-FIRST-CENTURY USED-CAR LOT	140
THE COURTS OF JAMSHYD	163
PRODUCTION PROBLEM	170
LITTLE RED SCHOOLHOUSE	172
WRITTEN IN THE STARS	188
A DRINK OF DARKNESS	195
YOUR GHOST WILL WALK . . .	211

INTRODUCTION

HE LIVES IN A HOUSE by the shore of a Great Lake, from which, on days as clear as those he writes about so lovingly, he can see Canada—a sight on which he is sometimes reluctantly obliged to draw the curtain in order to continue writing. He knows people, books, machinery, as well as scenery, and—equally lovingly—this knowledge is reflected in his writing. I'm writing about Robert F. Young, a man known to and appreciated by the editors, publishers, and readers of science fiction. One reason why this book is a good thing is that it will acquaint a lot of people with him who perhaps don't often read the *genre*. There are, of course, many good reasons for *not* reading it; you won't find any of them here, though. No cowboy or knighthood-gone-to-seed stories set on Betelgeuse, no tonight-we-overthrow-the-23rd-century-Caligula yarns, no accounts of computers Taking Over, thousand-times-twice-told tales of Doomsday and The Bomb, not a single insectoid or reptilian Earth-conquering monster—with or without bug-eyes. None.

What you *will* find, though, is—as I've said above—love. Calm. Compassion. Rational imagination. Laughter. Sense. Excitement. Scorn. Integrity. And hope. *There's the sun and the moon, and night and day, brother—all good things. . . . There's the wind on the heath, brother. I could gladly live for that.*

Nor, in dealing with Some Aspects of the Future, has Mr. Young ignored certain musty corners of the present. Quasi-compulsory conformity and consumption, quiz shows, symbiosis on several times six cylinders, planet-plundering, and quite a few others—all are carried to a logical confusion in sentences which never stumble over one another. If Mr. Young, like the personal aides of Gulliver's Laputa, thwacks us now and then with a pea-filled bladder, it is to waken the dozers among us from their daze. No tax-free foundations subsidize him to give the world yet another damned dull book, nor is his eye forever on the word rate. Once, in the dear, dead days when I was an editor, I said of someone that *He writes with love.* Someone else wrote in, promptly and tartly, *Ink would be better.* Robert F. Young uses both.

—AVRAM DAVIDSON

THE GIRL
WHO MADE TIME STOP

LITTLE DID Roger Thompson dream when he sat down on the park bench that Friday morning in June that in a celibate sense his goose was already in the oven and that soon it would be cooked. He may have had an inkling of things to come when he saw the tall brunette in the red sheath walking down the winding walk some several minutes later, but that inkling could not conceivably have apprised him of the vast convolutions of time and space which the bowing out of his bachelorhood would shortly set in motion.

The tall brunette was opposite the bench, and it was beginning to look as though Roger's goose was in no imminent danger of being roasted after all when one of those incidents that so much inspire our boy-meets-girl literature occurred: one of her spike heels sank into a crevice in the walk and brought her to an abrupt halt. Our hero rose to the occasion admirably—especially in view of the fact that he was in the midst of a brown study concerning a particularly abstruse phase of the poetic analysis of science which he was working on and was even less aware of girls than usual. In a millisecond he was at her side; in another he had slipped his arm around her waist. He freed her foot from the shoe, noticing as he did so that there were three narrow golden bands encircling her bare leg just above her ankle, and helped her over to the bench. "I'll have it out of there in a jiffy," he said.

He was as good as his word, and seconds later he slipped the shoe back upon the girl's dainty foot. "Oh, thank you, Mr. . . . Mr. . . ." she began.

Her voice was husky, her face was oval; her lips were red and full. Looking into the pearly depths of her gray eyes, he had the feeling that he was falling—as in a sense he was— and he sat dizzily down beside her. "Thompson," he said. "Roger Thompson."

The pearly depths grew deeper still. "I'm glad to meet you, Roger. My name is Becky Fisher."

"I'm glad to meet *you*, Becky."

So far, so good. Boy has met girl, and girl has met boy. Boy is suitably smitten; girl is amenable. Both are young. The month is June. A romance is virtually bound to blossom, and soon a romance does. Nevertheless it is a romance that will never be recorded in the annals of time.

Why not? you ask.

You'll see.

They spent the rest of the day together. It was Becky's day off from the Silver Spoon, where she waited on tables. Roger, who was sweating out the sixth application he had tendered since graduating from the Lakeport Institute of Technology, had every day off for the moment. That evening they dined in a modest café, and afterward they played the jukebox and danced. The midnight moment upon the steps of the apartment house where Becky lived was a precious one, and their first kiss was so sweet and lingering on Roger's lips that he did not even wonder, until he reached his hotel room, how a young man such as himself —who saw love as an impediment to a scientific career— could have fallen so deeply into it in so short a span of time.

In his mind's eye the bench in the park had already taken on the aspect of a shrine, and the very next morning saw him walking down the winding walk, eager to view the sacred object once again. Consider his chagrin when he rounded the last curve and saw a girl in a blue dress sitting on the very section of the hallowed object that his goddess had consecrated the most!

He sat down as far away from her as the length of the bench permitted. Perhaps if she had been glamorous he wouldn't have minded so much. But she wasn't. Her face was too thin, and her legs were too long. Compared with the red dress Becky had worn, hers was a lackluster rag, and as for her feather-cut titian hair, it was an insult to cosmetology.

She was writing something in a little red notebook and didn't appear to notice him at first. Presently, however, she glanced at her wrist watch, and then—as though the time of day had somehow apprised her of his presence—she looked in his direction.

It was a rather mild—if startled—look, and did not in the least deserve the dirty one he squelched it with. He had a glimpse, just before she hastily returned her attention to her notebook, of a dusting of golden freckles, a pair of eyes the hue of bluebirds and a small mouth the color of sumac leaves after the first hard frost. He wondered idly if his initial reaction to her might not have been different if he had used a less consummate creature than Becky for a criterion.

Suddenly he became aware that she was looking at him again. "How do you xpell matrimony?" she asked.

He gave a start. "Matrimony?"

"Yex. How do you xpell it?"

"M-a-t-r-i-m-o-n-y," Roger said.

"Thankx." She made a correction in her notebook, then she turned toward him again. "I'm a very poor xpeller—expecially when it comex to foreign wordx."

"Oh, you're from another country, then?" That would explain her bizarre accent.

"Yex, from Buzenborg. It'x a xmall provinxe on the xouthernmoxt continent of the xixth planet of the xtar you call Altair. I juxt arrived on earth thix morning."

From the matter-of-fact way she said it, you'd have thought that the southernmost continent of Altair VI was no more remote from Lakeport than the southernmost continent of Sol III and that spaceships were as common as automobiles. Small wonder that the scientist in Roger was incensed. Small wonder that he girded himself immediately to do battle.

His best bet, he decided, would be a questions-and-answers campaign designed to lure her into deeper and deeper water until finally she went under. "What's your name?" he began casually.

"Alayne. What'x yourx?"

He told her. Then: "Don't you have a surname?"

"No. In Buzenborg we dixpenxed with xurnamex xenturiex ago."

He let that go by. "All right, then, where's your spaceship?"

"I parked it by a barn on a dexerted farm a few milex outxide the xity. With the forxe field turned on, it lookx xomething like a xilo. People never notixe an obvioux object, even if it'x right under their noxex, xo long ax it blendx in with itx xurroundingx."

"A xilo?"

"Yex. A—a silo. I see I've been getting my 'X's' mixed up with my 'S's' again. You see," she went on, pronouncing each word carefully, "in the Buzenborg alphabet the nearest sound to the 'S' sound is the 'X' sound, so if I don't watch myself, whenever I say 'S' it comes out 'X,' unless it is followed or preceded by a letter that softens its sibilance."

Roger looked at her closely. But her blue eyes were disarming, and not so much as a smidgin of a smile disturbed the serene line of her lips. He decided to humor her. "What you need is a good diction teacher," he said.

She nodded solemnly. "But how do I go about getting one?"

"The phone directory is full of them. Just call one up and make an appointment." Probably, he thought cynically, if he had met her before Becky swam into his ken he would have thought her accent charming and have advised her not to go to a diction teacher. "But let's get back to what we were talking about," he went on. "You say you left your ship in plain sight because people never notice an obvious object so long as it doesn't clash with its surroundings, which means that you want to keep your presence on Earth a secret. Right?"

"Yes, that's right."

"Then why," Roger pounced, "are you sitting here in broad daylight practically throwing the secret in my face?"

"Because the law of obviousness works with people too. The surest way to make everybody believe I'm not from Altair VI is to keep saying that I am."

"O.K., we'll let that pass." Eagerly Roger launched Phase Two of his campaign. "Let's consider your trip instead."

Inwardly he gloated. He was sure he had her now. However, as matters turned out, he didn't have her at all, for in drawing up his plans to lure her into deeper and deeper water he had overlooked a very pertinent possibility—the possibility that she might be able to swim. And not only could she swim, she was even more at home in the scientific sea than he was.

For instance, when he pointed out that, owing to the ratio between the mass and the velocity of a moving body, the speed of light cannot be equaled and that therefore her journey from Altair VI to Earth must have required more than the sixteen years needed by light to travel the same distance, she said, "You're not taking the Lorentz transformation into consideration. Moving clocks slow down with reference to stationary clocks, so if I traveled at just under the velocity of light my journey wouldn't have lasted over a few hours."

For instance, when he pointed out that more than sixteen years would still have gone by on Altair VI, and that her family and friends would be that much older, she said, "Yes, but you're only assuming that the speed of light can't be equaled. As a matter of fact, it can be doubled, tripled and quadrupled. True, the mass of a moving body increases in proportion to its velocity, but not when a demassifier—a device invented by our scientists to cancel out mass—is used."

For instance, when he conceded for the sake of argument that the velocity of light could be exceeded and pointed out that if she had traveled a little in excess of twice its velocity she not only would have traveled backward in time but would have finished her journey before she began it, thereby giving birth to a rather awkward paradox, she said, "There wouldn't be a paradox because the minute one became imminent a cosmic time shift would cancel it. Anyway, we don't use faster-than-light drives any more. We used to, and our ships are still equipped with them, but we aren't supposed to resort to them except in cases of emergency because too many time shifts occurring simultaneously could disrupt the space-time continuum."

And for instance, when he demanded how she *had* made her trip then, she said, "I took the short cut, the same as anyone else on Altair VI does when he wishes to travel vast distances. Space is warped, just as your own scientists have theorized, and with the new warp drive our Altairian VI scientists have developed it's no trick at all, even for an amateur to travel to any place he wants to in the galaxy in a matter of just a few days."

It was a classic dodge, but dodge or not, it was still unassailable. Roger stood up. He knew when he was beaten. "Well, don't take any wooden meteorites," he said.

"Where—where are you going, Roger?"

"To a certain tavern I know of for a sandwich and a beer, after which I'm going to watch the New York–Chicago game on TV."

"But—but aren't you going to ask me to come with you?"

"Of course not. Why should I?"

A transformation Lorentz had never dreamed of took place in her eyes, leaving them a misted and an incredulous blue. Abruptly she lowered them to her wrist watch. "I—I can't understand it. My wodget registers ninety, and even eighty is considered a high-compatibility reading."

A tear the size of a large dewdrop rolled down her cheek and fell with a soundless splash upon her blue bodice. The scientist in Roger was unmoved, but the poet in him was touched. "Oh, all right, come along if you want to," he said.

The tavern was just off Main Street. After phoning a diction teacher at the request of Alayne of Altair and making an appointment for her for four-thirty that afternoon, he chose a booth that afforded an unobstructed view of the TV screen and ordered two roast beefs on *kümmelweck* and two glasses of beer.

Alayne of Altair's sandwich disappeared as fast as his did. "Like another one?" he asked.

"No, thanks. Though the beef was really quite tasty considering the low chlorophyllic content of Earth grass."

"So you've got better grass than we have. I suppose you've got better cars and better TV sets too!"

"No, they're about the same. Except for its phenomenal advance in space travel, our technology is practically parallel with yours."

"How about baseball? Do you have that too?"

"What's baseball?" Alayne of Altair wanted to know.

"You'll see," said Roger of Earth gloatingly. Pretending to be from Altair VI was one thing, but pretending to be ignorant of baseball was quite another. She was bound to betray herself by at least one slip of the tongue before the afternoon was very much older.

However, she did nothing of the sort. As a matter of fact, her reactions strengthened rather than weakened her claim to extraterrestrialism. "Why do they keep shouting, 'Go, go, go, Aparicio'?" she asked during the bottom half of the fourth.

"Because Aparicio is famous for his base stealing. Watch him now—he's going to try to steal second."

Aparicio not only tried, he made it too. "See?" Roger said.

It was clear from the befuddled expression on Alayne of Altair's face that she did not see. "It doesn't make any sense," she said. "If he's so good at stealing bases, why didn't he steal first base instead of standing there swinging at that silly sphere?"

Roger gaped at her. "Look, you're not getting this at all. You can't steal *first* base."

"But suppose somebody did steal it. Would they let him stay there?"

"But you can't steal first base. It's impossible!"

"Nothing is impossible," Alayne of Altair said.

Disgusted, Roger let it go at that, and throughout the rest of the game he ignored her. However, he was a White Sox fan, and when his idols came through with a 5–4 win his disgust dissipated like mist on a summer morning, and so great was his euphoria that he told her he'd walk uptown with her to the diction teacher's studio. On the way he talked about his poetic analysis of science, and he even quoted a few lines from a Petrarchan sonnet he had done on the atom. Her warm enthusiasm sent his euphoria soaring even higher. "I hope you had a pleasant afternoon," he said when they paused in front of the building in which the diction teacher's studio was located.

"Oh, I did!" Excitedly she wrote something down in her notebook, tore out the page and handed it to him. "My Earth address," she explained. "What time are you going to call for me tonight, Rog?"

Abruptly his euphoria vanished. "Whatever gave you the idea we had a date for tonight?"

"I—I took it for granted. According to my wodget—"

"Stop!" Roger said. "I've had all I can take for one day of wodgets and demassifiers and faster-than-light drives. Besides, it just so happens that I've got a date for tonight, and it also just so happens that the girl I've got the date with is the girl I've been unconsciously searching for all my life and didn't find till yesterday morning, and . . ."

He paused. Sudden sadness had roiled the blue depths of Alayne of Altair's eyes, and her mouth was quivering like a frost-kissed sumac leaf in a November wind. "I—I understand now," she said. "Wodgets react to compatibility of body chemistry and intellectual proclivities. They aren't sensitive enough to detect superficial emotional attachments. I—I guess I came a day too late."

"You can't prove it by me. Well, give my regards to the Buzenborgians."

"Will—will you be in the park tomorrow morning?"

He opened his mouth to deliver an emphatic no—and saw the second tear. It was even larger than the first one had been and glimmered like a transparent pearl in the corner of her left eye. "I suppose so," he said resignedly.

"I'll be waiting for you on the bench."

He killed three hours in a movie house and picked up Becky at her apartment at seven-thirty. She was wearing a black sheath that made her shape shout, and a pair of pointed shoes with metal tips that matched the three golden bands around her ankle. He took one look into her gray eyes and knew then and there that he was going to propose to her before the evening ended.

They dined in the same café. When they were halfway through their meal, Alayne of Altair walked in the door on the arm of a sartorially elegant young man with a lean, hungry face and a long bushy tail. Roger nearly fell out of his chair.

She spotted him right away and brought her escort over to the table. "Roger, this is Ashley Ames," she said excitedly. "He invited me out to dinner so he could continue my diction lesson. Afterward he's going to take me to his apartment and show me his first edition of *Pygmalion*." She got her eyes on Becky then and gave a start. Abruptly her gaze traveled floorward to where Becky's trim ankles were visible just beneath the tablecloth, and when she raised her eyes again they had transmuted from blue to green. "Three down and one to go," she said. "I should have known it would be one of *you!*"

Becky's eyes had undergone a metamorphosis too. They were yellow now instead of gray. "I saw him first, and you know the rules as well as I do. So lay off!"

"Come on," Alayne of Altair said haughtily to Ashley Ames, who was hovering predatorily just behind her. "There must be better restaurants on Earth than this!"

Bewildered, Roger watched them leave. All he could think of was Little Red Riding Hood and the wolf. "Do you know her?" he asked Becky.

"She's a real gone crackpot with an outer-space complex who comes in the Silver Spoon sometimes and babbles about life on other planets. Let's change the subject, shall we?"

Roger did so. Dinner over, he took Becky to a show, and afterward he suggested a walk in the park. She squeezed his arm in an eloquent answer. The sacred bench stood like an island in a tarn of purest moonlight, and they waded through the silvery shallows to its iron-wrought shores and sat down upon its shelving hills. Her second kiss made the first seem sisterly, and when it was over Roger knew he would never be the same again. "Will you marry me, Becky?" he blurted.

She didn't seem particularly surprised. "Do you really want me to?"

"I'll say! Just as soon as I get a job and—"

"Kiss me, Roger."

He didn't get back to the subject till they were standing on her apartment-house steps. "Why, of course I'll marry you, Roger," she said. "Tomorrow we'll take a drive into the country and make plans."

"Fine! I'll rent a car, and we'll take a lunch and—"

"Never mind a lunch. Just pick me up at two." She kissed him so hard that his toes turned up. "Good night, Roger."

"See you tomorrow at two," he said when his breath came back.

"Maybe I'll ask you in for a cocktail."

His feet never touched the ground once all the way back to the hotel. He came back down to earth with a jar, though, when he read the letter the night clerk handed him. The wording was different from that of the five others he had received in answer to his five other applications, but the essential message was the same: "Don't call us, we'll call you."

He went upstairs sadly and undressed and got into bed. After five failures in a row he should have known better than to tell the sixth interviewer about his poetic analysis of science. Modern industrial corporations wanted men with hard unadorned facts in their heads, not frustrated poets seeking symmetry in the microcosm. But, as usual, his enthusiasm had carried him away.

It was a long time before he fell asleep. When he finally did so he dreamed a long and involved dream about a girl in an Alice-blue gown, a wolf in a Brooks Brothers suit and a siren in a black sheath.

True to her word, Alayne of Altair was sitting on the bench when he came down the walk the next morning. "Hi, Rog," she said brightly.

He sat glumly down beside her. "How was Ashley's first edition?"

"I didn't see it yet. Last night after we had dinner I was so tired I told him to take me straight home. He's going to show it to me tonight. We're going to dine by candlelight in his apartment." She hesitated for a moment—then, with a rush: "She's not the one for you, Rog. Becky, I mean."

He sat up straight on the bench. "What makes you think so?"

"I—I tracked you last night on my fleglinder. It's a little TV receiver that you beam in on whoever you want to see and hear. Last—last night I beamed it in on you and Becky."

"You followed us, you mean! Why, you snooping little—"

"Please don't get mad at me, Roger. I was worried about you. Oh, Rog, you've fallen into the clutches of a witch-woman from Muggenwort!"

It was too much. He stood up to leave, but she grabbed his arm and pulled him back down again. "Now you listen to me, Rog," she went on. "This is serious. I don't know what she told you about me, but whatever it was, it's a lie. Girls from Muggenwort are mean and cruel and crafty and will do anything to further their evil ends. They come to Earth in spaceships just as we girls from Buzenborg do—only their spaceships are big enough to hold five people instead of only two—then they take an assumed name, get a job where they'll come into contact with lots of men and start filling their quota of four husbands—"

"Are you sitting there in broad daylight trying to tell me that the girl I'm going to marry is a witch from Muggenwort who came to Earth to collect four husbands?"

"Yes—to collect them and take them back to Muggenwort with her. You see, Muggenwort is a small matriarchal province near the Altair VI equator, and their mating customs are as different from ours as they are from yours. All Muggenwort women have to have four husbands in order to be accepted into Muggenwort society, and as there are no longer enough men in Muggenwort to go around, they have to travel to other planets to get them. But that's not the worst of it. After they capture them and bring them back to Muggenwort, they put them to work twelve hours a day in the kritch fields while they lie around all day in their air-conditioned barkenwood huts chewing rutenstuga nuts and watching TV!"

Roger was more amused than angry now. "And how about the husbands? I suppose they take to all this docilely and don't mind in the least sharing their wife with three other men!"

"But you don't understand!" Alayne of Altair was becoming more agitated by the second. "The husbands have no choice. They're bewitched—the same way Becky is bewitching you. Do you think it was your idea to ask her to marry you? Well, it wasn't! It was her idea, planted in your mind by hypnosis. Didn't you notice those gleaming gray eyes of hers? She's a witch, Roger, and once she gets you completely in her clutches you will be her slave for life, and she must be pretty sure of you already or she wouldn't be taking you out to her spaceship this afternoon!"

"What about her other three husbands-to-be? Are they going to accompany us on our drive into the country?"

"Of course not. They're already in the ship, hopelessly bewitched, waiting for her. Didn't you notice the three anklets on her leg? Well, each of them stands for a man she has conquered. It's an old Muggenwort custom. Probably today she is wearing four. Didn't you ever wonder what happens to all the men who disappear from the face of the Earth each year, Roger?"

"No, I never did," Roger said. "But there is one thing I'm wondering about. Why did *you* come to Earth?"

Alayne of Altair's bluebird eyes dropped to his chin. "I—I was coming to that," she said. "You see, in Buzenborg, girls chase boys instead of boys chasing girls."

"That seems to be a standard operating procedure on Altair VI."

"That's because the man shortage isn't confined to Muggenwort alone but encompasses the whole planet. When push-button-type spaceships became available, Buzenborg as well as Muggenwort girls began renting them and traveling to other planets in search of husbands, and Buzenborg as well as Muggenwort girls' schools started teaching alien languages and customs. The information was easily available because the Altair VI world government has been sending secret anthropological expeditions to Earth, and planets like it, for years, so that we will be ready to make contact with you when you finally lick space travel and qualify for membership in the League of Super Planets."

"What's the Buzenborg husband quota?" Roger asked acidly.

"One. That's why we Buzenborg girls wear wodgets.

We're not like those witches from Muggenwort. They don't care whom they get, just so they have strong backs; but we girls from Buzenborg do. Anyway, when my wodget registered ninety, I knew that you and I were ideally suited for each other, and that's why I struck up a conversation with you. I—I didn't know at the time that you were half bewitched."

"Suppose your wodget had been right. What then?"

"Why, I'd have taken you back to Buzenborg with me, of course. Oh, you'd have loved it there, Rog," she rushed on. "Our industrial corporations would be crazy about your poetic analysis of science, and you could have got a swell job, and my folks would have built us a house and we could have settled down and raised—and—raised—" Her voice grew sad. "But I guess I'll have to settle for Ashley instead. He only registers sixty on my wodget, but sixty is better than nothing."

"Are you naïve enough to believe that if you go to his apartment tonight he'll marry you and return to Buzenborg with you?"

"I have to take a chance. I only had enough money to rent the ship for a week. What do you think I am—a rich witch from Muggenwort?"

She had raised her eyes to his, and he searched them vainly for the deceit that should have been in them. There must be some way he could trap her. She had eluded his time trap and his baseball trap and—

Wait a minute! Maybe she hadn't eluded his time trap after all. If she was telling the truth and really did want to cut Becky out and really did have a spaceship equipped with faster-than-light drive, she was overlooking a very large ace up her sleeve.

"Did you ever hear the limerick about Miss Bright?" he asked. She shook her head. "It goes something like this:

> There was a young lady named Bright,
> Whose speed was far faster than light;

> She set out one day
> In a relative way,
> And returned home the previous night.*

"Let me elaborate," Roger went on. "I met Becky a little less than twenty-four hours before I met you, and I met her the same as I did you—on the very bench we're sitting on now. So if you're telling the truth you really don't have a problem at all. All you have to do is make a round trip to Altair VI enough in excess of the velocity of light to bring you back to Earth twenty-four hours before your original arrival. Then you simply come walking down the walk to where I'm sitting on the bench, and if your wodget is worth a plugged nickel I'll feel the same way toward you as you feel toward me."

"But that would involve a paradox, and the cosmos would have to create a time shift to compensate for it," Alayne of Altair objected. "The millisecond I attained the necessary velocity and the extent of the paradox became evident, time would go *whoom!* And you, I and everybody else in the cosmos would be catapulted back to the moment when the paradox began, and we'd have no memory of the last few days. It would be as though I'd never met you, as though you'd never met me—"

"And as though I'd never met Becky. What more do you want?"

She was staring at him. "Why—why, it just might work at that. It—it would be sort of like Aparicio stealing first base. Let me see now, if I take a bus out to the farm, I'll get there in less than an hour. Then if I set the grodgel for Lapse Two, and the borque for—"

"Oh, for Pete's sake," Roger said, "come off it, will you!"

"Sh-sh!" Alayne of Altair said. "I'm trying to think."

He stood up. "Well, think then! I'm going back to my room and get ready for my date with Becky!"

---

* By Arthur H. R. Buller; © by *Punch*.

Angrily he walked away. In his room, he laid his best suit out on the bed. He shaved and showered leisurely and spent a long time getting dressed. Then he went out, rented a car and drove to Becky's apartment. It was 2:00 p.m. on the nose when he rang her bell. She must have been taking a shower, because when she opened the door all she had on was a terry-cloth towel and three anklets. No, four.

"Hi, Roger," she said warmly. "Come on in."

Eagerly he stepped across the threshold and made a—

Whoom! Time went.

Little did Roger Thompson dream when he sat down on the park bench that Friday morning in June that in a celibate sense his goose was already in the oven and that soon it would be cooked. He may have had an inkling of things to come when he saw the cute blonde in the blue dress walking down the winding walk some several seconds later, but that inkling could not conceivably have apprised him of the vast convolutions of time and space which the bowing out of his bachelorhood had already set in motion.

The cute blonde sat down at the other end of the bench, produced a little red notebook and began writing in it. Presently she glanced at her wrist watch. Then she gave a start and looked over at him.

He returned the look cordially. He saw a dusting of golden freckles, a pair of eyes the hue of bluebirds and a small mouth the color of sumac leaves after the first hard frost.

A tall brunette in a red sheath came down the walk. Roger hardly even noticed her. Just as she was opposite the bench one of her spike heels sank into a crevice and brought her to an abrupt halt. She slipped her foot out of the shoe and, kneeling down, jerked the shoe free with her hands. Then she put it back on, gave him a dirty look and continued on her way.

The cute blonde had returned her attention to her notebook. Now she faced him again. Roger's heart turned three somersaults and made an *entrechat*.

"How do you xpell matrimony?" she said.

ADDED INDUCEMENT

THE ELECTRICAL APPLIANCE STORE was one of many that had sprung up in and around the city, seemingly overnight. There were half a dozen TV sets in the window, marked at amazingly low prices, and a window-wide sign boasted: WE'RE PRACTICALLY *giving* THEM AWAY! "This is the place we've been looking for," Janice said, and she pulled Henry through the entrance and into the store proper.

They hadn't gone two steps beyond the entrance when they came to a common standstill. Before them stood a huge and dazzling console with a 24-inch screen, and if you were TV hunting, you couldn't go by it any more than a hungry mouse could go by a new mouse trap baited with his favorite cheese.

"We can never afford that one," Henry said.

"But, darling, we can afford to look, can't we?"

So they looked. They looked at the sleek mahogany cabinet and the cute little double doors that you could close when you weren't watching your programs; at the screen and the program in progress; at the company's name at the base of the screen—BAAL—

"Must be a new make," Henry said. "Never heard of it before."

"That doesn't mean it isn't any good," Janice said.

—at the array of chrome-plated dials beneath the company's name and the little round window just below the middle dial—

"What's *that* for?" Janice asked, pointing at the window.

Henry leaned forward. "The dial above it says 'popcorn' but that *can't* be."

"Oh, yes it can!" a voice behind them said.

Turning, they beheld a small, mild-looking man with a pronounced widow's peak. He had brown eyes, and he was wearing a brown pin-striped suit.

"Do you work here?" Henry asked.

The small man bowed. "I'm Mr. Krull, and this is my establishment. . . . Do you like popcorn, sir?"

Henry nodded. "Once in a while."

"And you, madam?"

"Oh, yes," Janice said. "Very much!"

"Allow me to demonstrate."

Mr. Krull stepped forward and tweaked the middle dial halfway around. Instantly, the little window lighted up, revealing a shining inbuilt frying pan with several thimble-sized aluminum cups suspended above it. As Henry and Janice watched, one of the cups upended itself and poured melted butter into the pan; shortly thereafter, another followed suit, emitting a Lilliputian cascade of golden popcorn kernels.

You could have heard a pin drop—or, more appropriately, you could have heard a popcorn kernel pop—the room was so quiet; and after a moment, Henry and Janice and Mr. Krull did hear one pop. Then another one popped, and then another, and pretty soon the machine-gun fire of popcorn in metamorphosis filled the room. The window now was like one of those little glass paperweights you pick up and shake and the snow starts falling, only this wasn't snow—it was popcorn—the whitest, liveliest, fluffiest popcorn that Henry and Janice had ever seen.

"Well, did you ever!" Janice gasped.

Mr. Krull held up his hand. The moment was a dramatic

one. The popcorn had subsided into a white, quivering mound. Mr. Krull tweaked the dial the rest of the way around and the pan flipped over. Abruptly a little secret door beneath the window came open, a tiny red light began blinking on and off, and a buzzer started to buzz; and there, sitting in the newly revealed secret cubicle, was a fat round bowl brim-full with popcorn, and with little painted bluebirds flying happily around its porcelain sides.

Henry was entranced. "Well, what'll they think of next!"

"How utterly charming!" Janice said.

"It's good popcorn too," Mr. Krull said.

He bent over and picked up the bowl, and the little red light went out and the buzzer became silent. "Have some?"

Henry and Janice took some, and Mr. Krull took some himself. There was a reflective pause while everybody munched. Presently: "Why, it's delicious!" Janice said.

"Out of this world," said Henry.

Mr. Krull smiled. "We grow our own. Nothing's too good for Baal Enterprises. . . . And now, if I may, I'd like to demonstrate some of our other special features."

"I don't know," Henry said. "You see—"

"Oh, let him!" Janice interrupted. "It won't hurt us to watch, even if we can't afford such an expensive model."

Mr. Krull needed no more encouragement. He began with a discourse on the cabinet, describing where the wood had been cut, how it had been cured, shaped, worked, polished, and fitted together; then he went into a mass of technical details about the chassis, the inbuilt antenna, the high-fidelity speaker—

Suddenly Henry realized that the paper that had somehow got into his left hand was a contract and that the object that had somehow slipped into his right was a fountain pen. "Wait a minute," he said. "Wait a minute! I can't afford anything like this. We were just look—"

"How do you know you can't afford it?" Mr. Krull asked reasonably. "I haven't even mentioned the price yet."

"Then don't bother mentioning it. It's bound to be too high."

"You might find it too high, and then again you might not. It's a rather relative figure. But even if you do find it too high, I'm sure the terms will be agreeable."

"All right," Henry said. "What *are* the terms?"

Mr. Krull smiled, rubbed the palms of his hands together. "*One,*" he said, "the set is guaranteed for life. *Two,* you get a lifetime supply of popcorn. *Three,* you pay nothing down. *Four,* you pay no weekly, monthly, quarterly, or annual installments—"

"Are you *giving* it to us?" Janice's hazel eyes were incredulous.

"Well, not exactly. You have to pay for it—on one condition."

"Condition?" Henry asked.

"On the condition that you come into a certain amount of money."

"How much money?"

"One million dollars," Mr. Krull said.

Janice swayed slightly. Henry took a deep breath, blew it out slowly. "And the price?"

"Come now, sir. Surely you know what the price is by now. And surely you know who I am by now."

For a while Henry and Janice just stood there. Mr. Krull's widow's peak seemed more pronounced than ever, and there was a hint of mockery in his smile. For the first time, and with something of a shock, Henry realized that his ears were pointed.

Finally he got his tongue loose from the roof of his mouth. "You're not, you can't be—"

"Mr. Baal? Of course not! I'm merely one of his representatives—though, in this instance, 'dealer' would be a more appropriate term."

There was a long pause. Then: "Both—both our souls?" Henry asked.

"Naturally," Mr. Krull said. "The terms are generous enough to warrant both of them, don't you think? . . . Well, what do you say, sir? Is it a deal?"

Henry began backing through the doorway. Janice backed with him, though not with quite the same alacrity.

Mr. Krull shrugged philosophically. "See you later then," he said.

Henry followed Janice into their apartment and closed the door. "I can't believe it," he said. "It *couldn't* have happened!"

"It happened all right," Janice said. "I can still taste the popcorn. You just don't want to believe it, that's all. You're afraid to believe it."

"Maybe you're right. . . ."

Janice fixed supper, and after supper they sat in the living room and watched *Gunfire, Feud, Shoot-'em-Up Henessey,* and the news, on the old beat-up TV set they'd bought two years ago when they were married to tide them over till they could afford a better one. After the news, Janice made popcorn in the kitchen and Henry opened two bottles of beer.

The popcorn was burned. Janice gagged on the first mouthful, pushed her bowl away. "You know, I almost think it would be worth it," she said. "Imagine, all you have to do is turn a dial and you can have popcorn any time you want without missing a single one of your programs!"

Henry was aghast. "You can't be serious!"

"Maybe not, but I'm getting awful sick of burned popcorn and picture trouble! And besides, who'd ever give *us* a million dollars anyway!"

"We'll look around again tomorrow afternoon," Henry said. "There must be other makes of sets besides Baal that have inbuilt popcorn poppers. Maybe we'll find one if we look long enough."

But they didn't. They started looking as soon as they got through work in the pants-stretcher factory, but the only sets they found with inbuilt popcorn poppers were stamped unmistakably with the name BAAL, and stood in the new electrical appliance stores that had sprung up, seemingly overnight, along with Mr. Krull's.

"I can't understand it," said the last orthodox dealer they visited. "You're the fiftieth couple to come in here today looking for a TV set with a popcorn window and an inbuilt popcorn popper. Why, I never heard of such a thing!"

"You will," Henry said.

They walked home disconsolately. A truck whizzed by in the street. They read the big red letters on its side—BAAL ENTERPRISES—and they saw the three new TV consoles jouncing on the truckbed, and the three little popcorn windows twinkling in the summer sunshine.

They looked at each other, then looked quickly away. . . .

The truck was parked in front of their apartment building when they got home. Two of the sets had already been delivered and the third was being trundled down the nearby alley to the freight elevator. When they reached their floor they saw the set being pushed down the hall, and they lingered in their doorway long enough to learn its destination.

"Betty and Herb!" Janice gasped. "Why, I never thought they'd—"

"Humph!" Henry said. "Shows what their values amount to."

They went in, and Janice fixed supper. While they were eating they heard a noise outside the door, and when they looked out they saw another Baal set being delivered across the hall.

Next morning, three more were delivered on the same floor, and when Janice looked out the window after fixing breakfast, she saw two Baal trucks in the street and half a dozen consoles being trundled into the alley that led to the freight elevator. She beckoned to Henry, and he came over and stood beside her.

She pointed down at the trucks. "I'll bet we're the only people left on the whole block who still pop popcorn in their kitchen. Mr. and Mrs. Neanderthal—that's us!"

"But at least we can still call our souls our own," Henry said, without much conviction.

"I suppose you're right. But it would be so nice to pop popcorn in the living room for a change. And such good popcorn too. . . ."

They put in a miserable day at the pants-stretcher factory. On the way home they passed Mr. Krull's store. There was a long line of people standing in front of it, and a new sign graced the window where the dummy come-on sets still stood: GOING OUT OF BUSINESS—THIS MAY BE YOUR LAST CHANCE TO OWN A TV–POPCORN CONSOLE!

Janice sighed. "We'll be the only ones," she said. "The only ones in the whole city who pop popcorn in the kitchen and watch their favorite programs on a stone-age TV set!"

When Henry didn't answer, she turned toward where she thought he was. But he wasn't there any more. He was standing at the end of the line and waving to her to join him.

Mr. Krull was beaming. He pointed to the two little dotted lines, and Henry and Janice signed their names with eager fingers. Then Henry wrote down their street and number in the space marked ADDRESS and handed the contract back to Mr. Krull.

Mr. Krull glanced at it, then turned toward the back of the store. "Henry and Janice Smith, sir," he called. "111 Ibid Street, Local."

They noticed the tall man then. He was standing at the back of the store, jotting down something in a little red notebook. You could tell just by looking at him that he was a businessman, and you didn't have to look twice to see that he was a successful one. He was wearing a neat charcoal-gray suit and a pair of modern horn-rimmed glasses. His hair was quite dark, but his temples were sprinkled becomingly with gray. When he noticed Henry and Janice staring at him, he smiled at them warmly and gave a little laugh. It was an odd kind of a laugh. "Ha ha ha ha," it went, then dropped abruptly way down the scale: "HO HO HO HO! . . ."

ADDED INDUCEMENT

"Incidentally," Mr. Krull was saying, "if a million dollars *does* come your way, you have to accept it, you know—even though you won't get a chance to spend it. Not only that, if you get an opportunity to *win* a million dollars, you've got to take advantage of it. It's all stipulated in the contract."

Janice repressed a nervous giggle. "Now who in the world would give *us* a million dollars!"

Mr. Krull smiled, then frowned. "Sometimes I just can't understand people at all," he said. "Why, if I'd approached our prospective customers directly, in my capacity as Mr. Baal's representative, and had offered each of them a brand-new TV console—or even a million dollars—for his or her soul, I'd have been laughed right off the face of the earth! If you want to be a success today, no matter what business you're in, you've got to provide an added inducement. Oh, good night, sir."

The tall man was leaving. At Mr. Krull's words, he paused in the doorway and turned. The final rays of the afternoon sun gave his face a reddish cast. He bowed slightly. "Good night, Krull," he said. "Good night, Janice and Henry." He appended to his words another measure of his unusual laughter.

"Who—who was that?" Henry asked.

"That was Mr. Baal. He's preparing a list of contestants for his new TV program."

"His TV program!"

Mr. Krull's smile was the quintessence of innocence. "Why, yes. It hasn't been announced yet, but it will be soon. . . . It's a giveaway show—and quite a unique one, too. Mr. Baal has everything arranged so that none of the contestants can possibly lose."

Janice was tugging at Henry's arm. Her face was pale. "Come on, darling. Let's go home."

But Henry hung back. "What—what's the name of the show?" he asked.

"*Make a Million,*" Mr. Krull said.

HOPSOIL

(TRANSLATOR'S NOTE: *The following story came into my possession through certain hitherto inaccessible channels, the nature of which I am not at liberty to divulge. It is, to the best of my knowledge, the first Martian science-fiction story ever to reach Earth, and, while it makes its own point, there are a number of other points that can be inferred from its pages: (1) Martians are pretty much like us; (2) their civilization is pretty much like our own; (3) all the while Earth science-fiction writers have been using Mars to mirror the foibles of our society, Martian science-fiction writers have been using Earth to mirror the foibles of Martian society; (4) the mirror business has been overdone on Mars as well as on Earth, and certain Martian science-fiction writers have started parodying other Martian science-fiction writers; and (5) the story itself falls into this latter category.*)

The ship came down out of the abysmal immensities and settled like a dark and wingless bird on the blue sands of Earth.

Captain Frimpf opened the door. He stepped out into the sparkling sunshine and filled his lungs with the clean sweet air. All around him the blue sands stretched away to the hazy horizon. In the distance the broken buildings of a long-dead city iridesced like upthrust shards of colored glass. High above him fat little clouds played tag on the big blue playground of the sky.

His eyes misted. Earth, he thought. Earth at last!

The three enlisted men, who made up the rest of the historic crew, came out of the ship and stood beside him. They, too, stared at the land with misted eyes.

"Blue," breathed Birp.

"Blue," murmured Fardel.

"Blue!" gasped Pempf.

"Well, of course, blue," said the captain gently. "Haven't our astronomers maintained all along that the blueness of Earth could not be wholly attributable to the light-absorbent properties of its atmosphere? The soil *had* to be blue!"

He knelt down and scooped up a handful of the wondrous substance. It trickled through his fingers like blue mist. "The blue sands of Earth," he whispered reverently.

He straightened up and took off his hat and stood in the sparkling sunlight and let the clean Earth wind blow through his hair. In the distance the city tinkled like glass chimes, and the wind wafted the sound across the blue sands to his ears, and he thought of warm Martian summers and long lazy days, and hot afternoons, drinking lemonade on Grandmother Frimpf's front porch.

Presently he became aware that someone was breathing down the back of his neck. He turned irritably. "What is it, Birp?"

Birp cleared his throat. "Beg pardon, sir," he said, "but don't you think the occasion calls for—I mean to say, sir, that it's been a long voyage, and Pempf and Fardel and myself, we're a little thir—I mean, we're a little tense, and we thought—"

He quailed before the scorn in the captain's eyes. "Very well," the captain said coldly. "Open up a case of the rotgut. But only one, understand? And if I find a single empty bottle defiling this virgin landscape I'll clap every one of you in the brig!"

Birp had started off at a gallop toward the ship. He paused at the captain's admonition. "But what'll we do with them, sir? If we put them back in the ship, it'll take just that much more fuel to blast off, and we're already short of fuel as it is."

The captain pondered for a moment. It was not a particularly abstruse problem, and he solved it with a minimum of difficulty. "Bury them," he said.

While the crew chug-a-lugged their beer the captain stood a little to one side, staring at the distant city. He pictured himself telling his wife about it when he got back to Mars, and he saw himself sitting at the dinner table, describing the pastel towers and the shining spires and the sad and shattered buildings.

In spite of himself, he saw his wife, too. She was sitting across the table from him, listening and eating. Mostly eating. Why, she was even fatter now than she'd been when he left. For the thousandth time he found himself wondering why wives had to get so fat—so fat sometimes that their husbands had to wheel them around in wife-barrows. Why couldn't they get up and move around once in a while instead of going in whole hog for every labor-saving device the hucksters put on the market? Why did they have to eat, eat, eat, all the time?

The captain's face paled at the thought of the grocery bill he would have to pay upon his return, and presently the grocery bill directed his mind to other equally distressing items, such as the national sales tax, the road tax, the tree tax, the gas tax, the grass tax, the air tax, the first-world-war tax, the second-world-war tax, the third-world-war tax and the fourth-world-war tax.

He sighed. It was enough to drive a man to drink, paying for wars your father, your grandfather, your great-grandfather and your great-great-grandfather had fought in! He looked enviously at Birp and Pempf and Fardel. *They* weren't worried about *their* taxes. *They* weren't worried about anything. They were dancing around the empty beer case like a trio of barbarians, and already they had made up a dirty song about the blue sands of Earth.

Captain Frimpf listened to the words. His ears grew warm, then hot. "All right, men, that's enough!" he said abruptly. "Bury your bottles, burn the case and turn in. We've got a hard day ahead of us tomorrow."

Obediently, Birp and Pempf and Fardel dug four rows of little holes in the blue soil and covered up their dead soldiers one by one. Then, after burning the case and saying good night to the captain, they went back into the ship.

The captain lingered outside. The moon was rising, and such a moon! Its magic radiance turned the plain into a vast midnight-blue tablecloth and transformed the city into a silvery candelabrum. He was captivated all over again.

The mystery of those distant empty buildings and silent forsaken streets crept across the plain and touched his marrow. What had happened to the inhabitants? he wondered. What had happened to the inhabitants of the other broken cities he had seen while the ship was orbiting in?

He shook his head. He did not know, and probably he never would. His ignorance saddened him, and suddenly he could no longer endure the poignancy of the plain and the uninterrupted silence of the night, and he crept into the ship and closed the door behind him. For a long time he lay in the darkness of his stateroom, thinking of the people of Earth; of the noble civilization that had come and gone its way and had left nothing behind it but a handful of crystal memories. Finally he slept.

When he went outside the next morning there were twenty-four beer trees growing in front of the ship.

The classification had leaped automatically into Captain Frimpf's mind. He had never seen beer trees before, in fact he had never even heard of them; but what better name could you give to a group of large woody plants with bottles of amber fluid hanging from their branches like fruit ready to be plucked?

Some of the fruit had already been plucked, and there was a party in progress in the young orchard. Moreover, judging from the row of little hummocks along the orchard's edge, more seed had been planted.

The captain was dumfounded. How could any kind of soil—even Earth soil—grow beer trees overnight from empty bottles? He began to have a glimmering of what might have happened to the people of Earth.

Pempf came up to him, a bottle in each hand. "Here, try some, sir," he said enthusiastically. "You never tasted anything like it!"

The captain put him in his place with a scathing glance. "I'm an officer, Pempf. Officers don't drink *beer!*"

"Oh. I—I forgot, sir. Sorry."

"You should be sorry. You and those other two! Who gave you permission to eat—I mean to drink—Earth fruit?"

Pempf hung his head just enough to show that he was repentant, but not any more repentant than his inferior status demanded. "No one, sir. I—I guess we kind of got carried away."

"Aren't you even curious about how these trees happened to come up? You're the expedition's chemist—why aren't you testing the soil?"

"There wouldn't be any point in testing it, sir. A topsoil with properties in it capable of growing trees like this out of empty beer bottles is the product of a science a million years ahead of our own. Besides, sir, I don't think it's the soil alone that's responsible. I think that the sunlight striking on the surface of the moon combines with certain lunar radiations and gives the resultant moonlight the ability to replenish and to multiply anything planted on the planet."

The captain looked at him. "*Anything,* you say?"

"Why not, sir? We planted empty beer bottles and got beer trees, didn't we?"

"Hmm," the captain said.

He turned abruptly and re-entered the ship. He spent the day in his stateroom, lost in thought, the busy schedule he had mapped out for the day completely forgotten. After the sun had set, he went outside and buried all the credit notes he had brought with him in back of the ship. He regretted that he hadn't had more to bring, but it didn't make any difference really, because as soon as the credit trees bloomed he would have all the seed he needed.

That night, for the first time in years, he slept without dreaming about his grocery bill and his taxes.

But the next morning when he hurried outside and ran around the ship he found no credit trees blooming in the sunlight. He found nothing but the little hummocks he himself had made the night before.

At first his disappointment stunned him. And then he thought, *Perhaps with money it takes longer. Money is probably as hard to grow as it is to get.* He walked back around the ship and looked at the orchard. It was three times its former size and fronted the ship like a young forest. Wonderingly he walked through the sun-dappled aisles, staring enviously at the clusters of amber fruit.

A trail of beer-bottle caps led him to a little glade where a new party was in progress. Perhaps whingding would have been a better word. Pempf and Fardel and Birp were dancing around in a circle like three bearded woodland nymphs, waving bottles and singing at the top of their voices. The dirty song about the blue sands of Earth now had a second verse.

They came to a startled stop when they saw him; then, after regarding him blearily for a moment, they resumed festivities again. Abruptly Captain Frimpf wondered if they had gone to bed at all last night. He was inclined to doubt it, but whether they had or hadn't, it was painfully clear that discipline was deteriorating rapidly. If he wanted to save the expedition he would have to act quickly.

But for some reason his initiative seemed to have deserted him. The thought of saving the expedition made him think of going back to Mars, and the thought of going back to Mars made him think of his fat wife, and the thought of his fat wife made him think of the grocery bill, and the thought of the grocery bill made him think of his taxes, and for some unfathomable reason the thought of his taxes made him think of the liquor cabinet in his stateroom and of the unopened bottle of bourbon that stood all alone on its single shelf.

He decided to put off reprimanding the crew till tomorrow. Surely, by then, his credit trees would have broken through the soil, thereby giving him some idea of how long he would have to wait before he could harvest his first crop and plant his second. Once his fortune was assured he would be able to cope more competently with the beer-tree problem.

But in the morning the little hummocks behind the ship were still barren. The beer orchard, on the other hand, was a phenomenon to behold. It stretched halfway across the plain in the direction of the dead city, and the sound of the wind in its fruit-laden branches brought to mind a bottling works at capacity production.

There was little doubt in Captain Frimpf's mind now of the fate that had overtaken the people of Earth. But what, he asked himself, had happened to the trees *they* had planted? He was not an obtuse man, and the answer came presently: The people of Earth had performed a function similar to that performed by the bees on Mars. In drinking the fluid fruit they had in effect pollinated the crystal seed-shells that enclosed it, and it was the pollinating as well as the planting of the shells that had caused new trees to grow.

It must have been a pleasant ecology while it lasted, the captain reflected. But like all good things it had been run into the ground. One by one the people had become heavy pollinators, and finally they had pollinated themselves to death, and the trees, unable any longer to reproduce themselves, had become extinct.

A tragic fate, certainly. But was it any more tragic than being taxed to death?

The captain spent the day in his stateroom trying to figure out a way to pollinate money, his eyes straying, with increasing frequency, to the little paneled door of his liquor cabinet. Toward sunset Birp and Fardel and Pempf appeared and asked for an audience with him.

Fardel was spokesman. "Shir," he said, "we've made up our minds. We aren't going to go back to Marsh."

The captain wasn't surprised, but for some reason he was annoyed. "Oh, go on back to your damned orchard and stop bothering me!" he said, turning away from them.

After they left he went over to his liquor cabinet and opened the paneled door. He picked up the forlorn bottle sitting on the shelf. Its two empty companions had long ago gone down the disposal tube and were somewhere in orbit between Earth and Mars.

"Good thing I saved one," the captain said. He opened it up and pollinated it; then he staggered outside and buried it behind the ship and sat down to watch it grow.

Maybe his credit trees would come up and maybe they wouldn't. If they didn't he was damned if he was going back to Mars, either. He was sick of his fat wife and he was sick of the grocery bill and he was sick of the national sales tax, the road tax, the tree tax, the gas tax, the grass tax, the air tax, the first-world-war tax, the second-world-war tax, the third-world-war tax and the fourth-world-war tax. Most of all he was sick of being a self-righteous martinet with a parched tongue.

Presently the moon came up and he watched delightedly while the first shoot of his whiskey tree broke the surface of the blue sands of Earth.

FLYING PAN

MARIANNNE SUMMERS worked in a frying-pan factory. For eight hours every day and for five days every week she stood by a production-line conveyor and every time a frying pan went by she put a handle on it. And all the while she stood by one conveyor she rode along on another—a big conveyor with days and nights over it instead of fluorescent tubes, and months standing along it instead of people. And every time she passed a month it added something to her or took something away, and as time went by she became increasingly aware of the ultimate month—the one standing far down the line, waiting to put a handle on her soul.

Sometimes Marianne sat down and wondered how she could possibly have gotten into such a rut, but all the while she wondered she knew that she was only kidding herself, that she knew perfectly well why. Ruts were made for untalented people, and if you were untalented you ended up in one; moreover, if you were untalented and were too stubborn to go home and admit you were untalented, you stayed in one.

There was a great deal of difference between dancing on TV and putting handles on frying pans: the difference between being graceful and gawky, lucky and unlucky, or

—to get right back to the basic truth again—the difference between being talented and untalented. No matter how hard you practiced or how hard you tried, if your legs were too fat, no one wanted you and you ended up in a rut or in a frying-pan factory, which was the same thing, and you went to work every morning and performed the same tasks and you came home every night and thought the same thoughts, and all the while you rode down the big conveyor between the merciless months and came closer and closer to the ultimate month that would put the final touches on you and make you just like everybody else. . . .

Mornings were getting up and cooking breakfasts in her small apartment and taking the bus to work. Evenings were going home and cooking lonely suppers and afterward TV. Weekends were writing letters and walking in the park. Nothing ever changed and Marianne had begun to think that nothing ever would. . . .

And then one night when she came home, she found a flying frying pan on her window ledge.

It had been a day like all days, replete with frying pans, superintendents, boredom and tired feet. Around ten o'clock the maintenance man stopped by and asked her to go to the Halloween Dance with him. The Halloween Dance was a yearly event sponsored by the company and was scheduled for that night. So far, Marianne had turned down fifteen would-be escorts.

A frying pan went by and she put a handle on it. "No, I don't think so," she said.

"Why?" the maintenance man asked bluntly.

It was a good question, one that Marianne couldn't answer honestly because she wasn't being honest with herself. So she told the same little white lie she had told all the others: "I—I don't like dances."

"Oh." The maintenance man gave her the same look his fifteen predecessors had given her, and moved on. Marianne shrugged her shoulders. *I don't care what they think, she* told herself. Another frying pan went by, and another and another.

After a while, noon came, and Marianne and all the other employees ate frankfurters and sauerkraut in the company cafeteria. The parade of frying pans recommenced promptly at 12:30.

During the afternoon she was approached twice more by would-be escorts. You'd have thought she was the only girl in the factory. Sometimes she hated her blue eyes and round pink face, and sometimes she even hated her bright yellow hair, which had some of the properties of a magnet. But hating the way she looked didn't solve her problems—it only aggravated them—and by the time 4:30 came she had a headache and she heartily despised the whole world.

Diminutive trick-or-treaters were already making the rounds when she got off the bus at the corner. Witches walked and goblins leered, and pumpkin candles sputtered in the dusk. But Marianne hardly noticed.

Halloween was for children, not for an embittered old woman of twenty-two who worked in a frying-pan factory.

She walked down the street to the apartment building and picked up her mail at the desk. There were two letters, one from her mother, one from—

Marianne's heart pounded all the way up in the elevator and all the way down the sixth-floor corridor to her apartment. But she forced herself to open her mother's letter first. It was a typical letter, not essentially different from the last one. The grape crop had been good, but what with the trimming and the tying and the disking and the horse-hoeing, and paying off the pickers, there wasn't going to be much left of the check—if and when it came; the hens were laying better, but then they always did whenever egg prices dropped; Ed Olmstead was putting a new addition on his general store (it was high time!); Doris Hickett had just given birth to a 7 lb. baby boy; Pa sent his love, and please forget your foolish pride and come home. P.S.—Marianne should see the wonderful remodeling job Howard King was doing on his house. It was going to be a regular palace when he got done.

Marianne swallowed the lump in her throat. She opened the other letter with trembling fingers:

DEAR MARIANNE,

I said I wasn't going to write you any more, that I'd already written you too many times asking you to come home and marry me and you never gave me an answer one way or the other. But sometimes a fellow's pride don't amount to much.

I guess you know I'm remodeling the house and I guess you know the reason why. In case you don't it's the same reason I bought the house in the first place, because of you. I only got one picture window and I don't know whether I should put it in the parlor or in the kitchen. The kitchen would be fine, but all you can see from there is the barn and you know how the barn looks, but if I put it in the parlor the northwest wind would be sure to crack it the first winter though you'd get a good view of the road and the willows along the creek. I don't know what to do.

The hills behind the south meadow are all red and gold the way you used to like them. The willows look like they're on fire. Nights I sit on the steps and picture you coming walking down the road and stopping by the gate and then I get up and walk down the path and I say, "I'm glad you've come back, Marianne. I guess you know I still love you." I guess if anybody ever heard me they'd think I was crazy because the road is always empty when I get there, and there's no one ever standing by the gate.

HOWARD

There had been that crisp December night with the sound of song and laughter intermingling with the crackling of the ice beneath the runners and the chug-chugging of the tractor as it pulled the hay-filled sleigh, and the stars so bright and close they touched the topmost branches of the silhouetted trees, and the snow, pale and clean in the starlight, stretching away over the hills, up and up, into the first dark fringe of the forest; and herself, sitting on the tractor with Howard instead of in the hay with the rest of the party, and the tractor lurching and bumping, its headbeams lighting the way over the rutted country road—

Howard's arm was around her and their frosty breaths blended as they kissed. "I love you, Marianne," Howard said, and she could see the words issuing from his lips in little silvery puffs and drifting away into the darkness, and suddenly she saw her own words, silver too, hovering tenuously in the air before her, and presently she heard them in wondrous astonishment: "I love you, too, Howie. I love you, too. . . ."

She didn't know how long she'd been sitting there crying before she first became aware of the ticking sound. A long time, she guessed, judging by the stiffness of her limbs. The sound was coming from her bedroom window and what it made her think of most was the common pins she and the other kids used to tie on strings and rig up so they'd keep swinging against the windowpanes of lonely old people sitting alone on Halloween.

She had lit the table lamp when she came in, and its beams splashed reassuringly on the living-room rug. But beyond the aura of the light, shadows lay along the walls, coalesced in the bedroom doorway. Marianne stood up, concentrating on the sound. The more she listened the more she doubted that she was being victimized by the neighborhood small fry: the ticks came too regularly to be ascribed to a pin dangling at the end of a string. First there would be a staccato series of them, then silence, then another series. Moreover, her bedroom window was six stories above the street and nowhere near a fire escape.

But if the small fry weren't responsible for the sound, who

was? There was an excellent way to find out. Marianne forced her legs into motion, walked slowly to the bedroom doorway, switched on the ceiling light and entered the room. A few short steps brought her to the window by her bed.

She peered through the glass. Something gleamed on the window ledge but she couldn't make out what it was. The ticking noise had ceased and traffic sounds drifted up from below. Across the way, the warm rectangles of windows made precise patterns in the darkness, and down the street a huge sign said in big blue letters: SPRUCK'S CORN PADS ARE THE BEST.

Some of Marianne's confidence returned. She released the catch and slowly raised the window. At first she didn't recognize the gleaming object as a flying saucer; she took it for an upside-down frying pan without a handle. And so ingrained was the habit by now that she reached for it instinctively, with the unconscious intention of putting a handle on it.

"Don't touch my ship!"

That was when Marianne saw the spaceman. He was standing off to one side, his diminutive helmet glimmering in the radiance of SPRUCK'S CORN PADS. He wore a gray, form-fitting space suit replete with ray guns, shoulder tanks, and boots with turned-up toes, and he was every bit of five inches tall. He had drawn one of the ray guns (Marianne didn't know for sure they were ray guns, but judging from the rest of his paraphernalia, what else could they be?) and was holding it by the barrel. It was clear to Marianne that he had been tapping on the window with it.

It was also clear to Marianne that she was going, or had gone, out of her mind. She started to close the window—

"Stop, or I'll burn you!"

Her hands fell away from the sash. The voice had seemed real enough, a little on the thin side, perhaps, but certainly audible enough. Was it possible? Could this tiny creature be something more than a figment?

He had changed his gun to his other hand, she noticed, and its minute muzzle pointed directly at her forehead. When she made no further move, he permitted the barrel to drop slightly and said, "That's better. Now if you'll behave yourself and do as I say, maybe I can spare your life."

"Who are you?" Marianne asked.

It was as though he had been awaiting the question. He stepped dramatically into the full radiance of the light streaming through the window and sheathed his gun. He bowed almost imperceptibly, and his helmet flashed like the tinsel on a gum wrapper. "Prince Moy Trehano," he said majestically, though the majesty was marred by the thinness of his voice, "Emperor of 10,000 suns, Commander of the vast space fleet which is at this very moment in orbit around this insignificant planet you call 'Earth'!"

"Wh—why?"

"Because we're going to bomb you, that's why!"

"But why do you want to bomb us?"

"Because you're a menace to galactic civilization! Why else?"

"Oh," Marianne said.

"We're going to blow your cities to smithereens. There'll be so much death and destruction in our wake that you'll never recover from it . . . Do you have any batteries?"

For a moment Marianne thought she had misunderstood. "Batteries?"

"Flashlight batteries will do." Prince Moy Trehano seemed embarrassed, though it was impossible to tell for sure because his helmet completely hid his face. There was a small horizontal slit where, presumably, his eyes were, but that was the only opening. "My atomic drive's been acting up," he went on. "In fact, this was a forced landing. Fortunately, however, I know a secret formula whereby I can convert the energy in a dry-cell battery into a controlled chain reaction. Do you have any?"

"I'll see," Marianne said.

"Remember now, no tricks. I'll burn you right through the walls with my atomic ray gun if you try to call anyone!"

"I—I think there's a flashlight in my bed-table drawer."

There was. She unscrewed the base, shook out the batteries and set them on the window sill. Prince Moy Trehano went into action. He opened a little door on the side of his ship and rolled the batteries through. Then he turned to Marianne. "Don't you move an inch from where you are!" he said. "I'll be watching you through the viewports." He stepped inside and closed the door.

Marianne held her terror at bay and peered at the spaceship more closely. They aren't really flying *saucers* at all, she thought; they're just like frying pans . . . flying frying pans. It even had a little bracket that could have been the place where the handle was supposed to go. Not only that, its ventral regions strongly suggested a frying-pan cover.

She shook her head, trying to clear it. First thing you knew, everything she saw would look like a frying pan. She remembered the viewports Prince Moy Trehano had mentioned, and presently she made them out—a series of tiny crinkly windows encircling the upper part of the saucer. She leaned closer, trying to see into the interior.

"Stand back!"

Marianne straightened up abruptly, so abruptly that she nearly lost her kneeling position before the window and toppled back into the room. Prince Moy Trehano had reemerged from his vessel and was standing imperiously in the combined radiance of the bedroom light and SPRUCK'S CORN PADS.

"The technical secrets of my stellar empire are not for the likes of you," he said. "But as a recompense for your assistance in the repairing of my atomic drive I am going to divulge my space fleet's target areas.

"We do not contemplate the complete destruction of humanity. We wish merely to destroy the present civilization, and to accomplish this it is our intention to wipe out every city on Earth. Villages will be exempt, as will small towns with populations of less than 20,000 humans. The bombings will begin as soon as I get back to my fleet—a matter of four or five hours—and if I do not return, they will begin in four or five hours anyway. So if you value your life, go ho— I mean leave the city at once. I, Prince Moy Trehano, have spoken!"

Once again the bow, and the iridescing of the tinselly helmet, and then Prince Moy Trehano stepped into the spaceship and slammed the door. A whirring sound ensued, and the vessel began to shake. Colored lights went on in the viewports—a red one here, a blue one there, then a green one—creating a Christmas-tree effect.

Marianne watched, entranced. Suddenly the door flew open and Prince Moy Trehano's head popped out. "Get back!" he shouted. "Get back! You don't want to get burned by the jets, do you?" His head disappeared and the door slammed again.

Jets? Were flying saucers jet-propelled? Even as she instinctively shrank back into her bedroom, Marianne pondered the question. Then, as the saucer rose from the window ledge and into the night, she saw the little streams of fire issuing from its base. They were far more suggestive of sparks from a Zippo lighter than they were of jets, but if Prince Moy Trehano had said they were jets, then jets they were. Marianne was not inclined to argue the point.

When she thought about the incident afterward she remembered a lot of points that she could have argued—if she'd wanted to. Prince Moy Trehano's knowledge of the English language, for one, and his slip of the tongue when he started to tell her to go home, for another. And then there was the matter of his atomic drive. Certainly, Marianne reflected later, if the bombs his fleet was supposed to have carried were as technically naïve as his atomic drive, the world had never had much to worry about.

But at the moment she didn't feel like arguing any points. Anyway, she was too busy to argue. Busy packing. Under ordinary circumstances Prince Moy Trehano's threatened destruction of the cities of Earth would never have been reason enough to send her scurrying to the sticks. But Lord, when you were so sick of the pinched little channels of blue that city dwellers called a sky, of the disciplined little plots of grass that took the place of fields, of bored agents who sneered at you just because you had fat legs; when, deep in your heart, you wanted an excuse to go home—then it was reason enough.

More than enough.

At the terminal she paused long enough to send a telegram:

DEAR HOWIE: PUT THE PICTURE WINDOW IN THE KITCHEN, I DON'T MIND THE BARN. WILL BE HOME ON THE FIRST TRAIN.
MARIANNE

When the lights of the city faded into the dark line of the horizon, Prince Moy Trehano relaxed at the controls. His mission, he reflected, had come off reasonably well.

Of course there had been the inevitable unforeseen complication. But he couldn't blame anyone for it besides himself. He should have checked the flashlight batteries before he swiped them. He knew well enough that half the stock in Olmstead's general store had been gathering dust for years, that Ed Olmstead would rather die than throw away anything that some unwary customer might buy. But he'd been so busy rigging up his ship that he just hadn't thought.

In a way, though, his having to ask Marianne's help in the repairing of his improvised motor had lent his story a conviction it might otherwise have lacked. If he'd said right out of a clear blue sky that his "fleet" was going to bomb the cities and spare the villages, it wouldn't have sounded right. Her giving him the batteries had supplied him with a motivation. And his impromptu explanation about converting their energy into a controlled chain reaction had been a perfect cover-up. Marianne, he was sure, didn't know any more about atomic drives than he did.

Prince Moy Trehano shifted to a more comfortable position on his match-box pilot's seat. He took off his tinfoil helmet and let his beard fall free. He switched off the Christmas-tree lights beneath the Saran Wrap viewports and looked out at the village-bejeweled countryside.

By morning he'd be home, snug and secure in his miniature mansion in the willows. First, though, he'd hide the frying pan in the same rabbit hole where he'd hidden the handle, so no one would ever find it. Then he could sit back and take it easy, comforted by the knowledge of a good deed well done—and by the happy prospect of his household chores being cut in half.

A witch went by on a broom. Prince Moy Trehano shook his head in disgust. Such an outmoded means of locomotion! It was no wonder humans didn't believe in witches any more. You had to keep up with the times if you expected to stay in the race. Why, if he were as old-fashioned and as antiquated as his contemporaries he might have been stuck with a bachelor for the rest of his life, and a shiftless bachelor—when it came to housework, anyway—at that. Not that Howard King wasn't a fine human being; he was as fine as they came. But you never got your dusting and your sweeping done mooning on the front steps like a sick calf, talking to yourself and waiting for your girl to come home from the city.

When you came right down to it, you *had* to be modern. Why, Marianne wouldn't even have *seen* him, to say nothing of hearing what he'd had to say, if he'd worn his traditional clothing, used his own name and employed his normal means of locomotion. Twentieth-century humans were just as imaginative as eighteenth-century and nineteenth-century humans: they believed in creatures from black lagoons and monsters from 20,000 fathoms and flying saucers and beings from outer space—

But they didn't believe in brownies. . . .

EMILY

AND THE BARDS SUBLIME

EMILY MADE THE ROUNDS of her charges every weekday morning as soon as she arrived at the museum. Officially, she was assistant curator, in charge of the Hall of Poets. In her own mind, however, she was far more than a mere assistant curator: she was a privileged mortal, thrown into happy propinquity to the greatest of the Immortals—*the bards sublime,* in the words of one of their number, *whose distant footsteps echo through the corridors of Time.*

The poets were arranged alphabetically rather than chronologically, and Emily would begin with the pedestals on the left of the hall—the A's—and make her way around the imposing semicircle. That way she was always able to save Alfred, Lord Tennyson till the last, or very nearly the last. Lord Alfred was her favorite.

She had a pleasant good-morning for each of the poets, and each of them responded characteristically; but for Lord Alfred she had a pleasant phrase or two as well, such as, "Isn't it a beautiful day for writing?" or "I do hope the *Idyls* don't give you any more trouble!" Of course she knew that Alfred wasn't really going to do any writing, that the old-fashioned pen and the ream of period paper on the little escritoire beside his chair were there just for show, and that anyway his android talents did not go beyond reciting the poetry which his flesh-and-blood prototype had written centuries ago; but just the same, it did no harm to pretend, especially when his Tennyson tapes responded with something like, "*In the Spring a livelier iris changes on the burnish'd dove; in the Spring a young man's fancy lightly turns to thoughts of love—*" or, "*Queen rose of the rosebud garden of girls, come hither, the dances are done, in gloss of satin and glimmer of pearls, Queen lily and rose in one—*"

When Emily had first taken over the Hall of Poets she had had great expectations. She, like the museum directors who had conceived of the idea, had devoutly believed that poetry was *not* dead, and that once the people found out that they could listen to the magic words rather than having to read them in dusty books, and, moreover, listen to them falling from the lips of an animated life-size model of their creator, neither hell nor high taxes would be able to keep the people away. In this, both she and the museum directors had been out of tune.

The average twenty-first-century citizen remained as immune to Browning-brought-to-life as he had to Browning-preserved-in-books. And as for the dwindling literati, *they* preferred *their* poetic dishes served the old-fashioned way, and in several instances stated publicly that investing animated dummies with the immortal phrases of the Grand Old Masters was a technological crime against the humanities.

But in spite of the empty years, Emily remained faithfully at her desk, and up until the morning when the poetic sky collapsed, she still believed that someday someone would take the right-hand corridor out of the frescoed foyer (instead of the left which led to the Hall of Automobiles, or the one in the middle which led to the Hall of Electrical Appliances) and walk up to her desk and say, "Is Leigh Hunt around? I've always wondered *why* Jenny kissed him and I thought maybe he'd tell me if I asked," or "Is Bill Shakespeare busy right now? I'd like to discuss the melancholy Dane with him." But the years flew by and the only people

EMILY AND THE BARDS SUBLIME

who ever took the right-hand corridor besides Emily herself were the museum officials, the janitor and the night watchman. Consequently, she came to know the bards sublime very well, and to sympathize with them in their ostracism. In a way she was in the same boat as they were. . . .

On the morning when the poetic sky collapsed, Emily made her rounds as usual, unaware of the imminent calamity. Robert Browning had his customary *"Morning's at seven; the hill-side's dew-pearl'd"* in answer to her greeting, and William Cowper said briskly, *"The twentieth year is well-nigh past since first our sky was overcast!"* Edward Fitzgerald responded (somewhat tipsily, Emily thought) with his undeviating *"Before the phantom of False morning died, methought a Voice within the Tavern cried, 'When all the Temple is prepared within, why lags the drowsy Worshipper outside?'"* Emily walked past his pedestal rather brusquely. She'd never seen eye to eye with the museum directors with regard to the inclusion of Edward Fitzgerald in the Hall of Poets. In her mind he had no real claim to immortality. True, he had infiltrated his five translations of Omar with an abundance of original imagery, but that didn't make him a genuine poet. Not in the sense that Milton and Byron were poets. Not in the sense that Tennyson was a poet.

Emily's step quickened at the thought of Lord Alfred, and two undernourished roses bloomed briefly on her thin cheeks. She could hardly wait till she reached his pedestal and heard what he had to say. Unlike the tapes of so many of the other poets, his tapes always came up with something different—possibly because he was one of the newer models, though Emily disliked thinking of her charges as models.

She came at last to the treasured territory and looked up into the youthful face (all of the androids were patterned after the poets as they had looked in their twenties). "Good morning, Lord Alfred," she said.

The sensitive synthetic lips formed a lifelike smile. The

tapes whirred soundlessly. The lips parted, and soft words emerged:

> *"For a breeze of morning moves,*
> *And the planet of Love is on high,*
> *Beginning to faint in the light that she loves*
> *On a bed of daffodil sky—"*

Emily raised one hand to her breast, the words gamboling in the lonely woodland of her mind. She was so enchanted that she couldn't think of any of her usual pleasantries on the exigencies of writing poetry and she stood there silently instead, staring at the figure on the pedestal with a feeling akin to awe. Presently she moved on, murmuring abstracted good-mornings to Whitman, Wilde, Wordsworth, Yeats—

She was surprised to see Mr. Brandon, the curator, waiting at her desk. Mr. Brandon rarely visited the Hall of Poets; he concerned himself almost exclusively with the technological displays and left the management of the bards to his assistant. He was carrying a large book, Emily noticed, and that was another source of surprise: Mr. Brandon wasn't much of a reader.

"Good morning, Miss Meredith," he said. "I have some good news for you."

Immediately Emily thought of Percy Bysshe Shelley. The present model had a tape deficiency and she had mentioned the matter to Mr. Brandon several times, suggesting that he write Androids, Inc. and demand a replacement. Perhaps he had finally done so, perhaps he had received an answer. "Yes, Mr. Brandon?" she said eagerly.

"As you know, Miss Meredith, the Hall of Poets has been somewhat of a letdown to all of us. In my own opinion it was an impractical idea in the first place, but being a mere curator I had nothing to say in the matter. The Board of Directors wanted a roomful of verse-happy androids, so we ended up with a roomful of verse-happy androids. Now, I am happy to say, the members of the board have finally come to their senses. Even they have finally realized that poets, as far as the public is concerned, are dead and that the Hall of Poets—"

"Oh, but I'm sure the public's interest will be awakened soon," Emily interrupted, trying to shore up the trembling sky.

"The Hall of Poets," Mr. Brandon repeated relentlessly, "is a constant and totally unnecessary drain on the museum's financial resources and is pre-empting space desperately needed by our expanding display in the Hall of Automobiles. I'm even happier to say that the Board has finally come to a decision: starting tomorrow morning the Hall of Poets will be discontinued to make room for the Chrome Age period of the Automobile display. It's by far the most important period and—"

"But the poets," Emily interrupted again. "What about the poets?" The sky was falling all around her now, and intermingled with the shards of blue were the tattered fragments of noble words and the debris of once proud phrases.

"Why, we'll put them in storage, of course." Mr. Brandon's lips gave brief tenure to a sympathetic smile. "Then, if the public's interest ever is awakened, all we'll need to do is uncrate them and—"

"But they'll smother! They'll die!"

Mr. Brandon looked at her sternly. "Don't you think you're being a little bit ridiculous, Miss Meredith? How can an android smother? How can an android die?"

Emily knew her face had reddened, but she held her ground. "Their words will be smothered if they can't speak them. Their poetry will die if nobody listens to it."

Mr. Brandon was annoyed. There was a touch of pinkness in his sallow cheeks and his brown eyes had grown dark. "You're being very unrealistic about this, Miss Meredith. I'm very disappointed in you. I thought you'd be delighted to be in charge of a progressive display for a change, instead of a mausoleum filled with dead poets."

"You mean I'm going to be in charge of the Chrome Age period?"

Mr. Brandon mistook her apprehension for awe. Instantly his voice grew warm. "Why, of course," he said. "You didn't think I'd let someone else take over your domain, did you?" He gave a little shudder, as though the very thought of such a consideration was repugnant. In a sense it was: someone else would demand more money. "You can take over your new duties first thing tomorrow, Miss Meredith. We've engaged a moving crew to transfer the cars tonight, and a gang of decorators will be here in the morning to bring the hall up to date. With luck, we'll have everything ready for the public by the day after tomorrow. . . . Are you familiar with the Chrome Age, Miss Meredith?"

"No," Emily said numbly, "I'm not."

"I thought you might not be, so I brought you this." Mr. Brandon handed her the big book he was carrying. *"An Analysis of the Chrome Motif in Twentieth Century Art.* Read it religiously, Miss Meredith. It's the most important book of our century."

The last of the sky had fallen and Emily stood helplessly in the blue rubble. Presently she realized that the heavy object in her hands was *An Analysis of the Chrome Motif in Twentieth Century Art* and that Mr. Brandon had gone. . . .

Somehow she got through the rest of the day, and that night, just before she left, she said farewell to the poets. She was crying when she slipped through the electronic door into the September street and she cried all the way home in the aircab. Her apartment seemed cramped and ugly, the way it had seemed years ago, before the bards sublime had come into her life; and the screen of her video set stared out of the shadows at her like the pale and pitiless eye of a deep-sea monster.

She ate a tasteless supper and went to bed early. She lay in the empty darkness looking through her window at the big sign across the street. The big sign kept winking on and off, imparting a double message. On the first wink it said: TAKE SOMI-TABLETS. On the second: ZZZZZZZZZZZZZZZZZ. She lay there sleepless for a long while. Part of the time she was the Lady of Shalott, robed in snowy white, floating down the river to Camelot, and the rest of the time she was holding her breath again beneath the surface of the swimming hole, desperately hoping that the neighborhood boys, who had caught her swimming bare, would tire of their cruel laughter and their obscene words and go away so that she could crawl out of the cold water and get her clothes. Finally, after she had buried her flaming face for the sixth time, they did go away, and she stumbled, blue and trembling, up the bank, and struggled furiously into the sanctuary of her dacron dress. And then she was running, wildly running, back to the village, and yet, strangely, she wasn't running at all, she was floating instead, lying in the boat and robed in snowy white, floating down the river to Camelot. *A gleaming shape she floated by, dead-pale between the houses high, silent into Camelot.* And the knights and the people came out upon the wharf, the way they always did, and read her name upon the prow, and presently Lancelot appeared—Lancelot or Alfred, for sometimes he was one and sometimes he was the other and lately he had come to be both. "*She has a lovely face,*" Lancelot-Alfred said, and Emily of Shalott heard him clearly even though she was supposed to be dead: "*God in His mercy lend her grace, the lady of Shalott. . . .*"

The moving crew had worked all night and the Hall of Poets was unrecognizable. The poets were gone, and in their places stood glittering representations of twentieth-century art. There was something called a "Firedome 8" where Robert Browning had sat dreaming of E.B.B., and a long, low, sleek object with the improbable name of "Thunderbird" pre-empted the space that Alfred, Lord Tennyson had made sacred.

Mr. Brandon approached her, his eyes no less bright than

the chrome décor he had come to love. "Well, Miss Meredith, what do you think of your new display?"

Emily almost told him. But she held her bitterness back. Getting fired would only estrange her from the poets completely, while, if she continued to work in the museum, she would at least have the assurance that they were near. "It's —it's dazzling," she said.

"You think it's dazzling now, just wait till the interior decorators get through!" Mr. Brandon could barely contain his enthusiasm. "Why, I almost envy you, Miss Meredith. You'll have the most attractive display in the whole museum!"

"Yes, I guess I will," Emily said. She looked bewilderedly around at her new charges. Presently: "Why did they paint them such gaudy colors, Mr. Brandon?" she asked.

The brightness in Mr. Brandon's eyes diminished somewhat. "I see you didn't even open the cover of *An Analysis of the Chrome Motif in Twentieth Century Art*," he said reprovingly. "Even if you'd as much as glanced at the jacket flap you'd know that color design in the American automobile was an inevitable accompaniment to the increase in chrome accouterments. The two factors combined to bring about a new era in automobile art that endured for more than a century."

"They look like Easter eggs," Emily said. "Did people actually *ride* in them?"

Mr. Brandon's eyes had regained their normal hue and his enthusiasm lay at his feet like a punctured balloon. "Why, of course they rode in them! I think you're being deliberately difficult, Miss Meredith, and I don't approve of your attitude at all!" He turned and walked away.

Emily hadn't meant to antagonize him and she wanted to call him back and apologize. But for the life of her she couldn't. The transition from Tennyson to the Thunderbird had embittered her more than she had realized.

She put in a bad morning, helplessly watching the decorators as they went about refurbishing the hall. Gradually, pastel walls acquired a brighter hue, and mullioned windows disappeared behind chrome Venetian blinds. The indirect lighting system was torn out and blazing fluorescents were suspended from the ceiling; the parqueted floor was mercilessly overlaid with synthetic tile. By noon the hall had taken on some of the aspects of an oversized lavatory. All that was lacking, Emily thought cynically, was a row of chrome commodes.

She wondered if the poets were comfortable in their crates, and after lunch she ascended the stairs to the attic storeroom to find out. But she found no crated poets in the big dusty loft; she found nothing that had not been there before—the outoutdated relics that had accumulated through the years. A suspicion tugged at the corner of her mind. Hurriedly she descended the stairs to the museum proper and sought out Mr. Brandon. "Where are the poets?" she demanded when she found him directing the alignment of one of the automobiles.

The guilt on Mr. Brandon's face was as unmistakable as the rust spot on the chrome bumper before which he was standing. "Really, Miss Meredith," he began, "don't you think you're being a little un—"

"Where are they?" Emily repeated.

"We—we put them in the cellar." Mr. Brandon's face was almost as red as the incarnadine fender he had just been sighting along.

"Why?"

"Now, Miss Meredith, you're taking the wrong attitude toward this. You're—"

"Why did you put them in the cellar?"

"I'm afraid there was a slight change in our original plans." Mr. Brandon seemed suddenly absorbed in the design in the synthetic tile at his feet. "In view of the fact that public apathy in poetical matters is probably permanent, and in view of the additional fact that the present redecorating project is more of a drain upon our finances than we anticipated, we—"

"You're going to sell them for scrap!" Emily's face was white. Furious tears coalesced in her eyes, ran down her cheeks. "I hate you!" she cried. "I hate you and I hate the directors. You're like crows. If something glitters you pick it up and hoard it away in your old nest of a museum and throw out all the good things to make room for it. I hate you I hate you I hate you!"

"Please, Miss Meredith, try to be realistic . . ." Mr. Brandon paused when he discovered that he was talking to unoccupied air. Emily was a flurry of footsteps and a prim print dress far down the row of cars. Mr. Brandon shrugged. But the shrug was a physical effort, not at all casual. He kept thinking of the time, years ago, when the thin girl with the big haunted eyes and the shy smile had approached him in the Hall of Electrical Appliances and asked him for a job. And he thought of how shrewd he had been—only "shrewd" didn't seem to be the right word now—in making her assistant curator, which was an empty title that no one else wanted because it rated less than janitor's wages, and in foisting the Hall of Poets on her so that he himself could spend his time in pleasanter surroundings. And he remembered the inexplicable change that had come over her in the ensuing years, how the haunted quality had gradually disappeared from her eyes, how her step had quickened, how bright her smile had become, especially in the morning.

Angrily, Mr. Brandon shrugged again. His shoulders felt as though they were made of lead.

The poets were piled in an unsung corner. Afternoon sunlight eked through a high cellar window and lay palely on their immobile faces. Emily sobbed when she saw them.

It was some time before she found and extricated Alfred. She propped him up on a discarded twentieth-century chair and sat down facing him in another. He regarded her almost questioningly with his android eyes. "'Locksley Hall,'" she said.

> "*Comrades, leave me here a little, while as
> yet 'tis early morn:
> Leave me here, and when you want me,
> sound upon the bugle horn—*"

When he had finished reciting "Locksley Hall," Emily said: "'Morte d'Arthur,'" and when "Morte d'Arthur" was over, she said: "'The Lotus-Eaters.'" And all the while he recited, her mind was divided into two parts. One part was absorbed with the poetry, the other with the dilemma of the poets.

It wasn't until the middle of "Maud" that Emily became aware of the passage of time. With a start she realized that she could no longer see Alfred's face, and, glancing up at the window, she saw that it was gray with twilight. Alarmed, she got to her feet and made her way to the cellar stairs. She found the light switch in the darkness and climbed the stairs to the first floor, leaving Alfred alone with "Maud." The museum was in darkness, except for a night light burning in the foyer.

Emily paused in the dim aura of the light. Apparently no one had seen her descend into the cellar, and Mr. Brandon, assuming that she had gone home, had turned the place over to the night watchman and gone home himself. But where was the night watchman? If she wanted to get out she would have to find him and ask him to open the door. But did she want to get out?

Emily pondered the question. She thought of the poets piled ignominiously in the cellar and she thought of the glittering vehicles usurping the hallowed ground that was rightfully theirs. At the crucial moment her eyes caught the glint of metal coming from a small display beside the door.

It was an ancient firemen's display, showing the fire-fighting equipment in use a century ago. There was a chemical fire extinguisher, a miniature hook and ladder, a coiled canvas hose, an ax . . . It was the light ricocheting from the burnished blade of the ax that had first attracted her attention.

Hardly conscious of what she was doing, she walked over to the display. She picked up the ax, hefted it. She found that she could wield it easily. A mist settled over her mind and her thoughts came to a halt. Carrying the ax, she moved down the corridor that once had led to the Hall of Poets. She found the switch in the darkness and the new fluorescents exploded like elongated novæ, blazed harshly down on twentieth-century man's contribution to art.

The cars stood bumper to bumper in a large circle, as though engaged in a motionless race with each other. Just before Emily was a bechromed affair in gray—an older model than its color-bedaubed companions, but good enough for a starter. Emily approached it purposefully, raised the ax, and aimed for the windshield. And then she paused, struck by a sense of wrongness.

She lowered the ax, stepped forward, and peered into the open window. She looked at the imitation leopard-skin seat covers, the bedialed dashboard, the driving wheel. . . . Suddenly she realized what the wrongness was.

She moved on down the circle. The sense of wrongness grew. The cars varied as to size, color, chrome décor, horsepower and seating capacity, but in one respect they did not vary at all. Every one of them was empty.

Without a driver, a car was as dead as a poet in a cellar.

Abruptly Emily's heart began pounding. The ax slipped from her fingers, fell unnoticed to the floor. She hurried back along the corridor to the foyer. She had just opened the door to the cellar when a shout halted her. She recognized the night watchman's voice and waited impatiently till he came close enough to identify her.

"Why, it's Miss Meredith," he said when he came up to her. "Mr. Brandon didn't say anybody was working overtime tonight."

"Mr. Brandon probably forgot," Emily said, marveling at the ease with which the lie slipped from her lips. Then a thought struck her: why stop at one lie? Even with the aid of the freight elevator, her task wasn't going to be easy. Why indeed! "Mr. Brandon said for you to give me a hand if I needed any help," she said. "And I'm afraid I'm going to need lots of help!"

The night watchman frowned. He considered quoting the union clause appropriate to the situation—the one stipulating that a night watchman should never be expected to engage in activities detrimental to the dignity of his occupation—in other words, to work. But there was a quality about Emily's face that he had never noticed before—a cold determined quality not in the least amenable to labor-union clauses. He sighed. "All right, Miss Meredith," he said.

"Well, what do you think of them?" Emily asked.

Mr. Brandon's consternation was a phenomenon to behold. His eyes bulged slightly and his jaw had dropped a good quarter of an inch. But he managed a reasonably articulate "Anachronistic."

"Oh, that's because of the period clothes," Emily said. "We can buy them modern business suits later on, when the budget permits."

Mr. Brandon stole a look into the driver's seat of the aquamarine Buick beside which he was standing. He made an effort to visualize Ben Jonson in twenty-first-century pastels. To his surprise he found the effort rewarding. His eyes settled back in place and his vocabulary began to come back.

"Maybe you've got something here at that, Miss Meredith," he said. "And I think the Board will be pleased. We didn't really want to scrap the poets, you know; it's just that we couldn't find a practical use for them. But now—"

Emily's heart soared. After all, in a matter of life and death, practicality was a small price to have to pay. . . .

After Mr. Brandon had gone, she made the rounds of her charges. Robert Browning had his usual "*Morning's at seven; the hill-side's dew-pearl'd*" in response to her greeting, though his voice sounded slightly muffled coming from the interior of his 1958 Packard, and William Cowper said briskly from his new upholstered eminence: "*The twentieth year is well-nigh past since first our sky was overcast!*" Edward Fitzgerald gave the impression that he was hurtling along at breakneck speed in his 1960 Chrysler, and Emily frowned severely at his undeviating reference to Khayyám's tavern. She saved Alfred, Lord Tennyson till the last. He looked quite natural behind the wheel of his 1965 Ford, and a casual observer would have assumed that he was so preoccupied with his driving that he saw nothing but the chrome-laden rear end of the car ahead of him. But Emily knew better. She knew that he was really seeing Camelot, and the Island of Shalott, and Lancelot riding with Guinevere over a burgeoning English countryside.

She hated to break into his reverie, but she was sure he wouldn't mind.

"Good morning, Lord Alfred," she said.

The noble head turned and the android eyes met hers. They seemed brighter, for some reason, and his voice, when he spoke, was vibrant and strong:

"The old order changeth, yielding place to new,
And God fulfills Himself in many ways. . . ."

THE DANDELION GIRL

THE GIRL on the hill made Mark think of Edna St. Vincent Millay. Perhaps it was because of the way she was standing there in the afternoon sun, her dandelion-hued hair dancing in the wind; perhaps it was because of the way her old-fashioned white dress was swirling around her long and slender legs. In any event, he got the definite impression that she had somehow stepped out of the past and into the present; and that was odd, because as things turned out, it wasn't the past she had stepped out of, but the future.

He paused some distance behind her, breathing hard from the climb. She had not seen him yet, and he wondered how he could apprise her of his presence without alarming her. While he was trying to make up his mind, he took out his pipe and filled and lighted it, cupping his hands over the bowl and puffing till the tobacco came to glowing life. When he looked at her again, she had turned around and was regarding him curiously.

He walked toward her slowly, keenly aware of the nearness of the sky, enjoying the feel of the wind against his face. He should go hiking more often, he told himself. He had been tramping through woods when he came to the hill, and now the woods lay behind and far below him, burning gently with the first pale fires of fall, and beyond the woods lay the little lake with its complement of cabin and fishing pier. When his wife had been unexpectedly summoned for jury duty, he had been forced to spend alone the two weeks he had saved out of his summer vacation and he had been leading a lonely existence, fishing off the pier by day and reading the cool evenings away before the big fireplace in the raftered living room; and after two days the routine had caught up to him, and he had taken off into the woods without purpose or direction and finally he had come to the hill and had climbed it and seen the girl.

Her eyes were blue, he saw when he came up to her—as blue as the sky that framed her slender silhouette. Her face was oval and young and soft and sweet. It evoked a *déjà vu* so poignant that he had to resist an impulse to reach out and touch her wind-kissed cheek; and even though his hand did not leave his side, he felt his finger tips tingle.

Why, I'm forty-four, he thought wonderingly, *and she's hardly more than twenty. What in heaven's name has come over me?* "Are you enjoying the view?" he asked aloud.

"Oh, yes," she said and turned and swept her arm in an enthusiastic semicircle. "Isn't it simply marvelous!"

He followed her gaze. "Yes," he said, "it is." Below them the woods began again, then spread out over the lowlands in warm September colors, embracing a small hamlet several miles away, finally bowing out before the first outposts of the suburban frontier. In the far distance, haze softened the serrated silhouette of Cove City, lending it the aspect of a sprawling medieval castle, making it less of a reality than a dream. "Are you from the city too?" he asked.

"In a way I am," she said. She smiled at him. "I'm from the Cove City of two hundred and forty years from now."

The smile told him that she didn't really expect him to believe her, but it implied that it would be nice if he would pretend. He smiled back. "That would be A.D. twenty-two hundred and one, wouldn't it?" he said. "I imagine the place has grown enormously by then."

"Oh, it has," she said. "It's part of a megalopolis now and

extends all the way to there." She pointed to the fringe of the forest at their feet. "Two Thousand and Fortieth Street runs straight through that grove of sugar maples," she went on, "and do you see that stand of locusts over there?"

"Yes," he said, "I see them."

"That's where the new plaza is. Its supermarket is so big that it takes half a day to go through it, and you can buy almost anything in it from aspirins to aerocars. And next to the supermarket, where that grove of beeches stands, is a big dress shop just bursting with the latest creations of the leading *couturiers*. I bought this dress I'm wearing there this very morning. Isn't it simply beautiful?"

If it was, it was because she made it so. However, he looked at it politely. It had been cut from a material he was unfamiliar with, a material seemingly compounded of cotton candy, sea foam and snow. There was no limit any more to the syntheses that could be created by the miracle-fiber manufacturers—nor, apparently, to the tall tales that could be created by young girls. "I suppose you traveled here by time machine," he said.

"Yes. My father invented one."

He looked at her closely. He had never seen such a guileless countenance. "And do you come here often?"

"Oh, yes. This is my favorite space-time co-ordinate. I stand here for hours sometimes and look and look and look. Day before yesterday I saw a rabbit, and yesterday a deer, and today, you."

"But how can there be a yesterday," Mark asked, "if you always return to the same point in time?"

"Oh, I see what you mean," she said. "The reason is because the machine is affected by the passage of time the same as anything else, and you have to set it back every twenty-four hours if you want to maintain exactly the same co-ordinate. I never do because I much prefer a different day each time I come back."

"Doesn't your father ever come with you?"

Overhead, a v of geese was drifting lazily by, and she

watched it for some time before she spoke. "My father is an invalid now," she said finally. "He'd like very much to come if he only could. But I tell him all about what I see," she added hurriedly, "and it's almost the same as if he really came. Wouldn't you say it was?"

There was an eagerness about the way she was looking at him that touched his heart. "I'm sure it is," he said; then: "It must be wonderful to own a time machine."

She nodded solemnly. "They're a boon to people who like to stand on pleasant leas. In the twenty-third century there aren't very many pleasant leas left."

He smiled. "There aren't very many of them left in the twentieth. I guess you could say that this one is sort of a collector's item. I'll have to visit it more often."

"Do you live near here?" she asked.

"I'm staying in a cabin about three miles back. I'm supposed to be on vacation, but it's not much of one. My wife was called to jury duty and couldn't come with me, and since I couldn't postpone it, I've ended up being a sort of reluctant Thoreau. My name is Mark Randolph."

"I'm Julie," she said. "Julie Danvers."

The name suited her. The same way the white dress suited her—the way the blue sky suited her, and the hill and the September wind. Probably she lived in the little hamlet in the woods, but it did not really matter. If she wanted to pretend she was from the future, it was all right with him. All that really mattered was the way he had felt when he had first seen her, and the tenderness that came over him every time he gazed upon her gentle face. "What kind of work do you do, Julie?" he asked. "Or are you still in school?"

"I'm studying to be a secretary," she said. She took a half step and made a pretty pirouette and clasped her hands before her. "I shall just love to be a secretary," she went on. "It must be simply marvelous working in a big important office and taking down what important people say. Would you like me to be your secretary, Mr. Randolph?"

"I'd like it very much," he said. "My wife was my secretary once—before the war. That's how we happened to meet." Now, why had he said that? he wondered.

"Was she a good secretary?"

"The very best. I was sorry to lose her; but then when I lost her in one sense, I gained her in another, so I guess you could hardly call that losing her."

"No, I guess you couldn't. Well, I must be getting back now, Mr. Randolph. Dad will be wanting to hear about all the things I saw, and I've got to fix his supper."

"Will you be here tomorrow?"

"Probably. I've been coming here every day. Goodbye now, Mr. Randolph."

"Goodbye, Julie," he said.

He watched her run lightly down the hill and disappear into the grove of sugar maples where, two hundred and forty years hence, Two Thousand and Fortieth Street would be. He smiled. What a charming child, he thought. It must be thrilling to have such an irrepressible sense of wonder, such an enthusiasm for life. He could appreciate the two qualities all the more fully because he had been denied them. At twenty he had been a solemn young man working his way through law school; at twenty-four he had had his own practice, and, small though it had been, it had occupied him completely—well, not quite completely. When he had married Anne, there had been a brief interim during which making a living had lost some of its immediacy. And then, when the war had come along, there had been another interim—a much longer one this time—when making a living had seemed a remote and sometimes even a contemptible pursuit. After his return to civilian life, though, the immediacy had returned with a vengeance, the more so because he now had a son as well as a wife to support, and he had been occupied ever since, except for the four vacation weeks he had recently been allowing himself each year, two of which he spent with Anne and Jeff at a resort of their choosing and two of which he spent with Anne, after Jeff returned to college, in their cabin by the lake. This year, though, he was spending the second two alone. Well, perhaps not quite alone.

His pipe had gone out some time ago, and he had not even noticed. He lighted it again, drawing deeply to thwart the wind, then he descended the hill and started back through the woods toward the cabin. The autumnal equinox had come and the days were appreciably shorter. This one was very nearly done, and the dampness of evening had already begun to pervade the hazy air.

He walked slowly, and the sun had set by the time he reached the lake. It was a small lake, but a deep one, and the trees came down to its edge. The cabin stood some distance back from the shore in a stand of pines, and a winding path connected it with the pier. Behind it a gravel drive led to a dirt road that gave access to the highway. His station wagon stood by the back door, ready to whisk him back to civilization at a moment's notice.

He prepared and ate a simple supper in the kitchen, then went into the living room to read. The generator in the shed hummed on and off, but otherwise the evening was unsullied by the usual sounds the ears of modern man are heir to. Selecting an anthology of American poetry from the well-stocked bookcase by the fireplace, he sat down and thumbed through it to "Afternoon on a Hill." He read the treasured poem three times, and each time he read it he saw her standing there in the sun, her hair dancing in the wind, her dress swirling like gentle snow around her long and lovely legs; and a lump came into his throat, and he could not swallow.

He returned the book to the shelf and went out and stood on the rustic porch and filled and lighted his pipe. He forced himself to think of Anne, and presently her face came into focus—the firm but gentle chin, the warm and compassionate eyes with that odd hint of fear in them that he had never been able to analyze, the still-soft cheeks, the gentle smile—and each attribute was made more compelling by the memory of her vibrant light-brown hair and her tall, lithe gracefulness. As was always the case when he thought of her, he found himself marveling at her agelessness, marveling how she could have continued down through the years as lovely as she had been that long-ago morning when he had looked up, startled, and seen her standing timidly before his desk. It was inconceivable that a mere twenty years later he could be looking forward eagerly to a tryst with an overimaginative girl who was young enough to be his daughter. Well, he wasn't—not really. He had been momentarily swayed—that was all. For a moment his emotional equilibrium had deserted him, and he had staggered. Now his feet were back under him where they belonged, and the world had returned to its sane and sensible orbit.

He tapped out his pipe and went back inside. In his bedroom he undressed and slipped between the sheets and turned out the light. Sleep should have come readily, but it did not; and when it finally did come, it came in fragments interspersed with tantalizing dreams.

"*Day before yesterday I saw a rabbit,*" she had said, "*and yesterday a deer, and today, you.*"

On the second afternoon she was wearing a blue dress, and there was a little blue ribbon to match tied in her dandelion-colored hair. After breasting the hill, he stood for some time, not moving, waiting till the tightness of his throat went away; then he walked over and stood beside her in the wind. But the soft curve of her throat and chin brought the tightness back, and when she turned and said, "Hello, I didn't think you'd come," it was a long while before he was able to answer.

"But I did," he finally said, "and so did you."

"Yes," she said. "I'm glad."

A nearby outcropping of granite formed a bench of sorts, and they sat down on it and looked out over the land. He filled his pipe and lighted it and blew smoke into the wind. "My father smokes a pipe too," she said, "and when he lights it, he cups his hands the same way you do, even when there isn't any wind. You and he are alike in lots of ways."

"Tell me about your father," he said. "Tell me about yourself too."

And she did, saying that she was twenty-one, that her father was a retired Government physicist, that they lived in a small apartment on Two Thousand and Fortieth Street and that she had been keeping house for him ever since her mother had died four years ago. Afterward he told her about himself and Anne and Jeff—about how he intended to take Jeff into partnership with him someday, about Anne's phobia about cameras and how she had refused to have her picture taken on their wedding day and had gone on refusing ever since, about the grand time the three of them had had on the camping trip they'd gone on last summer.

When he had finished, she said, "What a wonderful family life you have. Nineteen-sixty-one must be a marvelous year in which to live!"

"With a time machine at your disposal, you can move here any time you like."

"It's not quite that easy. Even aside from the fact that I wouldn't dream of deserting my father, there's the time police to take into consideration. You see, time travel is limited to the members of Government-sponsored historical expeditions and is out of bounds to the general public."

"You seem to have managed all right."

"That's because my father invented his own machine, and the time police don't know about it."

"But you're still breaking the law."

She nodded. "But only in their eyes, only in the light of their concept of time. My father has his own concept."

It was so pleasant hearing her talk that it did not matter really what she talked about, and he wanted her to ramble on, no matter how farfetched her subject. "Tell me about it," he said.

"First I'll tell you about the official concept. Those who

endorse it say that no one from the future should participate physically in anything that occurred in the past, because his very presence would constitute a paradox, and future events would have to be altered in order for the paradox to be assimilated. Consequently the Department of Time Travel makes sure that only authorized personnel have access to its time machines, and maintains a police force to apprehend the would-be generation-jumpers who yearn for a simpler way of life and who keep disguising themselves as historians so they can return permanently to a different era.

"But according to my father's concept, the book of time has already been written. From a macrocosmic viewpoint, my father says, everything that is going to happen has already happened. Therefore, if a person from the future participates in a past event, he becomes a part of that event —for the simple reason that he was a part of it in the first place—and a paradox cannot possibly arise."

Mark took a deep drag on his pipe. He needed it. "Your father sounds like quite a remarkable person," he said.

"Oh, he is!" Enthusiasm deepened the pinkness of her cheeks, brightened the blueness of her eyes. "You wouldn't believe all the books he's read, Mr. Randolph. Why, our apartment is bursting with them! Hegel and Kant and Hume; Einstein and Newton and Weizsäcker. I've—I've even read some of them myself."

"I gathered as much. As a matter of fact, so have I."

She gazed raptly up into his face. "How wonderful, Mr. Randolph," she said. "I'll bet we've got just scads of mutual interests!"

The conversation that ensued proved conclusively that they did have—though the transcendental aesthetic, Berkeleianism and relativity were rather incongruous subjects for a man and a girl to be discussing on a September hilltop, he reflected presently, even when the man was forty-four and the girl was twenty-one. But happily there were compensations. Their animated discussion of the transcendental aesthetic did more than elicit a priori and a posteriori conclusions—it also elicited microcosmic stars in her eyes; their breakdown of Berkeley did more than point up the inherent weaknesses in the good bishop's theory—it also pointed up the pinkness of her cheeks; and their review of relativity did more than demonstrate that E invariably equals mc^2—it also demonstrated that, far from being an impediment, knowledge is an asset to feminine charm.

The mood of the moment lingered far longer than it had any right to, and it was still with him when he went to bed. This time he didn't even try to think of Anne; he knew it would do no good. Instead he lay there in the darkness and played host to whatever random thoughts came along—and all of them concerned a September hilltop and a girl with dandelion-colored hair.

Day before yesterday I saw a rabbit, and yesterday a deer, and today, you.

Next morning he drove over to the hamlet and checked at the post office to see if he had any mail. There was none. He was not surprised. Jeff disliked writing letters as much as he did, and Anne, at the moment, was probably incommunicado. As for his practice, he had forbidden his secretary to bother him with any but the most urgent of matters.

He debated whether to ask the wizened postmaster if there was a family named Danvers living in the area. He decided not to. To have done so would have been to undermine the elaborate make-believe structure which Julie had built, and even though he did not believe in the structure's validity, he could not find it in his heart to send it toppling.

That afternoon she was wearing a yellow dress the same shade as her hair, and again his throat tightened when he saw her, and again he could not speak. But when the first moment passed and words came, it was all right, and their thoughts flowed together like two effervescent brooks and coursed gaily through the arroyo of the afternoon. This time when they parted, it was she who asked, "Will you be here tomorrow?"—though only because she stole the question from his lips—and the words sang in his ears all the way back through the woods to the cabin and lulled him to sleep after an evening spent with his pipe on the porch.

Next afternoon when he climbed the hill it was empty. At first his disappointment numbed him, and then he thought, *She's late, that's all. She'll probably show up any minute.* And he sat down on the granite bench to wait. But she did not come. The minutes passed—the hours. Shadows crept out of the woods and climbed part way up the hill. The air grew colder. He gave up, finally, and headed miserably back toward the cabin.

The next afternoon she did not show up either. Nor the next. He could neither eat nor sleep. Fishing palled on him. He could no longer read. And all the while he hated himself—hated himself for behaving like a lovesick schoolboy, for reacting just like any other fool in his forties to a pretty face and a pair of pretty legs. Up until a few days ago he had never even so much as looked at another woman, and here in the space of less than a week he had not only looked at one but had fallen in love with her.

Hope was dead in him when he climbed the hill on the fourth day—and then suddenly alive again when he saw her standing in the sun. She was wearing a black dress this time, and he should have guessed the reason for her absence; but he didn't—not till he came up to her and saw the tears start from her eyes and the telltale trembling of her lip. "Julie, what's the matter?"

She clung to him, her shoulders shaking, and pressed her face against his coat. "My father died," she said, and somehow he knew that these were her first tears, that she had sat tearless through the wake and funeral and had not broken down till now.

He put his arms around her gently. He had never kissed her and he did not kiss her now, not really. His lips brushed her forehead and briefly touched her hair—that was all. "I'm sorry, Julie," he said. "I know how much he meant to you."

"He knew he was dying all along," she said. "He must

have known it ever since the Strontium 90 experiment he conducted at the laboratory. But he never told anyone—he never even told me. . . . I don't want to live. Without him there's nothing left to live for—nothing, nothing, nothing!"

He held her tightly. "You'll find something, Julie. Someone. You're young yet. You're still a child, really."

Her head jerked back, and she raised suddenly tearless eyes to his. "I'm not a child! Don't you dare call me a child!"

Startled, he released her and stepped back. He had never seen her angry before. "I didn't mean—" he began.

Her anger was as evanescent as it had been abrupt. "I know you didn't mean to hurt my feelings, Mr. Randolph. But I'm not a child, honest I'm not. Promise me you'll never call me one again."

"All right," he said. "I promise."

"And now I must go," she said. "I have a thousand things to do."

"Will—will you be here tomorrow?"

She looked at him for a long time. A mist, like the aftermath of a summer shower, made her blue eyes glisten. "Time machines run down," she said. "They have parts that need to be replaced—and I don't know how to replace them. Ours—mine may be good for one more trip, but I'm not sure."

"But you'll try to come, won't you?"

She nodded. "Yes, I'll try. And, Mr. Randolph?"

"Yes, Julie?"

"In case I don't make it—and for the record—I love you."

She was gone then, running lightly down the hill, and a moment later she disappeared into the grove of sugar maples. His hands were trembling when he lighted his pipe, and the match burned his fingers. Afterward he could not remember returning to the cabin or fixing supper or going to bed, and yet he must have done all of those things, because he awoke in his own room, and when he went into the kitchen there were supper dishes standing on the drainboard.

He washed the dishes and made coffee. He spent the morning fishing off the pier, keeping his mind blank. He would face reality later. Right now it was enough for him to know that she loved him, that in a few short hours he would see her again. Surely even a run-down time machine should have no trouble transporting her from the hamlet to the hill.

He arrived there early and sat down on the granite bench and waited for her to come out of the woods and climb the slope. He could feel the hammering of his heart and he knew that his hands were trembling. *Day before yesterday I saw a rabbit, and yesterday a deer, and today, you.*

He waited and he waited, but she did not come. She did not come the next day either. When the shadows began to lengthen and the air grow chill, he descended the hill and entered the grove of sugar maples. Presently he found a path and he followed it into the forest proper and through the forest to the hamlet. He stopped at the small post office and checked to see if he had any mail. After the wizened postmaster told him there was none, he lingered for a moment. "Is—is there a family by the name of Danvers living anywhere around here?" he blurted.

The postmaster shook his head. "Never heard of them."

"Has there been a funeral in town recently?"

"Not for nigh onto a year."

After that, although he visited the hill every afternoon till his vacation ran out, he knew in his heart that she would not return, that she was lost to him as utterly as if she had never been. Evenings he haunted the hamlet, hoping desperately that the postmaster had been mistaken; but he saw no sign of Julie, and the description he gave of her to the passers-by evoked only negative responses.

Early in October he returned to the city. He did his best to act toward Anne as though nothing had changed between them; but she seemed to know the minute she saw him that something had changed. And although she asked no questions, she grew quieter and quieter as the weeks went by, and the fear in her eyes that had puzzled him before became more and more pronounced.

He began driving into the country Sunday afternoons and visiting the hilltop. The woods were golden now, and the sky was even bluer than it had been a month ago. For hours he sat on the granite bench, staring at the spot where she had disappeared. *Day before yesterday I saw a rabbit, and yesterday a deer, and today, you.*

Then, on a rainy night in mid-November, he found the suitcase. It was Anne's, and he found it quite by accident. She had gone into town to play bingo, and he had the house to himself; and after spending two hours watching four jaded TV programs, he remembered the jigsaw puzzles he had stored away the previous winter.

Desperate for something—anything at all—to take his mind off Julie, he went up to the attic to get them. The suitcase fell from a shelf while he was rummaging through the various boxes piled beside it, and it sprang open when it struck the floor.

He bent over to pick it up. It was the same suitcase she had brought with her to the little apartment they had rented after their marriage, and he remembered how she had always kept it locked and remembered her telling him laughingly that there were some things a wife had to keep a secret even from her husband. The lock had rusted over the years, and the fall had broken it.

He started to close the lid, paused when he saw the protruding hem of a white dress. The material was vaguely familiar. He had seen material similar to it not very long ago—material that brought to mind cotton candy and sea foam and snow.

He raised the lid and picked up the dress with trembling fingers. He held it by the shoulders and let it unfold itself, and it hung there in the room like gently falling snow. He looked at it for a long time, his throat tight. Then, tenderly, he folded it again and replaced it in the suitcase and closed the lid. He returned the suitcase to its niche under the eaves. *Day before yesterday I saw a rabbit, and yesterday a deer, and today, you.*

Rain thrummed on the roof. The tightness of his throat was so acute now that he thought for a moment that he was going to cry. Slowly he descended the attic stairs. He went down the spiral stairway into the living room. The clock on the mantel said ten-fourteen. In just a few minutes the bingo bus would let her off at the corner, and she would come walking down the street and up the walk to the front door. Anne would . . . Julie would. Julianne?

Was that her full name? Probably. People invariably retained part of their original names when adopting aliases; and having completely altered her last name, she had probably thought it safe to take liberties with her first. She must have done other things, too, in addition to changing her name, to elude the time police. No wonder she had never wanted her picture taken! And how terrified she must have been on that long-ago day when she had stepped timidly into his office to apply for a job! All alone in a strange generation, not knowing for sure whether her father's concept of time was valid, not knowing for sure whether the man who would love her in his forties would feel the same way toward her in his twenties. She had come back all right, just as she had said she would.

Twenty years, he thought wonderingly, *and all the while she must have known that one day I'd climb a September hill and see her standing, young and lovely, in the sun, and fall in love with her all over again. She had to know because the moment was as much a part of her past as it was a part of my future. But why didn't she tell me? Why doesn't she tell me now?*

Suddenly he understood.

He found it hard to breathe, and he went into the hall and donned his raincoat and stepped out into the rain. He walked down the walk in the rain, and the rain pelted his face and ran in drops down his cheeks, and some of the drops were raindrops, and some of them were tears. How could anyone as agelessly beautiful as Anne—as Julie—was be afraid of growing old? Didn't she realize that in his eyes she couldn't grow old—that to him she hadn't aged a day since the moment he had looked up from his desk and seen her standing there in the tiny office and simultaneously fallen in love with her? Couldn't she understand that that was why the girl on the hill had seemed a stranger to him?

He had reached the street and was walking down it toward the corner. He was almost there when the bingo bus pulled up and stopped, and the girl in the white trench coat got out. The tightness of his throat grew knife-sharp, and he could not breathe at all. The dandelion-hued hair was darker now, and the girlish charm was gone; but the gentle loveliness still resided in her gentle face, and the long and slender legs had a grace and symmetry in the pale glow of the November street light that they had never known in the golden radiance of the September sun.

She came forward to meet him, and he saw the familiar fear in her eyes—a fear poignant now beyond enduring because he understood its cause. She blurred before his eyes, and he walked toward her blindly. When he came up to her, his eyes cleared, and he reached out across the years and touched her rain-wet cheek. She knew it was all right then, and the fear went away forever, and they walked home hand in hand in the rain.

THE STARS ARE CALLING,

MR. KEATS

HUBBARD had seen queegy birds before, but this was the first time he had ever seen a lame one.

However, if you discounted its crooked left leg, it didn't differ particularly from the other birds on display. It had the same bright yellow topknot and the same necklace of blue polka dots; it had the same royal-blue beads of eyes and the same pale-green breast; it had the same bizarre curvature of beak and the same outlandish facial expression. It was about six inches long, and it weighed in the neighborhood of one and a quarter ounces.

Hubbard realized that he had paused. The clerk, a high-breasted girl wearing one of the latest translucent dresses, was looking at him questioningly from the other side of the bird counter. He cleared his throat. "What happened to its leg?" he asked.

The girl shrugged. "Got broke during shipment. We marked him down but nobody'll buy him anyway. They want them in tip-top shape."

"I see," Hubbard said. Mentally he reviewed the little he knew about queegy birds: they were native to Queeg, a primitive province of the Venerian Tri-State Republic; they could remember practically anything if it was repeated to them once or twice; they responded to association words;

they were highly adaptable, but they refused to breed anywhere except in their native habitat, so the only way to commercialize them was by shipping them from Venus to Earth; fortunately they were sturdy enough to endure the acceleration and deceleration that shipment involved.

Shipment . . .

"It's been in space then!" Hubbard spoke the words before he thought.

The girl made a malicious *moue,* nodded. "I always said space was for the birds."

Hubbard knew he was supposed to laugh. He even tried to. After all, the girl had no way of knowing that he was an ex-spaceman. On the surface he looked just like any other middle-aged man wandering through a five-and-ten dollar store on a February afternoon. But he couldn't laugh. No matter how hard he tried.

The girl didn't seem to notice. She went on in the same vein: "I wonder why it is that eggheads are the only people who ever travel to the stars."

Because they're the only ones who can stand the loneliness and even they can stand it just so long, Hubbard almost said. Instead, he said, "What do you do with them when nobody wants them?"

"Oh, you mean the birds. Well, first you take a paper bag and pump some natural gas into it—you don't need very much—then you—"

"How much is it?"

"You mean the *lame* one?"

"Yes."

"You *are* a tesseract, aren't you! . . . Six ninety-five—plus seventeen-fifty for the cage."

"I'll take it," Hubbard said.

The cage was awkward to carry and the cover kept sliding off and every time it did the queegy bird gave a loud *cheep!* and the people on the airbus, and afterward on the suburban street, turned and stared, and Hubbard couldn't help feeling like a fool.

He'd had hopes of getting his purchase into the house and up the stairs to his room without his sister getting her eyes on it. He should have known better. Alice got her eyes on everything. "Now what have you gone and thrown your money away on?" she said, coming into the hall just as he closed the front door.

Hubbard turned toward her resignedly. "A queegy bird," he said.

"A *queegy* bird!" The look, which he had long ago classified as "compulsive-aggressive with frustration overtones," settled upon her face, flaring her nostrils, thinning her lips, giving an odd flattening effect to her cheeks. She snatched off the cover, peered into the cage. "Well what do you know," she said. "And a crippled one at that!"

"It isn't a monster," Hubbard said. "It's just a bird. Quite a small one, in fact. It won't take up much room and I'll make sure that it doesn't bother anybody."

Alice gave him a long, cold look. "You'd better!" she said. "I can just imagine what Jack's going to say when I tell him." Abruptly she turned and walked away. "Supper's at six," she said over her shoulder.

He ascended the stairs slowly. He felt tired, defeated. They were right when they said that the longer you lived in space, the more remote your chances became of ever being reaccepted by society. Space was big, and in space you thought big; in space you read big books written by big men. You changed, you grew different . . . and eventually, even your relatives got to hate you.

Though God knew, you tried to be just like everybody else on the surface. You tried to say the same things everybody else said; you tried to do the same things everybody else did. You made it a point never to call anyone a "fish." But there was always the inevitable slip of the tongue, the inevitable unorthodox action, and then the staring hostile faces and finally the inevitable ostracism. You couldn't quote Schweitzer in a society that conceived of God as a rosy-cheeked philanthropist piloting a winged Cadillac. You couldn't admit to liking Wagner in a civilization addicted to cowboy operettas.

You couldn't buy a crippled queegy bird in a world that had forgotten—if indeed it had ever known—the meaning of the phrase "reverence for life."

Twenty-five years, he thought. The best twenty-five years of my life. And all I've got to show for them are a lonely room and a pittance of a pension that won't even let me retain my self-respect.

And yet he didn't regret the years: the slow magnificent drifting of the stars; the indescribable moment when a new planet swam into your ken, grew from a gold or green or azure mote into a sphere that eclipsed the entire cosmos. And the coming in, with the new land rising up in green greeting, singing of splendors both beautiful and terrible, of strange horizons; of civilizations undreamed of by piscine man groping his uninspired way beneath his incalculable tons of atmosphere on the deep sea bottom of Earth.

No, he didn't regret the years, no matter what their price had been. You had to pay high prices for valuable things, and if you were afraid to pay, you went destitute all your life. Spiritually destitute, intellectually destitute.

The nothingness of the body and the all of mind, the pure flow of thought: the unhindered passages through the staid corridors of knowledge, the breathless sojourns in cathedrals built of phrase and word; the rare and shining moments when you glimpsed the star-patterned face of God.

Yes, and those other moments, too, the soul-shattering moments when you glimpsed, in your aloneness, the abysmal deeps of hell. . . .

He shuddered. Slowly he returned to the bottom of the sea, found himself facing the bleak façade of his bedroom door. Reluctantly his fingers closed upon the knob, turned.

Opposite the doorway, a bookcase burst with well-worn books. To the right was the battered article of furniture which he faithfully referred to as his desk but whose drawers held not papers nor pen nor log book, but underwear and socks and shirts and all the other bodily impedimenta that mortal man is heir to. His bed, narrow and hard the way he believed beds should be, stood like a stubborn Spartan by the window, the toes of his other shoes peeping from beneath the hem of the spread.

He set the cage on the desk and removed his hat and coat. The queegy bird, after a blue appraisal of its new surroundings, hopped lopsidedly down from its perch and went to work on one of the cups of *piwi* seeds that had been included with the cage. Hubbard watched for a while—before it occurred to him that it was impolite to watch somebody else eat, even when that somebody was a queegy bird; then he hung his coat and hat in the closet, went down the hall to the bathroom and washed up. By the time he returned, the queegy bird had finished its repast and was regarding itself contemplatively in its mirror.

"I think it's about time for your first lesson," Hubbard said. "Let's see what you can do with Keats: *'Beauty is truth, truth beauty—that is all ye know on Earth, and all ye need to know.'*"

The queegy bird regarded him obliquely with one blue eye. The seconds scampered by. "All right," Hubbard said presently, "let's try again: *'Beauty is truth—'*"

"*'—truth beauty—that is all ye know on Earth, and all ye need to know!'*"

Hubbard's weight settled back on his heels. The words had been uttered almost without intonation and in a rather gravelly voice. Nevertheless, they had been precise and clear, and marked the first time in his life he had ever heard anyone—outside of another spaceman—give utterance to anything that did not directly or indirectly concern a bodily need or function. He touched his cheek a little tremulously. Why, he wondered, hadn't he thought of buying a queegy bird a long time ago?

"I think," he said, "that before we go any farther, we'd better give you a name. Suppose we make it 'Keats,' as long as we started with him. Or, better yet, 'Mr. Keats,' since we've got to establish your sex one way or another. I admit it's a rather arbitrary way of doing so, but I never thought to ask whether you were a boy bird or a girl bird."

"Keats," Mr. Keats said.

"Fine! And now we'll try a line or two from Shelley." (In the background of his mind, Hubbard was aware of a car pulling into the drive, of voices in the downstairs hall; but in his absorption with Mr. Keats, he paid no attention.)

> " 'Tell me, thou Star, whose wings of light
> Speed thee in thy fiery flight,
> In what cavern of the night
> Will thy pinions close now?' "

" 'Tell me, thou Star—' " Mr. Keats began.

"Now I've really had it. A queegy bird reciting poetry!"

Reluctantly, Hubbard turned. His brother-in-law was standing in the doorway. Usually he kept his door closed. Tonight he had forgotten. "Yes," he said, "he recites poetry. Is there a law against it?"

" '—whose wings of light—' " Mr. Keats went on.

Jack shook his head. He was 35, looked 40 and thought 15. "No, there isn't," he said. "But there should be."

" 'Speed thee in thy fiery flight—' "

"I disagree," Hubbard said.

" 'In what cavern of the night—' "

"And there should also be a law against bringing them in human houses."

" 'Will thy pinions close now . . .' "

"Are you trying to tell me that I can't keep him?"

"Not exactly. But I'm telling you to keep him far away from me! They carry germs, you know."

"So do you," Hubbard said. He didn't mean to say it, but he couldn't resist.

Jack's nostrils flared, his lips thinned, his cheeks grew flat. Odd, Hubbard reflected, how twelve years of marriage could make the physical reactions of two people identical. "Just keep it away from me, that's all! And keep it away from the kids, too. I don't want it poisoning their minds with that claptrap talk you're teaching it!"

"I'll keep it away from them, don't worry about that," Hubbard said.

"Want your door closed?"

"Yes."

Abruptly the room trembled from the impact of wood on wood. Mr. Keats nearly jumped through the bars of his cage. Hubbard headed furiously for the hall.

He never reached it. What would be the sense, he asked himself, of giving them the one excuse they needed to evict him? His pension wasn't enough to enable him to live anywhere else—unless he hit Derelict Alley—and his temperament precluded his supplementing it through employment. Sooner or later he'd betray himself to his fellow workers, just as he always did, and be railroaded or ridiculed—it didn't matter which—off the job.

Miserably, he turned away from the door. Mr. Keats had calmed down somewhat, but his pale-green breast still rose and fell at an accelerated rhythm. Hubbard bent over the cage. "I'm sorry, Mr. Keats," he said. "I guess birds can't afford to be different any more than humans can."

He was late for supper. Jack, Alice, and the kids were already at the table when he entered the ration room, and Jack was saying, "I'm getting damned sick of his insolence. After all, if it wasn't for me, where would he be? Derelict Alley, that's where!"

"I'll speak to him," Alice said.

"Now's as good a time as any," Hubbard said, sitting down and opening his vacuumized supper-pak.

Alice gave him the injured look she reserved for such occasions. "Jack was just telling me how rude you were to him. I think you should apologize. After all, this is his house."

Hubbard was trembling inside. Usually he backed down whenever his obligations were thrown in his face. Tonight, somehow, he couldn't. "I'll concede," he said, "that you've given me a room to sleep in and that you feed me, and that I'm unable to pay you enough for either service to permit you to make a profit. But such munificence hardly entitles you to a slice of my soul every time I try to preserve my dignity as a human being."

Alice looked at him blankly for a moment. Then: "No one's asking you for a slice of your soul! Why do you talk that way, Ben?"

"He talks that way because he used to be a spaceman," Jack interrupted. "That's the way they talk in space—to themselves, of course. It keeps them from going crazy—or keeps them from knowing they're already crazy!"

Nancy, who was 8, and Jimmy, who was 11, broke into simultaneous giggles. Hubbard cut a small square of his near-steak. The trembling in him was worse than ever. Then he thought of Mr. Keats, and the trembling went away. He looked coldly around the table. For the first time in years he was not afraid. "If the present gathering is an index to the norm," he said, "perhaps we are crazy. Thank God for that! There may be hope!"

Jack's and Alice's faces were skintight masks. But neither of them said a word. Supper was resumed. Hubbard seldom ate very much. He was rarely hungry.

But tonight he had an excellent appetite.

The next day was Saturday. Usually Hubbard washed Jack's car Saturday morning. Not this Saturday morning. After breakfasting he retired to his room and spent the next three hours with Mr. Keats. Descartes, this time, and Nietzsche, and Hume. Mr. Keats didn't do quite so well with pure prose, though. A phrase or two on any one subject was about the extent of his abilities.

Apparently poetry was his forte.

In the afternoon Hubbard visited the spaceport, as was

his custom, and watched the shuttle-ships come and go. The *Flame* and the *Wanderer;* the *Promise* and the *Song*. The *Promise* was his favorite. He'd surfaced on that one himself —a long time ago, it seemed now, though it wasn't really. Two or three years, maybe—no more than that. . . . Taken up equipment and personnel to the orbiting freighters and brought back Centaurian bauxite and Martian ore and Sirian chrome and all the other elements man needed to perpetuate his complex civilization.

Piloting a shuttle-ship was a sort of prelude to piloting a freighter. It gave you a chance to find out whether you could take that awesome moment when you emerged from the depths and rode free on the star-isled sea of space. If you could take it, and could continue to take it, you were eligible for the big boats and the long runs.

Trouble was, when you grew older, your personal universe shrank, no matter what you did to stop it, and the aloneness of the long runs grew with you; grew to a point where even the corridors of knowledge and the cathedrals built of phrase and word no longer helped, grew till you psychoed out once too many times and were given the plank —consigned forever to the bottom of the sea. If piloting a freighter had been an operation complex enough to occupy your time, instead of a long and lonely vigil in a cockpit filled with self-operating controls and nothing else, or if Interstellar and the other space transportation outfits did not have to operate on so slender a margin of profit that payloads had to be computed down to the last pound, the situation might have been different.

If, Hubbard thought, standing in the snow outside the spaceport fence. If, he thought, watching the ships come in, watching the huge mobile docks trundle over to the pads and fill their ravenous bins with ore and bauxite and magnesium. If, he thought, watching the ships climb up beyond the blue where the freighters orbited on the soundless surface of the sea . . .

When the afternoon shadows lengthened and the daylight

began to dwindle, he debated, as usual, on whether to stop in and see McCaffrey, the port operations chief. As usual, and for the same reason, he decided not to. It was the same reason that made him avoid the company of other ex-spacemen like himself: the nostalgia such meetings evoked was too poignant for him to bear.

He turned away, walked along the fence to the gate, and, when the airbus came in, boarded it and went home.

March came, and winter blended into spring. Rains washed the snow away; gutters churned with muddy water, and lawns took on a naked look. The first robins began to appear.

Hubbard rigged up a perch for Mr. Keats in front of the bedroom window. Mr. Keats would sit there all day, flying back to his cage every now and then for a snack of *piwi* seeds. He liked the mornings best of all, the mornings with the sun breasting the rooftop of the house next door, all bright and golden, and when the brightness struck the window and washed all through the room, he would fly in swift ecstatic figure-eights and loops and spirals, chirping at the top of his voice, returning to his perch and miraculously realighting on one foot: a golden mote, winged and living, a part of the sun itself, a part of the morning; a feathered exclamation point emphasizing each new beauty the day divulged.

Under Hubbard's tutelage, his repertoire grew and grew. The most casual remark was bound to contain at least one association word capable of provoking a reaction, and the resultant quotation would range anywhere from Juvenal to Joyce, from Rousseau to Russell, or from Euripides to Eliot. He had a penchant for the first two lines of "Dover Beach," and often would recite them without any provocation at all.

During this period Hubbard's sister and brother-in-law left him pretty much alone. They did not even remark about his shirking his Saturday-morning car-wash job, nor even so much as mention Mr. Keats. Hubbard wasn't fooled. They were waiting, and he knew it: waiting till he gave them whatever opportunity they were looking for, waiting till he turned his back at the right moment.

He wasn't particularly surprised when he returned from the spaceport one Saturday afternoon and found Mr. Keats huddled forlornly in the corner of his cage, his feathers fluffed up, his blue eyes glazed with fear.

Later, at the supper table, he saw the cat lurking in the shadows of the ration room. But he said nothing. The cat was a psychological weapon: if your landlord permitted you to keep one species of pet, you could hardly object to his keeping a different species. Instead, Hubbard had bought a new lock for his bedroom door and installed it himself. Then he bought a new catch for the window and made sure that whenever he left the room, both means of ingress were securely fastened.

He sat back to wait for their next maneuver.

He didn't have to wait long. This time they didn't have to contrive a means for getting rid of Mr. Keats: one was thrown right in their laps.

Hubbard came down to supper one night and the minute he saw their faces, he knew. Even the kids showed it—not so much in the way they looked at him as in the way they kept looking away from him. The newspaper clipping Jack shoved under his nose was almost an anticlimax:

QUEEGY BIRD FEVER STRIKES FAMILY OF FIVE

Deetville, Mo., March 28, 2043—Dr. Otis Q. Farnham today diagnosed the illness which simultaneously afflicted Mr. and Mrs. Fred Krudlow and their three children as queegy bird fever.

Recently, Mrs. Krudlow purchased a pair of queegy birds at the local five-and-ten dollar store. Several days ago, the entire Krudlow family began complaining of sore throats and aching limbs, and Dr. Farnham was called.

"The fact that queegy bird fever is not a great deal more serious than the common cold should not affect our attitude toward this totally unnecessary disease," Dr. Farnham said, in a prepared statement. "I have long deplored the unsupervised sale of these extraterrestrial bird forms, and I intend, immediately, to recommend to the WMA a thorough examination of all birds being brought in from Venus, all birds now in department and five-and-ten dollar stores, as well as all birds already purchased and living in households throughout the world. They serve no useful purpose, and Earth will be better off without them."

Hubbard's eyes trailed away from the clipping, rested unseeingly on the table. In the back of his mind, Mr. Keats gave a despairing peep.

Jack was beaming. "I told you they carried germs," he said.

"So does Dr. Farnham," Hubbard said.

"Why, what an awful thing to say," Alice said. "What germs could a *doctor* carry?"

"The same germs all pompous and opportunistic people carry—the virii 'publicity-hunger,' 'ill-considered action,' and 'xenophobia,' to name a few. . . . He'll do anything to get out of his provincial rut. He'll exterminate every queegy bird in the system if he has to."

"You're not going to talk your way out of this one," Jack said. "That article says as clear as day that queegy birds are dangerous to have around."

"So are cats and dogs. . . . So are automobiles. If you read about a traffic accident occurring in Deetville, Missouri, would you get rid of your car?"

"You leave my car out of this!" Jack shouted. "And you get that damned bird out of here by tomorrow morning or get out yourself!"

Alice touched his arm. "Jack—"

"Shut up! I've had enough of his highfalutin talk. Just because he was a spaceman once, he thinks he's better than we are. He looks down on us because we stay on Earth." He confronted Hubbard, pointing at him with his finger. "All right, tell me this, then, you're so smart! Just how long do you think there'd *be* spacemen if there wasn't people like us staying here on Earth to consume and use what you bring back from your damned planets? Why, if it wasn't for the consumer there wouldn't be a ship in the whole sky. There wouldn't even be a civilization!"

Hubbard looked at him for a long time. Finally he got up and said the one word he had promised himself he would never say to an Earth-bound mortal—the ultimate epithet, in space argot, whose esoteric meaning was forever lost to the purblind creatures of the deep—

"Fish!" he said, and turned and left the room.

His hands were trembling when he reached the top of the stairs. He waited in the hall till they steadied. It would never do to let Mr. Keats see how upset he was.

He censored the thought. You could carry anthropomorphism too far. No matter how human Mr. Keats might seem to be, he was still nothing but a bird. He could talk, and he had a personality, and he had his likes and his dislikes; but he wasn't human.

Well, then, was Jack human?

Was Alice?

Were the kids?

Well . . . certainly.

Why, then, was Mr. Keats's company preferable to theirs?

Because Alice and Jack and the kids lived in a different world, a world Hubbard had left behind a long time ago and to which he could never return. Mr. Keats didn't belong in that world, either. He was a fellow outcast capable of supplying the one thing human beings needed most: Companionship.

And he weighed only one and one-quarter ounces. . . .

Hubbard had just reached his door and was fitting the new key into the new lock when the thought struck him and washed through him like clear, cold wine. Abruptly his hands began trembling again.

This time he didn't notice.

"Sit down, Hub," McCaffrey said. "Haven't seen you for millennia."

The long walk across the starlit tarmac and the long wait in the crowded anteroom, with the frosted door gleaming coldly in the foreground, had honeycombed his confidence. But McCaffrey was an old friend. If anybody could understand, McCaffrey could. If anybody would help, McCaffrey would.

Hubbard sat down. "I won't waste your time with a lot of irrelevant words, Mac," he said. "I want to go out again."

McCaffrey had a pencil between his fingers. He let the point fall to the desktop and the graphite tip made a brief series of taps on the azure formica. "I guess I don't need to tell you that you're forty-five, that you've already psychoed out more than the critical number of times, and that if you got up there and psychoed out again you'd lose your life and I'd lose my job."

"No, you don't have to tell me," Hubbard said. "You've known me for twenty years, Mac. Do you think I'd ask to go out if I didn't think I had a good chance of making it back?"

McCaffrey raised the pencil, let it fall again. The series of taps hung in the air long after the point had ceased vibrating. "Why do you think you've got a chance?"

"If I don't psycho, I'll tell you afterward. If I do psycho, you tell them I stole the ship. You can fix it easy."

"I can fix everything easy—except my conscience."

"What does it do to your conscience looking across your desk at me now, Mac?"

The pencil fell again. Da—da—da—da—da—da-da-dada-da . . .

"They tell me you own stock in Interstellar, Mac."

Da—da—da—da—da—da-dadadada . . .

"I left part of my soul in Interstellar. That means you own stock in me."

Da—da—da—da—da—da-dadadada . . .

"I know that one or two hundred pounds can spell the difference between profit and loss. I'm not blaming you for that, Mac. And I know that pilots are a dime a dozen. You don't need much technical training to learn how to push buttons. But even so, think of the money Interstellar could save over a period of time if they could use a man for forty years instead of twenty."

"You'd be able to tell right away," McCaffrey said reflectively. "The minute you surfaced."

"That's right. In five minutes I'd know, one way or the other. In half an hour, you'd know."

"There's a run open on the *Promise* . . ." Abruptly McCaffrey made up his mind. "Be here at 0600 tomorrow morning," he said. "On the dot."

Hubbard stood up. He touched his cheek and his finger came away wet. "Thanks, Mac. I'll never forget it."

"You hadn't better, you old buzzard! And you'd better get back here whole or I won't be able to live with myself for the rest of my life!"

"Be seeing you, Mac."

Hubbard let himself out. There was so much to do before 0600. A special box to make, a final talk with Mr. Keats . . .

Lord, it had been so long since he'd risen at dawn. You forgot the watermelon color of the eastern sky, the slow, cool, magnificent influx of light over the land. You forgot all the good things, over the years; you only thought you remembered them. You had to live them again to realize what you'd lost.

It was 0545 when the airbus set him down before the spaceport gate. The gateman was new and didn't know him. At Hubbard's request, he called Mac. Presently he waved Hubbard in. Hubbard started the long walk across the tarmac, trying not to look at the tall spires of the shuttle-ships standing like fairy castles against the citron sky. His space fatigues felt unnatural, after all the years, and he walked awkwardly in his heavy spaceboots. He kept his hands nestled deep in the voluminous pockets of his jacket.

Mac was standing on the edge of the *Promise*'s launching pad. "You'll rendezvous with the *Canaveral* at 0609," he said. That was all he said. There was nothing else to say.

The rungs of the ladder were numbingly cold. They seemed to go on and on forever. No, not quite forever. He stepped, winded, into the lock. He waved to Mac. He closed the outer door, stepped into the cramped control room. He closed the inner door. He sat down on the pilot's seat and strapped himself in. He took the perforated box out of his jacket pocket. He took Mr. Keats out of the box. He checked the tiny acceleration couch, then he put Mr. Keats back in the box, on the couch, and adjusted the small straps about the small bird-body. "The stars are calling, Mr. Keats," he said.

He activated the "all-clear" signal. Presently the tower technician began the countdown. 10 . . . Numbers, Hubbard thought . . . 9 . . . It was like counting the years . . . 8 . . . counting the years backward . . . 7 . . . The lonely, starless years . . . 6 . . . *Tell me, thou Star* . . . 5 . . . *whose wings of light* . . . 4 . . . *Speed thee in thy fiery flight* . . . 3 . . . *In what cavern of the night* . . . 2 . . . *Will thy pinions close now* . . . 1 . . .

And now you knew it in the flattened hugeness of your ponderous body and in the swift upthrusting of the jets; now you knew it in the nausea in your stomach and in the first fingers of fright clawing tentatively in your brain; now you knew it in the darkening of the viewport and in the first stabbing light of the stars.

Abruptly the *Promise* emerged from the depths and floated, bereft of apparent motion, on the surface of the sea of space. In the vast distances the stars shone like brilliant buoys, lighting the way to unimaginable shores.

There was a slight tremor as the artificial gravity unit murmured into life. Hubbard knew normalcy again. Looking through the viewport, he knew fear. Alone, he thought. Alone on the sea of space. He felt his fingers at his collar, tearing at the tightness and the swelling terror. *Alone.* The word was a white lance of pure panic imbedding itself deeper and deeper into his brain. ALONE. Say it, his mind shrieked. Say it! His fingers dropped away from his collar, down to the box on his lap, and fumbled with the tiny straps. *Say it!*

"Alone," he croaked.

"You are not alone," Mr. Keats said, hopping up from the little couch and perching on the rim of the box. "*I* am with you."

And slowly, excruciatingly, the white lance withdrew.

Mr. Keats flew over and perched on a quadrant vane in front of the viewport. He cast one bright blue bead of an eye at the cosmos. He ruffled his feathers. " '*I think, therefore I am,*' " he said. " '*Cogito, ergo sum.*' "

GODDESS IN GRANITE

WHEN HE REACHED the upper ridge of the forearm, Marten stopped to rest. The climb had not winded him but the chin was still miles away, and he wanted to conserve as much of his strength as possible for the final ascent to the face.

He looked back the way he had come—down the slope of the tapered forearm ridge to the mile-wide slab of the hand; down to the granite giantess-fingers protruding like sculptured promontories into the water. He saw his rented inboard bobbing in the blue bay between forefinger and thumb, and, beyond the bay, the shimmering waste of the southern sea.

He shrugged his pack into a more comfortable position and checked the climbing equipment attached to his web belt—his piton pistol in its self-locking holster, his extra clips of piton cartridges, the airtight packet that contained his oxygen tablets, his canteen. Satisfied, he drank sparingly from the canteen and replaced it in its refrigerated case. Then he lit a cigarette and blew smoke at the morning sky.

The sky was a deep, cloudless blue, and Alpha Virginis beat brightly down from the blueness, shedding its warmth and brilliance on the gynecomorphous mountain range known as the Virgin.

She lay upon her back, her blue lakes of eyes gazing

eternally upward. From his vantage point on her forearm, Marten had a good view of the mountains of her breasts. He looked at them contemplatively. They towered perhaps 8,000 feet above the chest-plateau, but, since the plateau itself was a good 10,000 feet above sea level, their true height exceeded 18,000 feet. However, Marten wasn't discouraged. It wasn't the mountains that he wanted.

Presently he dropped his eyes from their snow-capped crests and resumed his trek. The granite ridge rose for a while, then slanted downward, widening gradually into the rounded reaches of the upper arm. He had an excellent view of the Virgin's head now, though he wasn't high enough to see her profile. The 11,000-foot cliff of her cheek was awesome at this range, and her hair was revealed for what it really was—a vast forest spilling riotously down to the lowlands, spreading out around her massive shoulders almost to the sea. It was green now. In autumn it would be brown, then gold; in winter, black.

Centuries of rainfall and wind had not perturbed the graceful contours of the upper arm. It was like walking along a lofty promenade. Marten made good time. Still, it was nearly noon before he reached the shoulder-slope, and he realized that he had badly underestimated the Virgin's vastness.

The elements had been less kind to the shoulder-slope, and he had to go slower, picking his way between shallow gullies, avoiding cracks and crevices. In places the granite gave way to other varieties of igneous rock, but the over-all color of the Virgin's body remained the same—a grayish-white, permeated with pink, startlingly suggestive of the hue of human skin.

Marten found himself thinking of her sculptors, and for the thousandth time he speculated as to why they had sculptured her. In many ways, the problem resembled such Earth enigmas as the Egyptian pyramids, the Sacsahuaman Fortress, and the Baalbek Temple of the Sun. For one thing, it was just as irresolvable, and probably always would be, for the ancient race that had once inhabited Alpha Virginis IX had either died out centuries ago, or had migrated to the stars. In either case, they had left no written records behind them.

Basically, however, the two enigmas were different. When you contemplated the pyramids, the Fortress, and the Temple of the Sun, you did not wonder *why* they had been built —you wondered *how* they had been built. With the Virgin, the opposite held true. She had begun as a natural phenomenon—an enormous geological upheaval—and actually all her sculptors had done, herculean though their labor had undoubtedly been, was to add the finishing touches and install the automatic subterranean pumping system that, for centuries, had supplied her artificial lakes of eyes with water from the sea.

And perhaps therein lay the answer, Marten thought. Perhaps their only motivation had been a desire to improve upon nature. There certainly wasn't any factual basis for the theosophical, sociological and psychological motivations postulated by half a hundred Earth anthropologists (none of whom had ever *really* seen her) in half a hundred technical volumes. Perhaps the answer was as simple as that. . . .

The southern reaches of the shoulder-slope were less eroded than the central and northern reaches, and Marten edged closer and closer to the south rim. He had a splendid view of the Virgin's left side, and he stared, fascinated, at the magnificent purple-shadowed escarpment stretching away to the horizon. Five miles from its juncture with the shoulder-slope it dwindled abruptly to form her waist; three miles farther on it burgeoned out to form her left hip; then, just before it faded into the lavender distances, it blended into the gigantic curve of her thigh.

The shoulder was not particularly steep, yet his chest was tight, his lips dry, when he reached its summit. He decided to rest for a while, and he removed his pack and sat down and propped his back against it. He raised his canteen to his

lips and took a long cool draught. He lit another cigarette.
   From his new eminence he had a much better view of the Virgin's head, and he gazed at it spellbound. The mesa of her face was still hidden from him, of course—except for the lofty tip of her granite nose; but the details of her cheek and chin stood out clearly. Her cheekbone was represented by a rounded spur, and the spur blended almost imperceptibly with the chamfered rim of her cheek. Her proud chin was a cliff in its own right, falling sheerly—much too sheerly, Marten thought—to the graceful ridge of her neck.
   Yet, despite her sculptors' meticulous attention to details, the Virgin, viewed from so close a range, fell far short of the beauty and perfection they had intended. That was because you could see only part of her at a time: her cheek, her hair, her breasts, the distant contour of her thigh. But when you viewed her from the right altitude, the effect was altogether different. Even from a height of ten miles, her beauty was perceptible; at 75,000 feet, it was undeniable. But you had to go higher yet—had to find the exact level, in fact—before you could see her as her sculptors had meant her to be seen.
   To Marten's knowledge, he was the only Earthman who had ever found that level, who had ever seen the Virgin as she really was; seen her emerge into a reality uniquely her own—an unforgettable reality, the equal of which he had never before encountered.
   Perhaps being the only one had had something to do with her effect on him; that, plus the fact that he had been only 20 at the time—20, he thought wonderingly. He was 32 now. Yet the intervening years were no more than a thin curtain, a curtain he had parted a thousand times.
   He parted it again.

After his mother's third marriage he had made up his mind to become a spaceman, and he had quit college and obtained a berth as cabin boy on the starship *Ulysses*. The *Ulysses'* destination was Alpha Virginis IX; the purpose of its voyage was to chart potential ore deposits.

Marten had heard about the Virgin, of course. She was one of the seven hundred wonders of the galaxy. But he had never given her a second thought—till he saw her in the main viewport of the orbiting *Ulysses*. Afterward, he gave her considerable thought and, several days after planetfall, he "borrowed" one of the ship's life-rafts and went exploring. The exploit had netted him a week in the brig upon his return, but he hadn't minded. The Virgin had been worth it.

The altimeter of the life-raft had registered 55,000 feet when he first sighted her, and he approached her at that level. Presently he saw the splendid ridges of her calves and thighs creep by beneath him, the white desert of her stomach, the delicate cwm of her navel. He was above the twin mountains of her breasts, within sight of the mesa of her face, before it occurred to him that, by lifting the raft, he might gain a much better perspective.

He canceled his horizontal momentum and depressed the altitude button. The raft climbed swiftly—60,000 feet . . . 65,000 . . . 70,000. It was like focusing a telescreen—80,000 . . . His heart was pounding now—90,000 . . . The oxygen dial indicated normal pressure, but he could hardly breathe.

100,000, 101,000 . . . Not quite high enough. 102,300 . . . *Thou art beautiful, O my love, as Tirzah, Comely as Jerusalem, Terrible as an army with banners* . . . 103,211 . . . *The joints of thy thighs are like jewels, the work of the hands of a cunning workman* . . . 103,288 . . .

He jammed the altitude button hard, locking the focus. He could not breathe at all now—at least not for the first, ecstatic moment. He had never seen anyone quite like her. It was early spring, and her hair was black; her eyes were a springtime blue. And it seemed to him that the mesa of her face abounded in compassion, that the red rimrock of her mouth was curved in a gentle smile.

She lay there immobile by the sea, a Brobdingnagian beauty come out of the water to bask forever in the sun. The barren lowlands were a summer beach; the glittering ruins of a nearby city were an earring dropped from her ear; and the sea was a summer lake, the life-raft a metallic gull hovering high above the littoral.

And in the transparent belly of the gull sat an infinitesimal man who would never be the same again. . . .

Marten closed the curtain, but it was some time before the after-image of the memory faded away. When it finally did so, he found that he was staring with a rather frightening fixity toward the distant cliff of the Virgin's chin.

Roughly, he estimated its height. Its point, or summit, was on an approximate level with the crest of the cheek. That gave him 11,000 feet. To obtain the distance he had to climb to reach the face-mesa, all he had to do was to deduct the height of the neck-ridge. He figured the neck-ridge at about 8,000 feet; 8,000 from 11,000 gave him 3,000—3,000 feet!

It was impossible. Even with the piton pistol, it was impossible. The pitch was vertical all the way, and from where he sat he couldn't discern the faintest indication of a crack or a ledge on the granite surface.

He could never do it, he told himself. Never. It would be absurd for him even to try. It might cost him his life. And even if he could do it, even if he could climb that polished precipice all the way to the face-mesa, could he get back down again? True, his piton pistol would make the descent relatively easy, but would he have enough strength left? The atmosphere on Alpha Virginis IX thinned rapidly after 10,000 feet, and while oxygen tablets helped, they could keep you going only for a limited period of time. After that—

But the arguments were old ones. He had used them on himself a hundred, a thousand times. . . . He stood up resignedly. He shrugged his pack into place. He took a final look down the nine-mile slope of the arm to the giantess-fingers jutting into the sea, then he turned and started across the tableland of the upper chest toward the beginning of the neck-ridge.

The sun had long since passed its meridian when he came opposite the gentle col between the mountains. A cold wind breathed down the slopes, drifting across the tableland. The wind was sweet, and he knew there must be flowers on the mountains—crocuses, perhaps, or their equivalent, growing high on the snow-soft peaks.

He wondered why he did not want to climb the mountains, why it had to be the mesa. The mountains presented the greater difficulties and therefore the greater challenge. Why, then, did he neglect them for the mesa?

He thought he knew. The beauty of the mountains was shallow, lacked the deeper meaning of the beauty of the mesa. They could never give him what he wanted if he climbed them a thousand times. It was the mesa—with its blue and lovely lakes—or nothing.

He turned his eyes away from the mountains and concentrated on the long slope that led to the neck-ridge. The pitch was gentle but treacherous. He moved slowly. A slip could send him rolling, and there was nothing he could grasp to stop himself. He noticed the shortness of his breath and wondered at it, till he remembered the altitude. But he did not break into his oxygen tablets yet; he would have a much more poignant need for them later.

By the time he reached the ridge, the sun had half completed its afternoon journey. But he wasn't dismayed. He had already given up the idea of assaulting the chin-cliff today. He had been presumptuous in the first place to have imagined himself capable of conquering the Virgin in a single day.

It was going to take at least two.

The ridge was over a mile wide, its curvature barely perceptible. Marten made good time. All the while he advanced he was conscious of the chin-cliff looming higher and higher above him, but he did not look at it; he was afraid to look at it till it loomed so close that it occulted half the sky, and then he had to look at it, had to raise his eyes from the granite swell of the throat and focus them on the appalling wall that now constituted his future.

His future was bleak. It contained no hand- or footholds; no ledges, no cracks, no projections. In a way he was relieved, for if no means existed for him to climb the chin-cliff, then he couldn't climb it. But in another way he was overwhelmingly disappointed. Gaining the face-mesa was more than a mere ambition; it was an obsession, and the physical effort that the task involved, the danger, the obstacles—all were an integral part of the obsession.

He could return the way he had come, down the arm to his inboard and back to the isolated colony; and he could rent a flier from the hard-bitten, taciturn natives just as easily as he had rented the inboard. In less than an hour after takeoff, he could land on the face-mesa.

But he would be cheating, and he knew it. Not cheating the Virgin, but cheating himself.

There was one other way, but he rejected it now for the same reason he had rejected it before. The top of the Virgin's head was an unknown quantity, and, while the trees of her hair might make climbing easier, the distance to be climbed was still over three times the height of the chin-cliff, and the pitch was probably just as precipitous.

No, it was the chin-cliff or nothing. The way things looked now, it was nothing. But he consoled himself with the fact that he had examined only a relatively small section of the cliff. Perhaps the outlying sections would be less forbidding. Perhaps—

He shook his head. Wishful thinking would get him nowhere. It would be time to hope *after* he found a means of ascent, not before. He started along the base of the cliff, then paused. While he had stood there, staring at the stupendous wall, Alpha Virginis had descended unobtrusively into the molten sea. The first star was already visible in the east, and the hue of the Virgin's breasts had transmuted from gold to purple.

Reluctantly, Marten decided to postpone his investigation till tomorrow. The decision proved to be a sensible one. Darkness was upon him before he had his sleeping bag spread out, and with it came the penetrating cold for which the planet was notorious throughout the galaxy.

He set the thermostat on the sleeping bag, then he undressed and crawled into the warm interior. He munched a supper biscuit and allotted himself two swallows of water from his canteen. Suddenly he remembered that he had missed his midday meal—and had not even known the difference.

There was a parallel there somewhere, an element of *déjà vu*. But the connection was so tenuous that he could not pin the other moment down. It would occur to him later, he knew, but such was the nature of the human mind that it would occur seemingly as the result of another chain of associations, and he would not remember the original connection at all.

He lay there, staring at the stars. The dark mass of the Virgin's chin rose up beside him, hiding half the sky. He should have felt forlorn, frightened even. But he did not. He felt safe, secure. For the first time in many years he knew contentment.

There was an unusual constellation almost directly overhead. More than anything else, it made him think of a man astride a horse. The man carried an elongated object on his shoulder, and the object could have been any one of a number of things, depending on the way you looked at the stars that comprised it—a rifle, perhaps, or a staff; maybe even a fishing pole.

To Marten, it looked like a scythe. . . .

He turned on his side, luxuriating in his tiny oasis of warmth. The Virgin's chin was soft with starlight now, and the night slept in soft and silent splendor. . . . That was one of his own lines, he thought drowsily—a part of that fantastic hodgepodge of words and phrases he had put together eleven years ago under the title of *Rise Up, My Love!*

A part of the book that had brought him fame and fortune—and Lelia.

Lelia . . . She seemed so long ago, and in a way she was. And yet, in another way, a strange, poignant way, she was yesterday.

The first time he saw her she was standing in one of those little antique bars so popular then in Old York. Standing there all alone, tall, dark-haired, Junoesque, sipping her midafternoon drink as though women like herself were the most common phenomena in the galaxy.

He had been positive, even before she turned her head, that her eyes were blue, and blue they proved to be; blue with the blueness of mountain lakes in spring, blue with the beauty of a woman waiting to be loved. Boldly, he walked over and stood beside her, knowing it was now or never, and asked if he might buy her a drink.

To his astonishment, she accepted. She did not tell him till later that she had recognized him. He was so naïve at the time that he did not even know that he was a celebrity in Old York, though he should have known. His book certainly had been successful enough.

He had knocked it off the preceding summer—the summer the *Ulysses* returned from Alpha Virginis IX; the summer he quit his berth as cabin boy, forever cured of his ambition to be a spaceman. During the interim consumed by the voyage, his mother had remarried again; and when he found out, he rented a summer cottage in Connecticut as far away from her as he could get. Then, driven by forces beyond his ken, he sat down and began to write.

Rise Up, My Love! had dealt with the stellar odyssey of a young adventurer in search of a substitute for God and with his ultimate discovery of that substitute in a woman. The reviewers shouted "Epic!" and the Freudian psychologists who, after four centuries of adversity, still hadn't given up psychoanalyzing writers shouted "Death-wish!" The diverse appraisals combined happily to stir up interest in the limited literary world and to pave the way for a second printing and then a third. Overnight, Marten had become that most incomprehensible of all literary phenomena —a famous first-novelist.

But he hadn't realized, till now, that his fame involved physical recognition. "I read your book, Mr. Marten," the dark-haired girl standing beside him said. "I didn't like it."

"What's your name?" he asked. Then: "Why?"

"Lelia Vaughn . . . Because your heroine is impossible."

"I don't think she's impossible," Marten said.

"You'll be telling me next that she has a prototype."

"Maybe I will." The bartender served them, and Marten picked up his glass and sipped the cool blueness of his Martian julep. "Why is she impossible?"

"Because she's not a woman," Lelia said. "She's a symbol."

"A symbol of what?"

"I–I don't know. Anyway, she's not human. She's too beautiful, too perfect. She's a criterion, really."

"You look just like her," Marten said.

She dropped her eyes then, and for a while she was silent. Presently: "There's an ancient cliché that bears mentioning at this point," she said: "'I'll bet you tell that to all the girls—' But somehow I don't think you do."

"You're right," Marten said. "I don't." Then: "It's so close in here, can't we go walking somewhere?"

"All right."

Old York was an anachronism kept alive by a handful of literati who doted on the prestige lent by old buildings, old streets and old ways of life. It was a grim, canyonesque grotesquerie compared to its pretty new cousin on Mars; but during the years, parts of it had taken on some of the coloring and some of the atmosphere once associated with the Left Bank of Paris, and if the season was spring and you were falling in love, Old York was a lovely place in which to be.

They walked through the dreaming desuetude of ancient avenues, in the cool shadows of buildings mellowed by the passage of time. They lingered in the wilderness of Central

Park, and the sky was blue with spring, the trees adorned with the pale greenness of nascent leaves. . . . It had been the loveliest of afternoons and, afterward, the loveliest of evenings. The stars had never shone so brightly, nor had the moon ever been so full, the hours so swift, the minutes so sweet. Marten's head had been light, seeing Lelia home, his footsteps unsteady; but it wasn't till later, sitting on his apartment steps, that he had realized how hungry he was, and simultaneously realized that he hadn't eaten a morsel of food since morning. . . .

Deep in the alien night, Marten stirred, awakened. The strange star patterns shocked him for a moment, and then he remembered where he was and what he was going to do. Sleep tiptoed back around him and he turned dreamily in the warmth of his electronic cocoon. Freeing one arm, he reached out till his fingers touched the reassuring surface of the star-kissed cliff. He sighed.

Dawn wore a pink dress and crept across the land like a timid girl. Her sister Morning followed, dressed in blue, the sun a dazzling locket on her breast.

There was a tightness in Marten, a tightness compounded of anticipation and dread. He did not permit himself to think. Methodically he ate his concentrated breakfast, packed his sleeping bag. Then he began a systematic examination of the Virgin's chin.

In the morning light, the cliff did not seem nearly so awesome as it had the night before. But its pitch had not varied, nor had its sheer, smooth surface. Marten was both relieved and chagrined.

Then, near the western edge of the neck-ridge, he found the chimney.

It was a shallow fissure, perhaps twice the breadth of his body, created probably by a recent seismic disturbance. He remembered, suddenly, the other signs of recent seismic activity he had noticed in the colony but had not bothered to inquire about. A dozen or so ruptured dwellings were of little consequence when you were on the verge of resolving a complex that had plagued you for twelve years.

The chimney zigzagged upward as far as he could see, presenting, at least for the first thousand feet, a comparatively easy means of ascent. There were innumerable hand- and footholds, and occasional ledges. The trouble was, he had no way of knowing whether the holds and the ledges—or even the chimney itself—continued all the way to the summit.

He cursed himself for having neglected to bring binoculars. Then he noticed that his hands were trembling, that his heart was tight against his ribs; and he knew, all at once, that he was going to climb the chimney regardless, that nothing could stop him, not even himself—not even the knowledge, had it been available, that the chimney was a dead end.

He drew his piton pistol and inserted one of the dozen clips he carried in his belt. He aimed carefully, squeezed the trigger. The long hours he had spent practicing, while awaiting transportation from the spaceport to the colony, paid off, and the peg, trailing its almost invisible nylon line, imbedded itself in the lofty ledge he had selected for his first belay. The sound of the second charge caromed down and joined the fading sound of the first, and he knew that the steel roots of the peg had been forced deep into the granite, guaranteeing his safety for the initial 500 feet.

He replaced the pistol in its self-locking holster. From now till he reached the ledge, the line would take in its own slack, automatically rewinding itself in the chamber in pace with his ascent.

He began to climb.

His hands were steady now, and his heart had resumed its normal beat. There was a song in him, throbbing soundlessly through his whole being, imbuing him with a strength he had never known before, might never know again. The first 500 feet were almost ridiculously easy. Hand- and footholds were so numerous most of the way that it was like climbing a stone ladder, and in the few places where the projections petered out, the walls were ideally spaced for opposite pressure. When he reached the ledge, he wasn't even breathing hard.

He decided not to rest. Sooner or later the thinness of the atmosphere was going to catch up with him, and the higher he got, while he was still fresh, the better. He stood up boldly and drew and aimed the piton pistol. The new peg soared forth, trailing the new line and dislodging the old, arrowing into the base of another ledge some 200 feet above the one on which he stood. The range of the pistol was 1,000 feet, but the narrowness of the chimney and the awkwardness of his position posed severe limitations.

He resumed his ascent, his confidence increasing with each foot he gained. But he was careful not to look down. The chimney was so far out on the western edge of the neck-ridge that looking down entailed not only the distance he had already climbed, but the 8,000-foot drop from the ridge to the lowlands. He did not think his new confidence quite capable of assimilating the shock of so appalling a height.

The climb to the second ledge was as uneventful as the climb to the first. Again he decided not to rest, and, sinking another peg into a third ledge approximately 250 feet above the second, he resumed climbing. Halfway to the third ledge the first pangs of oxygen starvation manifested themselves in a heaviness in his arms and legs and a shortness of his breath. He slipped an oxygen tablet into his mouth and went on climbing.

The dissolving tablet revived him, and when he reached the third ledge he still did not feel like resting. But he forced himself to sit down on the narrow granite shelf and he lay his head back against the chimney wall and tried to relax. Sunlight smote his eyes, and with a shock he realized that the speed of his ascent had been subjective; actually, hours had passed since he had left the neck-ridge, and Alpha Virginis was already at meridian.

Then he couldn't rest; there was no time. He had to reach the face-mesa before nightfall, else he might never reach it at all. In an instant he was on his feet, piton pistol drawn and aimed.

For a while the climb took on a different character. His confidence never diminished and the soundless song throbbed through him in ever-increasing cadence; but the heaviness of his limbs and the shortness of his breath recurred at more and more frequent periods, lending a dreamlike quality to the adventure, and this quality, in turn, was interspersed by the brief but lucid intervals that began immediately whenever he took an oxygen tablet.

The character of the chimney, however, varied only slightly. It grew wider for a while, but he found that by bracing his back against one wall and his feet against the other, he could inch his way upward with a minimum of effort. Then the chimney narrowed again and he returned to his original mode of ascent.

Inevitably he became bolder. Up to now he had been using three-point suspension, never moving one appendage till he was certain the other three were firmly placed. But as his boldness increased, his caution diminished. He neglected three-point suspension more and more often, finally neglected it altogether. After all, he reassured himself, what difference did it make if he did slip? The piton line would stop him before he fell two feet.

And it would have too—if the particular cartridge he had just discharged had not been defective. In his haste he did not notice that the nylon line was not rewinding itself, and when the chockstone, on which he'd just put his entire weight, gave way beneath his foot, his instinctive terror was tempered by the thought that his fall would be brief.

It was not. It was slow at first, unreal. He knew instantly that something had gone wrong. Nearby, someone was screaming. For a moment he did not recognize his own voice. And then the fall was swift; the chimney walls blurred past his clawing hands, and dislodged rubble rained about his anguished face.

Twenty feet down he struck a projection on one side of the chimney. The impact threw him against the other side, then the ledge that he had left a short while before came up jarringly beneath his feet and he sprawled forward on his stomach, the wind knocked from him, blood running into his eyes from a cut on his forehead.

When his breath returned he moved each of his limbs carefully, testing them for broken bones. Then he inhaled deeply. Afterward he lay there on his stomach for a long time, content with the knowledge that he was alive and not seriously hurt.

Presently he realized that his eyes were closed. Without thinking, he opened them and wiped the blood away. He found himself staring straight down at the forest of the Virgin's hair, 10,000 feet below. He sucked in his breath, tried to sink his fingers into the ungiving granite of the ledge. For a while he was sick, but gradually his sickness left him and his terror faded away.

The forest spread out almost to the sea, flanked by the magnificent precipices of the neck and shoulder, the nine-mile ridge of the arm. The sea was gold and glittering in the midafternoon sunlight, and the lowlands were a green-gold beach.

There was an analogy somewhere. Marten frowned, trying to remember. Hadn't he, a long time ago, crouched on another ledge—or was it a bluff?—looking down upon another beach, a real beach? Looking down at—

Abruptly he remembered, and the memory set his face on fire. He tried to force the unwanted moment back into his subconscious, but it slipped through his mental fingers and came out and stood nakedly in the sun, and he had to confront it whether he wanted to or not, had to live it over again.

After their marriage, he and Lelia had rented the same cottage in Connecticut where *Rise Up, My Love!* was born, and he had settled down to write his second book.

The cottage was a charming affair, perched on a bluff overlooking the sea. Below it, accessible by a flight of winding stairs, was a narrow strip of white sand, protected from the prying eyes of civilization by the wooded arms of a small cove. It was here that Lelia spent her afternoons sunbathing in the nude, while Marten spent those same afternoons feeding empty words and uninspired phrases into the manuscript machine on his study desk.

The new book was going very badly. The spontaneity that had characterized the creation of *Rise Up, My Love!* was no longer with him. Ideas would not come, or, if they did come, he was incapable of coping with them. A part of his mood, he knew, could be ascribed to his marriage. Lelia was everything a bride should be, but there was something she was not, an intangible something that taunted him by night and haunted him by day. . . .

The August afternoon had been hot and humid. There was a breeze coming in over the sea, but while it was strong enough to ruffle the curtains of his study window, it wasn't quite strong enough to struggle through the intervening expanse of stagnant air to the doldrums of the study proper where he sat miserably at his desk.

As he sat there, fingering words and phrases, grappling with ideas, he became aware of the soft sound of the surf on the beach below, and an image of Lelia, lying dark and golden in the sun, intruded repeatedly on his thoughts.

Presently he found himself speculating on the positions she might be lying in. On her side, perhaps . . . or perhaps on her back, the golden sunlight raining down on her thighs, her stomach, her breasts.

There was a faint throbbing in his temples, a new nervousness in the fingers that toyed with the correction pencil on the desktop before him. Lelia lying immobile by the sea, her dark hair spread out around her head and shoulders, her blue eyes staring up into the sky . . .

How would she look from above? Say from the height of the bluff? Would she resemble another woman lying by another sea—a woman who had affected him in some mysterious way and lent him his literary wings?

He wondered, and as he wondered his nervousness grew and the throbbing in his temples thickened and slowed till it matched the rhythmic beat of the surf.

He looked at the clock on the study wall: 2:45. There was very little time. In another half hour she would be coming up to shower. Numbly, he stood up. He walked slowly across the study, stepped into the living room; he walked across the living room and out upon the latticed porch that fronted the green lawn and the brow of the bluff and the sparkling summer sea.

The grass was soft beneath his feet and there was a dreaminess about the afternoon sunlight and the sound of the surf. When he neared the bluff he got down on his hands and knees, feeling like a fool, and crept cautiously forward. Several feet from the brow he lowered himself to his elbows and thighs and crawled the rest of the way. He parted the long grass carefully and looked down to the white strip of beach below.

She was lying directly beneath him—on her back. Her left arm was flung out to the sea and her fingers dangled in the water. Her right knee was drawn upward, a graceful hillock of sun-gold flesh . . . and the smooth expanse of her stomach was golden too, as were the gentle mountains of her breasts. Her neck was a magnificent golden ridge leading to the proud precipice of her chin and the vast golden mesa of her face. The blue lakes of her eyes were closed in peaceful sleep.

Illusion and reality intermingled. Time retreated and space ceased to be. At the crucial moment, the blue eyes opened.

She saw him instantly. There was amazement on her face

at first, then understanding (though she hadn't understood at all). Finally her lips curved in a beckoning smile and she held out her arms to him. "Come down, darling," she called. "Come down and see me!"

The throbbing in his temples drowned out the sound of the surf as he descended the winding stairs to the beach. She was waiting there by the sea, waiting as she had always waited, waiting for him; and suddenly he was a giant striding over the lowlands, his shoulders brushing the sky, the ground shuddering beneath his Brobdingnagian footsteps.

Thou art beautiful, O my love, as Tirzah, Comely as Jerusalem, Terrible as an army with banners . . .

A breeze, born in the purple shadows between the mountains, wafted up to his eyrie, cooling his flushed face and reviving his battered body. Slowly he got to his feet. He looked up at the enigmatic walls of the chimney, wondering if they continued for the thousand-odd feet that still separated him from the summit.

He drew his piton pistol and ejected the defective cartridge; then he took careful aim and squeezed the trigger. When he replaced the pistol he experienced a wave of giddiness and he reached instinctively for the oxygen packet on his belt. Then he fumbled for the packet, frantically feeling every inch of the web surface, and finally he found the tiny rivets that had remained after the packet had been torn away during his fall.

For a while he did not move. He had but one logical course of action and he knew it: climb back down to the neck-ridge, spend the night there and return to the colony in the morning; then arrange for transportation to the spaceport, take the first ship back to Earth and forget about the Virgin.

He nearly laughed aloud. Logic was a fine word and an equally fine concept, but there were many things in heaven and earth that it did not encompass, and the Virgin was one of them.

He started to climb.

In the neighborhood of 2,200 feet, the chimney began to change.

Marten did not notice the change at first. Oxygen starvation had decimated his awareness and he moved in a slow, continuous lethargy, raising one heavy limb and then another, inching his ponderous body from one precarious position to another equally precarious—but slightly closer to his goal. When he finally did notice, he was too weary to be frightened, too numb to be discouraged.

He had just crawled upon the sanctuary of a narrow ledge and had raised his eyes to seek out another ledge at which to point his pistol. The chimney was palely lit by the last rays of the sinking sun and for a moment he thought that the diminishing light was distorting his vision.

For there were no more ledges.

There was no more chimney either, for that matter. It had been growing wider and wider for some time; now it flared abruptly into a concave slope that stretched all the way to the summit. Strictly speaking, there had never been a chimney in the first place. *In toto,* the fissure was far more suggestive of the cross section of a gigantic funnel: the part he had already climbed represented the tube, and the part he had yet to climb represented the mouth.

The mouth, he saw at a glance, was going to be bad. The slope was far too smooth. From where he sat he could not see a single projection, and while that didn't necessarily rule out the possible existence of projections, it did cancel out the likelihood of there being any large enough to enable him to use his piton pistol. He couldn't very well drive a piton if there was nothing for him to drive it into.

He looked down at his hands. They were trembling again. He started to reach for a cigarette, realized suddenly that he hadn't eaten since morning, and got a supper biscuit out of his pack instead. He ate it slowly, forced it down with a mouthful of water. His canteen was nearly empty. He smiled wanly to himself. At last he had a logical reason for climbing to the mesa—to replenish his water supply in the blue lakes.

He reached for a cigarette again and this time he pulled one out and lit it. He blew smoke at the darkening sky. He drew his feet up on the ledge and hugged his knees with his arms and rocked himself gently back and forth. He hummed softly to himself. It was an old, old tune, dating back to his early childhood. Abruptly he remembered where he had heard it and who had sung it to him, and he stood up angrily and flicked his cigarette into the deepening shadows and turned toward the slope.

He resumed his upward journey.

It was a memorable journey. The slope was just as bad as it had looked. It was impossible to ascend it vertically, and he had to traverse, zigzagging back and forth with nothing but finger-thick irregularities to support his weight. But his brief rest and his condensed meal had replenished his strength and at first he experienced no difficulties.

Gradually, however, the increasing thinness of the atmosphere caught up with him again. He moved slower and slower. Sometimes he wondered if he was making any progress at all. He did not dare lean his head back far enough to look upward, for his hand- and footholds were so tenuous that the slightest imbalance could dislodge them. And presently there was the increasing darkness to contend with too.

He regretted not having left his pack on the last ledge. It was an awkward burden and it seemed to grow heavier with each foot he gained. He would have loosened the straps and slipped it from his shoulders—if he had had hands to spare.

Repeatedly, sweat ran down into his eyes. Once he tried to wipe his wet forehead on the granite slope, but he only succeeded in reopening his cut, and the blood joined forces with the sweat and for a while he could not see at all. He began to wonder if the cliff was forever. Finally he managed to wipe his eyes on his sleeve, but still he could not see, for the darkness was complete.

Time blurred, ceased to be. He kept wondering if the stars were out, and when he found a set of hand- and footholds less tenuous than the preceding ones, he leaned his head back carefully and looked upward. But the blood and the sweat ran down into his eyes again and he saw nothing.

He was astonished when his bleeding fingers discovered the ledge. His reconnaissance had been cursory, but even so he had been certain that there were no ledges. But there was this one. Trembling, he inched his weary body higher till at last he found purchase for his elbows, then he swung his right leg onto the granite surface and pulled himself to safety.

It was a wide ledge. He could sense its wideness when he rolled over on his back and let his arms drop to his sides. He lay there quietly, too tired to move. Presently he raised one arm and wiped the blood and sweat from his eyes. The stars *were* out. The sky was patterned with the pulsing beauty of a hundred constellations. Directly above him was the one he had noticed the night before—the rider-with-the-scythe.

Marten sighed. He wanted to lie there on the ledge forever, the starlight soft on his face, the Virgin reassuringly close; lie there in blissful peace, eternally suspended between the past and the future, bereft of time and motion.

But the past would not have it so. Despite his efforts to stop her, Xylla parted its dark curtain and stepped upon the stage. And then the curtain dissolved behind her and the impossible play began.

After the failure of his third novel (the second had sold on the strength of the first and had enjoyed an ephemeral success), Lelia had gone to work for a perfume concern so that he could continue writing. Later on, to free him from the burden of household chores, she had hired a maid.

Xylla was an e.t.—a native of Mizar X. The natives of Mizar X were remarkable for two things: their gigantic bodies and their diminutive minds. Xylla was no exception. She stood over seven feet tall and she had an I.Q. of less than 40.

But for all her height she was well proportioned, even graceful. In fact, if her face had possessed any appeal at all, she could have passed for an attractive woman. But her face was flat, with big, bovine eyes and wide cheekbones. Her mouth was much too full, and its fullness was accentuated by a pendulous lower lip. Her hair, which, by contributing the right dash of color, might have rescued her from drabness, was a listless brown.

Marten took one look at her when Lelia introduced them, said, "How do you do?" and then dismissed her from his mind. If Lelia thought a giantess could do the housework better than he could, it was all right with him.

That winter Lelia was transferred to the West Coast, and rather than suffer the upkeep of two houses they gave up the Connecticut cottage and moved to California. California was as sparsely populated as Old York. The promised land had long since absconded starward, lay scattered throughout a thousand as yet unexploited systems. But there was one good thing about the average man's eternal hankering for green pastures: the pastures he left behind grew lush in his absence; there was plenty of space for the stay-at-homes and the stubborn; and Earth, after four centuries of opportunism, had finally settled down in its new role as the cultural center of the galaxy.

Lavish twenty-third-century villas were scattered all along the California coast. Almost all of them were charming and almost all of them were empty. Lelia chose a pink one, convenient to her work, and settled down into a routine identical, except for a change from the morning to the afternoon shift, to the routine she had left behind; and Marten settled down to write his fourth book.

Or tried to.

He had not been naïve enough to think that a change in scene would snap him out of his literary lethargy. He had known all along that whatever words and combinations thereof that he fed into his manuscript machine had to come from within himself. But he *had* hoped that two failures in a row (the second book was really a failure, despite its short-lived financial success) would goad him to a point where he would not permit a third.

In this he had been wrong. His lethargy not only persisted; it grew worse. He found himself going out less and less often, retiring earlier and earlier to his study and his books. But not to his manuscript machine. He read the great novelists. He read Tolstoy and Flaubert. He read Dostoevski and Stendhal. He read Proust and Cervantes. He read Balzac. And the more he read Balzac, the more his wonder grew, that this small, fat, red-faced man could have been so prolific, while he himself remained as sterile as the white sands on the beach below his study windows.

Around ten o'clock each evening Xylla brought him his brandy in the big snifter glass Lelia had given him on his last birthday, and he would lie back in his lazy-chair before the fireplace (Xylla had built a fire of pine knots earlier in the evening) and sip and dream. Sometimes he would drowse for a moment, and then wake with a start. Finally he would get up, cross the hall to his room and go to bed. (Lelia had begun working overtime shortly after their arrival and seldom got home before one o'clock.)

Xylla's effect upon him was cumulative. At first he was not even conscious of it. One night he would notice the way she walked—lightly, for so ponderous a creature, rhythmically, almost; and the next night, the virginal swell of her huge breasts; and the night after that, the graceful surge of her Amazonian thighs beneath her coarse skirt. The night finally came when, on an impulse, or so he thought at the time, he asked her to sit down and talk for a while.

"If you weesh, sar," she said, and sat down on the hassock at his feet.

He hadn't expected that, and at first he was embarrassed. Gradually, however, as the brandy began its swift infiltration of his bloodstream, he warmed to the moment. He noticed the play of the firelight on her hair, and suddenly he was surprised to find that it was something more than a dull brown after all; there was a hint of redness in it, a quiet, unassuming redness that offset the heaviness of her face.

They talked of various things—the weather mostly, sometimes the sea; a book Xylla had read when she was a little girl (the only book she had ever read); Mizar X. When she spoke of Mizar X, something happened to her voice. It grew soft and childlike, and her eyes, which he had thought dull and uninteresting, became bright and round, and he even detected a trace of blueness in them. The merest trace, of course, but it was a beginning.

He began asking her to stay every night after that, and she was always willing, always took her place dutifully on the hassock at his feet. Even sitting, she loomed above him, but he did not find her size disquieting any more, at least not disquieting in the sense that it had been before. Now her vast presence had a lulling effect upon him, lent him a peace of sorts. He began looking forward more and more to her nightly visits.

Lelia continued to work overtime. Sometimes she did not come in till nearly two. He had been concerned about her at first; he had even reprimanded her for working so hard. Somewhere along the line, though, he had stopped being concerned.

Abruptly he remembered the night Lelia had come home early—the night he had touched Xylla's hand.

He had been wanting to touch it for a long time. Night after night he had seen it lying motionless on her knee and he had marveled again and again at its symmetry and grace, wondered how much bigger than his hand it was, whether it was soft or coarse, warm or cold. Finally the time came when he couldn't control himself any longer, and he bent forward and reached out—and suddenly her giantess fingers were intertwined with his pygmy ones and he felt the warmth of her and knew her nearness. Her lips were very close, her giantess-face, and her eyes were a vivid blue now, a blue-lake blue. And then the coppices of her eyebrows brushed his forehead and the red rimrock of her mouth smothered his and melted into softness and her giantess-arms enfolded him against the twin mountains of her breasts—

Then Lelia, who had paused shocked in the doorway, said, "I'll get my things . . ."

The night was cold, and particles of hoarfrost hovered in the air, catching the light of the stars. Marten shivered, sat up. He looked down into the pale depths below, then he lifted his eyes to the breathless beauty of the twin mountains. Presently he stood up and turned toward the slope, instinctively raising his hands in search of new projections.

His hands brushed air.

He stared. There were no projections. There was no slope. There had never been a ledge, for that matter. Before him lay the mesa of the Virgin's face, pale and poignant in the starlight.

Marten moved across the mesa slowly. All around him the starlight fell like glistening rain. When he came to the rimrock of the mouth, he pressed his lips to the cold, ungiving stone. "Rise up, my love!" he whispered.

But the Virgin remained immobile beneath his feet, as he had known she would, and he went on, past the proud tor of her nose, straining his eyes for the first glimpse of the blue lakes.

He walked numbly, his arms hanging limply at his sides. He hardly knew he walked at all. The lure of the lakes, now that they were so close, was overwhelming. The lovely lakes with their blue beckoning deeps and their promise of eternal delight. No wonder Lelia, and later Xylla, had palled on him. No wonder none of the other mortal women he had slept with had ever been able to give him what he wanted.

No wonder he had come back, after twelve futile years, to his true love.

The Virgin was matchless. There were none like her. None.

He was almost to the cheekbone now, but still no starlit sweep of blue rose up to break the monotony of the mesa. His eyes ached from strain and expectation. His hands trembled uncontrollably.

And then, suddenly, he found himself standing on the lip of a huge, waterless basin. He stared, dumfounded. Then he raised his eyes and saw the distant coppice of an eyebrow outlined against the sky. He followed the line of the eyebrow to where it curved inward and became the barren ridge that once had been the gentle isthmus separating the blue lakes—

Before the water had drained away. Before the subterranean pumping system had ceased to function, probably as a result of the same seismic disturbance that had created the chimney.

He had been too impetuous, too eager to possess his true love. It had never occurred to him that she could have changed, that—

No, he would not believe it! Believing meant that the whole nightmarish ascent of the chin-cliff had been for nothing. Believing meant that his whole life was without purpose.

He lowered his eyes, half expecting, half hoping to see the blue water welling back into the empty socket. But all he saw was the bleak lake bottom—and its residue—

And such a strange residue. Scatterings of gray, sticklike objects, curiously shaped, sometimes joined together. Almost like—like—

Marten shrank back. He wiped his mouth furiously. He turned and began to run.

But he did not run far, not merely because his breath gave out, but because, before he ran any farther, he had to know what he was going to do. Instinctively he had headed for the chin-cliff. But would becoming a heap of broken bones on the neck-ridge be any different, basically, from drowning in one of the lakes?

He paused in the starlight, sank to his knees. Revulsion shook him. How could he have been so naïve, even when he was 20, as to believe that he was the only one? Certainly he was the only Earthman—but the Virgin was an old, old woman, and in her youth she had had many suitors, conquering her by whatever various means they could devise, and symbolically dying in the blue deeps of her eyes.

Their very bones attested to her popularity.

What did you do when you learned that your goddess had feet of clay? What did you do when you discovered that your true love was a whore?

Marten wiped his mouth again. There was one thing that you did *not* do—

You did not sleep with her.

Dawn was a pale promise in the east. The stars had begun to fade. Marten stood on the edge of the chin-cliff, waiting for the day.

He remembered a man who had climbed a mountain centuries ago and buried a chocolate bar on the summit. A ritual of some kind, meaningless to the uninitiated. Standing there on the mesa, Marten buried several items of his own. He buried his boyhood and he buried *Rise Up, My Love!* He buried the villa in California and he buried the cottage in Connecticut. Last of all—with regret, but with finality—he buried his mother.

He waited till the false morning had passed, till the first golden fingers of the sun reached out and touched his tired face. Then he started down.

PROMISED PLANET

THE EUROPEAN PROJECT *was a noble undertaking. It was the result of the efforts of a group of noble men who were acquainted with the tragic histories of countries like Czechoslovakia, Lithuania, Rumania and Poland—countries whose juxtaposition to an aggressive totalitarian nation had robbed them of the right to evolve naturally. The European Project returned that right to them by giving them the stars. A distant planet was set aside for each downtrodden nation, and spaceships blasted off for New Czechoslovakia, New Lithuania, New Rumania and New Poland, bearing land-hungry, God-fearing peasants. And this time the immigrants found still waters and green pastures awaiting them instead of the methane-ridden coal mines which their countrymen had found centuries ago in another promised land.*

There was only one mishap in the entire operation: the spaceship carrying the colonists for New Poland never reached its destination . . .
—RETROSPECT; Vol. 16, *The Earth Years* (Galactic History Files)

The snow was falling softly and through it Reston could see the yellow squares of light that were the windows of the community hall. He could hear the piano accordion picking up the strains of "*O Moja Dziewczyna Myje Nogi.*" "My Girl Is Washing Her Feet," he thought, unconsciously reverting to his half-forgotten native tongue; washing them here on *Nowa Polska* the way she washed them long ago on Earth.

There was warmth in the thought, and Reston turned contentedly away from his study window and walked across the little room to the simple pleasures of his chair and his pipe. Soon, he knew, one of the children would come running across the snow and knock on his door, bearing the choicest viands of the wedding feast—*kielbasa*, perhaps, and *golabki* and *pierogi* and *kiszki*. And after that, much later in the evening, the groom himself would come round with the *wódka*, his bride at his side, and he and Reston would have a drink together in the warm room, the snow white and all-encompassing without, perhaps still falling, and, if not still falling, the stars bright and pulsing in the *Nowa Polska* sky.

It was a good life, hard sometimes, but unfailing in its finer moments. In his old age Reston had everything he wanted, and above all he had the simple things which are all any man wants in the final analysis; and if he occasionally needed to apply a slightly different connotation to a familiar word or two in order to alleviate a recurrent sadness, he harmed no one, and he did himself much good. At sixty, he was a contented if not a happy man.

But contentment had not come to him overnight. It was a product of the years, an indirect result of his acceptance of a way of life which circumstance and society had forced upon him . . .

Abruptly he got up from his chair and walked over to the window again. There was a quality about the moment that he did not want to lose: the reassuring yellow squares of the community-hall windows were part of it, the lilting cadence of the piano accordion, the softly falling snow—

It had been snowing, too, on that night forty years ago when Reston had landed the emigration ship—not snowing softly, but with cold fury, the flakes hard and sharp and coming in on a strong north wind, biting and stinging the faces of the little group of immigrants huddled in the lee of the slowly disintegrating ship, biting and stinging Reston's face, too, though he had hardly noticed. He had been too busy to notice—

Busy rounding up the rest of his passengers, then hurrying the women out of the danger area and setting the men to work unloading the supplies and equipment from the hold, using signs and gestures instead of words because he could not speak their language. As soon as the hold was empty, he directed the rearing of a temporary shelter behind the protective shoulder of a hill; then he climbed to the top of the hill and stood there in the bitter wind and the insanely swirling snow, watching his ship die, wondering what it was going to be like to spend the rest of his life in a foreign colony that consisted entirely of young, newly married couples.

For a moment his bitterness overwhelmed him. Why should *his* ship have been the one to develop reactor trouble in mid-run? Why should the appalling burden of finding a suitable planet for a group of people he had never seen before have fallen upon *his* shoulders? He felt like shaking his fist at God, but he didn't. It would have been a theatrical gesture, devoid of any true meaning. For it is impossible to execrate God without first having accepted Him, and in all his wild young life the only deity that Reston had ever worshiped was the Faster-Than-Light-Drive that made skipping stones of stars.

Presently he turned away and walked back down the hill. He found an empty corner in the makeshift shelter and he spread his blankets for the first lonely night.

In the morning there were improvised services for the single casualty of the forced landing. Then, on leaden feet, the immigrants began their new life.

Hard work kept Reston occupied that first winter. The

original village had been transported from Earth, and it was assembled in a small mountain-encompassed valley. A river running through the valley solved the water problem for the time being, though chopping through its ice was a dreaded morning chore; and an adjacent forest afforded plenty of wood to burn till more suitable fuel could be obtained, though cutting it into cords and dragging the cords into the village on crude sleds was a task that none of the men looked forward to. There was a mild flu epidemic along toward spring, but thanks to the efficiency of the youthful doctor, who of course had been included as part of the basic structure of the new society, everybody pulled through nicely.

After the spring rains the first crops were planted. The soil of *Nowa Polska* turned out to be a rich dark loam, a gratifying circumstance to Reston, who had bled his ship of its last drop of energy in order to find the planet. It was already inhabited, of course—traces of the nomadic pilgrimages of the indigenes were apparent in several parts of the valley. At first Reston had some hope in that direction —until several of the natives walked into the village one morning, smiling hugely with their multiple mouths and pirouetting grotesquely on their multiple legs.

But at least they were friendly and, as it later developed, convenient to have around.

He helped with the planting that first spring. That was when he became aware that he was even less an integral part of the new culture than he had thought. Many times he found himself working alone while the immigrants worked in groups of twos and threes. He could not help thinking that he was being avoided. And several times he caught his fellow workers looking at him with unmistakable disapproval in their eyes. On such occasions he shrugged his shoulders. They could disapprove of him all they wanted to, but like him or not, they were stuck with him.

He loafed the summer away, fishing and hunting in the

idyllic foothills of the mountains, sleeping in the open sometimes, under the stars. Often he lay half the summer night through, thinking—thinking of many things: of the sweet taste of Earth air after a run, of scintillating Earth cities spread out like gigantic pinball machines just waiting to be played, of bright lights and lithe legs, and chilled wine being poured into tall iridescent glasses; but most of all thinking of his neighbors' wives.

In the fall he helped with the harvest. The indigenes' penchant for farm work was still an unknown factor and consequently had not yet been exploited. Again he saw disapproval in the immigrants' eyes. He could not understand it. If he knew the peasant mind at all, these people should have approved of his willingness to work, not disapproved of it. But again he shrugged his shoulders. They could go to hell as far as he was concerned, the whole self-righteous, God-fearing lot of them.

It was a bountiful harvest. To the immigrants, accustomed as they were to the scrawny yields of Old Country soil, it was unbelievable. Reston heard them talking enthusiastically about the fine *kapusta*, the enormous *ziemniaki*, the golden *pszenica*. He could understand most of what they said by then, and he could even make himself understood, though the thick *cz's* and *sz's* still bothered him.

But the language was the least of his troubles in the winter that followed.

After the way the immigrants had acted toward him in the fields, Reston had anticipated a winter of enforced isolation. But it was not so. There was scarcely an evening when he wasn't invited to the Andruliewiczs' or the Pyzykiewiczs' or the Sadowskis' to share a flavorful meal and to join in the discussion of whatever subject happened to be of most concern to the community at the moment—the fodder for the newly domesticated livestock, the shortcomings of the village's only generator, the proposed site for the church. Yet all the while he ate and talked with them he was conscious of an undercurrent of uneasiness, of an unnatural formality of speech. It was as though they could not relax in his presence, could not be themselves.

Gradually, as the winter progressed, he stayed home more and more often, brooding in his wifeless kitchen and retiring early to his wifeless bed, tossing restlessly in the lonely darkness while the wind gamboled round the house and sent the snow spraying against the eaves.

In a way, the babies had been the hardest thing of all to take. They began arriving late that second winter. By spring there was a whole crop of them.

There was one shining hope in Reston's mind, and that hope alone kept his loneliness from turning into bitterness —the hope that his S O S had been intercepted and that a rescue ship was already beamed on the co-ordinates he had scattered to the stars during the taut moments that had preceded planetfall. In a way it was a desperate hope, for if his S O S had *not* been intercepted it would be at least ninety years before the co-ordinates reached the nearest inhabited planet, and ninety years, even when you were twenty-one and believed that with half a chance you could live forever, was an unpleasant reality to contend with.

As the long somber days dragged on, Reston began to read. There was utterly nothing else for him to do. He had finally reached a point where he could no longer stand to visit the burgeoning young families and listen to the lusty squalling of youthful lungs; or endure another pitiful baptism, with the father stumbling through the ritual, embarrassed, humble, a little frightened, splashing water with clumsy hands on the new infant's wizened face.

All of the available books were in Polish, of course, and most of them, as is invariably the case with peasant literature, dealt with religious themes. A good eighty per cent of them were identical copies of the Polish Bible itself, and, finally annoyed by its omnipresence whenever he asked his neighbors for something to read, Reston borrowed a copy and browsed his way through it. He could read Polish easily by then, and he could speak it fluently, with far more clarity and with far more expression than the immigrants could themselves.

He found the Old Testament God naïve. Genesis amused him, and once, to alleviate a dull evening—and to prove to himself that he was still contemptuous of religious credos regardless of his situation—he rewrote it the way he thought the ancient Hebrews might have conceived of it had they possessed a more mature comprehension of the universe. At first he was rather proud of his new version, but after rereading it several times he came to the conclusion that except for the postulates that God had *not* created Earth first and had created a far greater multitude of stars than the ancient Hebrews had given Him credit for, it wasn't particularly original.

After reading the New Testament he felt more at peace than he had for a long time. But his peace was short-lived. Spring devastated it when it came. Meadow flowers were hauntingly beautiful that year and Reston had never seen bluer skies—not even on Earth. When the rains were over and gone he made daily treks into the foothills, taking the Bible with him sometimes, losing himself in intricate green cathedrals, coming sometimes into sudden sight of the high white breasts of the mountains and wondering why he didn't climb them, pass over them into another land and leave this lonely land behind, and all the while knowing, deep in his heart, the reason why he stayed.

It wasn't until early in summer, when he was returning from one of his treks, that he finally saw Helena alone.

There had been a flu epidemic that second winter, too, but it had not been quite as mild as the first one had been. There had been one death.

Helena Kuprewicz was the first *Nowa Polska* widow.

In spite of himself, Reston had thought about her constantly ever since the funeral, and he had wondered frequently about the mores of the new culture as they applied to the interval of time that had to elapse before a bereaved wife could look at another man without becoming a social outcast.

Helena was still wearing black when he came upon her in one of the meadows that flanked the village. But she was very fair, and black became the milk-whiteness of her oval face and matched the lustrous darkness of her hair. Helena was a beautiful woman, and Reston would have looked at her twice under *any* circumstances.

She was gathering greens. She stood up when she saw him approaching. "*Jak sie masz, Pan* Reston," she said shyly.

Her formality disconcerted him, though it shouldn't have. None of the immigrants had ever addressed him by his first name. He smiled at her. He tried to smile warmly, but he knew his smile was cold. It had been so long since he had smiled at a pretty girl. "*Jak sie macie, Pani* Kuprewicz."

They discussed the weather first, and then the crops, and after that there didn't seem to be anything left to discuss, and Reston accompanied her back to the village. He lingered by her doorstep, reluctant to leave. "Helena," he said suddenly, "I would like to see you again."

"Why, of course, *Pan* Reston. You are more than welcome to my house. . . . All spring I waited for you to come, but when you did not I knew that it was because you were not yet prepared, that you were not quite certain of the call."

He looked at her puzzledly. He had never asked a Polish girl for a date before, but he was reasonably sure that they didn't usually respond in quite so formal a manner, or in quite so respectful a tone of voice. "I mean," he explained, "that I would like to see you again because—" he floundered for words—"because I like you, because you are beautiful, because . . ." His voice trailed away when he saw the expression that had come over her face.

Then he stared uncomprehendingly as she turned away and ran into the house. The door slammed and he stood there for a long time, looking dumbly at the mute panels and the little curtained windows.

The enormity of the social crime he had apparently committed bewildered him. Surely no society—not even a society as pious and as God-fearing as the one he was involved in—would expect its widows to remain widows forever. But even granting that such were the case, the expression that had come over Helena's face was still inexplicable. Reston could have understood surprise, or even shock—

But not horror.

He was something besides just an odd number in the peasants' eyes. He was a grotesque misfit, a monster. But why?

He walked home slowly, trying to think, trying, for the first time, to see himself as the immigrants saw him. He passed the church, heard the sporadic hammering of the carpenters as they applied the finishing touches to the interior. He wondered suddenly why they had built it next door to the only heathen in the village.

He brewed coffee in his kitchen and sat down by the window. He could see the foothills, green and lazily rising, with the mountains chaste and white beyond them.

He dropped his eyes from the mountains and stared down at his hands. They were long, slender hands, sensitive from long association with the control consoles of half a hundred complex ships—the hands of a pilot, different, certainly, from the hands of a peasant, just as he was different, but, basically, intrinsically the same.

How *did* they see him?

The answer was easy: they saw him as a pilot. But why should their seeing him as a pilot so affect their attitude toward him that they could never relax in his presence, could never evince toward him the warmth and camaraderie, or even the resentment, which they evinced toward each other? A pilot, after all, was nothing but a human being. It was no credit to Reston that he had delivered them from persecution, no credit to him that *Nowa Polska* had become a reality.

Suddenly he remembered the *Book of Exodus*. He got up,

disbelievingly, and located the copy of the Bible he had borrowed during the winter. With mounting horror, he began to read.

He had crouched wearily on the little ledge. Above him the insurmountable cornice had obfuscated the sky.

He had looked down into the valley and he had seen the remote winking of tiny lights that symbolized his destiny. But they symbolized something more than just his destiny: they symbolized warmth and a security of sorts; they symbolized all there was of humanity on *Nowa Polska*. Crouching there on the ledge, in the mountain cold, he had come to the inevitable realization that no man can live alone, and that his own need for the immigrants was as great as their need for him.

He had begun the descent then, slowly, because of his weariness and because his hands were bloodied and bruised from the frenzy of the climb. It was morning when he reached the meadows, and the sun was shining brightly on the cross above the church.

Abruptly Reston left the window and returned to his chair. There was pain even in remembered conflict.

But the room was warm and pleasant, and his chair deep and comfortable, and gradually the pain left him. Very soon now, he knew, one of the children would come running across the snow bearing viands from the feast, and a knock would sound at his door, and there would come another one of the moments for which he lived, which, added together through the years, had made his surrender to his destiny more bearable.

His surrender had not immediately followed his return to the village. It had come about subtly with the passage of the years. It had been the natural result of certain incidents and crises, of unanticipated moments. He tried to remember the moment when he had first stepped briefly into the niche which circumstance and society preordained for him. Surely it must have been during the fourth winter when the little Andruliewicz girl had died.

It had been a dull wintry day, the sky somber, the frozen earth unsoftened as yet with snow. Reston had followed the little procession up the hill that had been set aside for the cemetery and he had stood with the gray-faced immigrants at the edge of the little grave. The casket was a crude wooden one, and the father stood over it awkwardly with the Bible in his hands, stumbling through the service, trying to say the words clearly and instead uttering them brokenly in his clumsy peasant's voice. Finally Reston could stand it no longer and he walked over the frozen ground to where the stricken man was standing and took the Bible into his own hands. Then he stood up straight against the bleak cold sky, tall and strong, and his voice was as clear as a cold wind, yet as strangely soft as a midsummer's day, and filled with the promise of springs yet to come, and the sure calm knowledge that all winters must pass.

"I am the Resurrection and the Life, saith the Lord: he that believeth in me, though he were dead, yet shall he live: and whosoever liveth and believeth in me shall never die . . ."

The knock finally sounded, and Reston got up from his chair and walked over to the door. Funny the way a simple, God-fearing people would regard a spaceman, he thought. Especially the particular spaceman who had delivered them from persecution and brought them to the Promised Land; who had nonchalantly manipulated a ship three acres long by one acre wide with nothing but his fingers; who had, in the course of Exodus, performed exploits that made Moses' cleaving of the waters of the Red Sea seem like a picayune miracle by comparison; and who had, after the Promised Land had been attained, made many wanderings into the Wilderness to commune with God, sometimes carrying the sacred Book itself.

But that attitude by itself would not have been enough to engender the social pressure that had shaped his way of life without the catalyst that the single casualty of planetfall had provided. Reston could still appreciate the irony in the fact that that single casualty should have involved the most essential pillar in the structure of the new society—the Polish priest himself.

He opened the door and peered out into the snow. Little Piotr Pyzykiewicz was standing on the doorstep, a huge dish in his arms. "Good evening, Father. I've brought you some *kielbasa* and some *golabki* and some *pierogi* and some *kiszki* and—"

Father Reston opened the door wide. Being a priest had its drawbacks, of course—maintaining peace in a monogamous society that refused to stay evenly balanced in the ways of sex, for one, and making certain that his sometimes too greedy flock did not overexploit the simple indigenes, for another. But it had its compensations, too. For, while Reston could never have children of his own, he had many, many children in a different sense of the word, and what harm could there be in an old man's pretending to a virility which circumstance and society had denied him?

"Come in, my *son*," he said.

ROMANCE IN A TWENTY-FIRST-CENTURY USED-CAR LOT

THE CAR-DRESS stood on a pedestal in the Big Jim display window, and a sign beneath it said:

THIS BEAUTIFUL NEW CHEMMY IS GOING GOING GONE FOR ONLY $6499.99! GENEROUS TRADE-IN ALLOWANCE ON YOUR PRESENT CAR-DRESS—HARDTOP HAT THROWN IN FREE!

Arabella didn't mean to slam on her brakes, but she couldn't help herself. She had never seen a car-dress quite so stunning. And for only $6499.99!

It was Monday afternoon and the spring street was filled with homeward-hurrying office workers, the April air with the beeping of horns. The Big Jim establishment stood near the corner next to a large used-car lot with a Cape Cod fence around it. The architecture of the building was American Colonial, but the effect was marred by a huge neon sign projecting from the façade. The sign said:

BERNIE, THE BIG JIM MAN.

The beeping of horns multiplied, and belatedly realizing that she was holding up traffic, Arabella cut in front of an old man wearing a fuchsia Grandrapids and pulled over on the concrete shoulder in front of the display window.

Seen at close range, the car-dress was less dazzling, but still irresistible to the eye. Its sleek turquoise flanks and its sequinned grille gleamed in the slanted rays of the sun. Its tailfinned bustle protruded like the twin wakes of a catamaran. It was a beautiful creation, even by modern manufacturing standards, and a bargain worth taking advantage of. Even so, Arabella would have let it go by if it hadn't been for the hardtop hat.

A dealer—presumably Bernie—wearing an immaculate two-toned Lansing de mille advanced to meet her when she drove in the door. "Can I help you, madam?" he asked, his voice polite, but his eyes, behind his speckless windshield, regarding the car-dress she was wearing with obvious contempt.

Shame painted Arabella's cheeks a bright pink. Maybe she *had* waited too long to turn the dress in for a new one at that. Maybe her mother was right: maybe she *was* too indifferent to her clothes. "The dress in the window," she said. "Do—do you really throw in a hardtop hat with it?"

"We most certainly do. Would you like to try it on?"

"Please."

The dealer turned around and faced a pair of double doors at the rear of the room. "Howard!" he called, and a moment later the doors parted and a young man wearing a denim-blue pickup drove in. "Yes, sir?"

"Take the dress in the window back to the dressing room and get a hardtop hat to match it out of the stockroom." The dealer turned around to Arabella. "He'll show you where to go, madam."

The dressing room was just beyond the double doors and to the right. The young man wheeled in the dress, then went to get the hat. He hesitated after he handed it to her, and an odd look came into his eyes. He started to say something, then changed his mind and drove out of the room.

She closed and locked the door and changed hurriedly.

The upholstery-lining felt deliciously cool against her body. She donned the hardtop hat and surveyed herself in the big three-way mirror. She gasped.

The tailfinned bustle was a little disconcerting at first (the models she was accustomed to did not stick out quite so far behind), but the chrome-sequinned grille and the flush fenders did something for her figure that had never been done for it before. As for the hardtop hat—well, if the evidence hadn't been right there before her eyes, she simply wouldn't have believed that a mere hat, even a hardtop one, could achieve so remarkable a transformation. She was no longer the tired office girl who had driven into the shop a moment ago; now she was Cleopatra . . . Bathsheba . . . Helen of Troy!

She drove self-consciously back to the display room. A look akin to awe crept into the dealer's eyes. "You're not *really* the same person I talked to before, are you?" he asked.

"Yes, I am," Arabella said.

"You know, ever since we got that dress in," the dealer went on, "I've been hoping someone would come along who was worthy of its lines, its beauty, its—its personality." He raised his eyes reverently. "Thank you, Big Jim," he said, "for sending such a person to our door." He lowered his eyes to Arabella's awed countenance. "Like to try it out?"

"Oh, yes!"

"Very well. But just around the block. I'll draw up the papers while you're gone. Not," he added hastily, "that you'll be in any way obligated to take it; but just in case you decide to, we'll be all ready to do business."

"How—how much allowance can you give me on my old dress?"

"Let's see, it's two years old, isn't it? Hmm." The dealer frowned for a moment, then: "Look, I'll tell you what I'll do. You don't look like the type of person who'd wear a dress very hard, so I'll allow you a good, generous one thousand and two dollars. How does that sound?"

"Not—not very good." (Maybe, if she went without eating lunch for a year . . .)

"Don't forget, you're getting the hardtop hat free."

"I know, but—"

"Try it out first, and then we'll talk," the dealer said. He got a dealer's plate out of a nearby cabinet and clamped it onto her rear end. "There, you're all set," he said, opening the door. "I'll get right to work on the papers."

She was so nervous and excited when she pulled into the street that she nearly collided with a young man wearing a white convertible, but she got control of herself quickly, and to demonstrate that she was really a competent driver, first impressions to the contrary, she overtook and passed him. She saw him smile as she went by, and a little song began in her heart and throbbed all through her. Somehow that very morning she'd just known that something wonderful was going to happen to her. A perfectly ordinary day at the office had somewhat dimmed her expectations, but now they shone forth anew.

She had to stop for a red light, and when she did so, the young man drove up beside her. "Hi," he said. "That's a swell dress you're wearing."

"Thank you."

"I know a good drive-in. Like to take in a movie with me tonight?"

"Why, I don't even know you!" Arabella said.

"My name is Harry Fourwheels. Now you know me. But I don't know you."

"Arabella. Arabella Grille . . . But I don't know you very well."

"That can be remedied. Will you go?"

"I—"

"Where do you live?"

"Six-eleven Macadam Place," she said before she thought.

"I'll stop by at eight."

"I—"

At that very moment the light changed, and before she could voice her objection the young man was gone. Eight, she thought wonderingly. Eight o'clock . . .

After that, she simply had to take the dress. There was no other alternative. Having seen her in such a resplendent model, what would he think if she was wearing her old bucket of bolts when he showed up to take her out? She returned to the display room, signed the papers and went home.

Her father stared at her through the windshield of his three-tone Cortez when she drove into the garage and parked at the supper table. "Well," he said, "it's about time you broke down and bought yourself a new dress!"

"I guess *so!*" said her mother, who was partial to station wagons and wore one practically all the time. "I was beginning to think you were never going to wise up to the fact that you're living in the twenty-first century and that in the twenty-first century you've got to be *seen.*"

"I'm—I'm only twenty-seven," Arabella said. "Lots of girls are still single at that age."

"Not if they dress the way they should," her mother said.

"Neither one of you has said whether you liked it yet or not," Arabella said.

"Oh, I like it fine," her father said.

"Ought to catch somebody's eye," said her mother.

"It already has."

"Well!" said her mother.

"At long last!" said her father.

"He's coming for me at eight."

"For heaven's sake, don't tell him you read books," her mother said.

"I won't. I don't, really—not any more."

"And don't mention any of those radical notions you used to have, either," said her father. "About people wearing cars because they're ashamed of the bodies God gave them."

"Now, Dad, you know I haven't said things like that in years. Not since, not since—"

Not since the Christmas office party, she went on to herself, when Mr. Upswept had patted her rear end and had said, when she repulsed him, "Crawl back into your history books, you creep. You don't belong in this century!"

"Not since ever so long ago," she finished lamely.

Harry Fourwheels showed up at eight sharp, and she hurried down the drive to meet him. They drove off side by side, turned into Blacktop Boulevard and left the town behind them. It was a lovely night, with just enough winter lingering in the skirts of spring to paint the gibbous moon a vivid silver and to hone the stars to pulsing brightness.

The drive-in was crowded but they found two places way in the rear, not far from the edge of a small woods. They parked close together, so close their fenders almost touched, and presently she felt Harry's hand touch her chassis and creep tentatively around her waist, just above her tailfinned bustle. She started to draw away, but remembering Mr. Upswept's words, she bit her lip and tried to concentrate on the movie.

The movie concerned a retired vermicelli manufacturer who lived in a boarding garage. He had two ungrateful daughters, and he worshiped the concrete they drove on, and did everything in his power to keep them in luxury. To accomplish this, he had to deny himself all but the barest essentials, and consequently he lived in the poorest section of the garage and dressed in used-car suits so decrepit they belonged in the junkyard. His two daughters, on the other hand, lived in the most luxurious garages available and wore the finest car-clothes on the market. A young engineering student named Rastignac also lived in the boarding garage, and the plot concerned his efforts to invade the upper echelons of modern society and to acquire a fortune in the process. To get himself started, he chiseled enough money from his sister to outfit himself in a new Washington convertible, and contrived an invitation, through a rich cousin, to a dealer's daughter's debut. There he met one of the vermicelli manufacturer's daughters and—

Despite her best efforts, Arabella's attention wandered. Harry Fourwheels' hand had abandoned her waist in favor of her headlights and had begun a tour of inspection. She tried to relax, but she felt her body stiffen instead and heard her tense voice whisper, "Don't, please don't!"

Harry's hand fell away. "After the show, then?"

It was a way out and she grabbed it. "After the show," she said.

"I know a swell spot up in the hills. Okay?"

"Okay," she heard her frightened voice say.

She shuddered and patted her headlights back in place. She tried to watch the rest of the movie, but it wasn't any use. Her mind kept drifting off to the hills and she kept trying to think of some excuse, any excuse, that would extricate her from her predicament. But she couldn't think of a single one, and when the movie ended she followed Harry through the exit and drove beside him down Blacktop Boulevard. When he turned off into a dirt road, she accompanied him resignedly.

Several miles back in the hills, the road paralleled the local nudist reservation. Through the high electric fence, the lights of occasional cottages could be seen twinkling among the trees. There were no nudists abroad, but Arabella shuddered just the same. Once she had felt mildly sympathetic toward them, but since the Mr. Upswept incident, she had been unable even to think of them without a feeling of revulsion. In her opinion Big Jim gave them a much better break than they deserved; but then, she supposed, he probably figured that some of them would repent someday and ask forgiveness for their sins. It was odd, though, that none of them ever did.

Harry Fourwheels made no comment, but she could sense his distaste, and even though she knew that it stemmed from a different source than hers did, she experienced a brief feeling of camaraderie toward him. Maybe he wasn't quite as predatory as his premature passes had led her to think. Maybe, at heart, he was as bewildered as she was by the codes of conduct that regulated their existence—codes that meant one thing in one set of circumstances and the diametrical opposite in another set. Maybe . . .

About a mile past the reservation Harry turned into a narrow road that wound among oaks and maples into a parklike clearing. Diffidently, she accompanied him, and when he parked beneath a big oak, she parked beside him. She regretted it instantly when she felt his hand touch her chassis and begin its relentless journey toward her headlights again. This time her voice was anguished: "Don't!"

"What do you mean, don't!" Harry said, and she felt the hard pressure of his chassis against hers and his fumbling fingers around her headlights. She managed, somehow, to wheel out of his grasp and find the road that led out of the clearing, but a moment later he was abreast of her, edging her toward the ditch. "Please!" she cried, but he paid no attention and moved in even closer. She felt his fender touch hers, and instinctively she shied away. Her right front wheel lost purchase, and she felt her whole chassis toppling. Her hardtop hat fell off, caromed off a rock and into a thicket. Her right front fender crumpled against a tree. Harry's wheels spun furiously and a moment later the darkness devoured the red dots of his headlights.

There was the sound of tree toad and katydid and cricket, and far away the traffic sound of Blacktop Boulevard. There was another sound too—the sound her sobs made as they wrenched free from her throat. Gradually, though, the sound subsided as the pain dulled and the wound began to knit.

It would never knit wholly, though. Arabella knew that. Any more than the Mr. Upswept wound had. She recovered her hardtop hat and eased back onto the road. The hat was dented on top, and a ragged scratch marred its turquoise sheen. A little tear ran down her cheek as she put it on and patted it into place.

But the hat represented only half her problem. There was the crumpled right fender to contend with too. What in the world was she going to do? She didn't dare show up at the office in the morning in such a disheveled state. Someone would be sure to turn her in to Big Jim if she did, and he'd find out how she'd been secretly defying him all these years by owning only one car outfit when he'd made it perfectly clear that he expected everybody to own at least two. Suppose he took her license away and relegated her to the nudist reservation? She didn't think he would for such a minor deviation, but it was a possibility that she had to take into consideration. The mere thought of such a fate surfeited her with shame.

In addition to Big Jim there were her parents to be considered too. What was she going to tell *them*? She could just see them when she came down to breakfast in the morning. She could hear them too. "So you wrecked it already!" her father said. "I've had hundreds of car-dresses in my life," said her mother, "and I never wrecked a single one, and here you go out and get one one minute and smash it up the next!"

Arabella winced. She couldn't possibly go through with it. Some way, somehow, she had to get the dress repaired tonight. But where? Suddenly she remembered a sign she'd noticed in the display window that afternoon—a sign which her preoccupation with the car-dress had crowded out of her awareness: 24-HOUR SERVICE.

She drove back to town as fast as she dared and made a beeline for the Big Jim building. Its windows were square wells of darkness and its street door was closed tight. Her disappointment became a sick emptiness in her stomach. Had she read the sign wrong? She could have sworn that it said 24-HOUR SERVICE.

She drove up to the display window and read it again.

She was right: it did say 24-HOUR SERVICE; but it also said, in smaller, qualifying letters, *After 6 P.M., apply at used-car lot next door.*

The same young man who had taken the dress out of the window drove up to meet her when she turned into the entrance. Howard, his name was, she remembered. He was still wearing the same denim-blue pickup, and the odd look she had noticed in his eyes before came back when he recognized her. She had suspected it was pity; now she knew it was. "My dress," she blurted, when he braked beside her. "It's ruined! Can you fix it, please?"

He nodded. "Sure, I can fix it." He pointed to a garagette at the back of the lot. "You can take it off in there," he said.

She drove hurriedly across the lot. Used car-dresses and -suits lay all about her in the darkness. She glimpsed her old model, and the sight of it made her want to cry. If only she'd held on to it! If only she hadn't let her better judgment be swayed by so tawdry an accouterment as a hardtop hat!

It was cold in the garagette, cold and damp. She slipped out of her dress and hat and shoved them through the doorway to Howard, being careful not to reveal herself. But she needn't have bothered, because he looked the other way when he took them. Probably he was used to dealing with modest females.

She noticed the cold much more now, without her dress, and she huddled in a corner trying to keep warm. Presently she heard someone pounding outside and she went to the single window and peeked out into the lot. Howard was working on her right front fender. She could tell from the way he was going about it that he must have straightened hundreds of them. Except for the sound of his rubber mallet, the night was silent. The street beyond the Cape Cod fence was empty, and save for a lighted window or two, the office buildings across the way were in darkness. Above the building tops, the huge Big Jim sign that pre-empted the public square in the center of town was visible. It was an alternating sign: WHAT'S GOOD ENOUGH FOR BIG JIM IS GOOD

ENOUGH FOR EVERYBODY, it said on the first circuit. IF IT WASN'T FOR BIG JIM, WHERE WOULD EVERYBODY BE? it asked on the second.

Hammer hammer hammer . . . Suddenly she thought of a TV musical—one of a series entitled *Opera Can Be Fun When Brought Up to Date*—she'd listened to once, called *Siegfried Roads,* and she remembered the opening act in which Siegfried had kept importuning a sawed-off mechanic—supposedly his father—named Mime to build him a hot-rod superior to the Fafner model owned by the villain so that he could beat the latter in a forthcoming race at Valhalla. The hammer motif kept sounding forth on the bongo drums while Mime worked desperately on the new hot-rod, and Siegfried kept asking over and over who his real father was. *Hammer hammer hammer* . . .

Howard had finished straightening her fender, and now he was working on her hardtop hat. Someone wearing a citron Providence passed in the street with a swish of tires, and a quality about the sound made her think of the time. She looked at her watch: 11:25. Her mother and father would be delighted when they asked her at breakfast what time she got in and she said, "Oh, around midnight." They were always complaining about her early hours.

Her thoughts came back to Howard. He had finished pounding out the dent in the hardtop hat and now he was touching up the scratch. Next, he touched up the scratches on the fender, and presently he brought both hat and dress back to the garagette and shoved them through the doorway. She slipped into them quickly and drove outside.

His eyes regarded her from behind his windshield. A gentle light seemed to emanate from their blue depths. "How beautiful with wheels," he said.

She stared at him. "What did you say?"

"Nothing, really. I was thinking of a story I read once."

"Oh." She was surprised. Mechanics didn't usually go in for reading—mechanics or anyone else. She was tempted to

tell him she liked to read too, but she thought better of it.
"How much do I owe you?" she asked.
"The dealer will send you a bill. I only work for him."
"All night?"
"Till twelve. I just came on when you saw me this afternoon."
"I—I appreciate your fixing my dress. I—I don't know what I would have done—" She left the sentence unfinished.
The gentle light in his eyes went out. Bleakness took its place. "Which one was it? Harry Fourwheels?"
She fought back her humiliation, forced herself to return his gaze. "Yes. Do—do you know him?"
"Slightly," Howard said, and she got the impression that slightly was enough. His face, in the tinselly radiance of the Big Jim sign, seemed suddenly older, and little lines she hadn't noticed before showed at the corners of his eyes. "What's your name?" he asked abruptly.
She told him. "Arabella," he repeated, "Arabella Grille." And then: "I'm Howard Highways."
They nodded to each other. Arabella looked at her watch. "I have to go now," she said. "Thank you very much, Howard."
"You're welcome," Howard said. "Good night."
"Good night."
She drove home through the quiet streets in the April darkness. Spring tiptoed up behind her and whispered in her ear: *How beautiful with wheels. How beautiful with wheels!* . . .

"Well," her father said over his eggs the following morning, "how was the double feature?"
"Double feature?" Arabella asked, buttering a slice of toast.
"Hah!" her father said. "So it wasn't a double feature!"
"In a way it probably was," said her mother. "Two drive-ins—one with movie and one without."

Arabella suppressed a shudder. Her mother's mind functioned with the directness of a TV commercial. In a way it matched the gaudy station wagons she wore. She had on a red one now, with a bulbous grille and swept-back fins and dark heavy wipers. Again Arabella suppressed a shudder. "I—I had a nice time," she said, "and I didn't do a thing wrong."

"That's news?" said her father.

"Our chaste little twenty-seven—almost twenty-eight—year-old daughter," said her mother. "Pure as the driven snow! I suppose you'll do penance now for having stayed out so late by staying in nights and reading books."

"I told you," Arabella said, "I don't read books any more."

"You might as well read them," her father said.

"I'll bet you told him you never wanted to see him again just because he tried to kiss you," said her mother. "The way you did with all the others."

"I did not!" Arabella was trembling now. "As a matter of fact I'm going out with him again tonight!"

"Well!" said her father.

"Three cheers!" said her mother. "Maybe now you'll start doing right by Big Jim and get married and raise your quota of consumers and share the burden of the economy with the rest of your generation."

"Maybe I will!"

She backed away from the table. She had never lied before and she was angry with herself. But it wasn't until she was driving to work that she remembered that a lie, once made, either had to be lived up to or admitted. And since admitting this one was unthinkable, she would have to live up to it . . . or at least give the impression that she was living up to it. That night she would have to go some place and remain there till at least midnight or her parents would suspect the truth.

The only place she could think of was a drive-in.

She chose a different one from the one Harry Fourwheels

had taken her to. The sun had set by the time she got there and the main feature was just beginning. It was a full-length animated fairy tale and concerned the adventures of a cute little teen-ager named Carbonella who lived with her stepmother and her two ugly stepsisters. She spent most of her time in a corner of the garage, washing and simonizing her stepmother's and stepsisters' car-dresses. They had all sorts of beautiful gowns—Washingtons and Lansings and Flints —while she, little Carbonella, had nothing but clunkers and old junk-heaps to wear. Finally, one day, the Big Jim dealer's son announced that he was going to throw a big whingding at his father's palatial garage. Immediately, the two stepsisters and the stepmother got out their best gowns for Carbonella to wash and simonize. Well, she washed and simonized them, and cried and cried because she didn't have a decent dress to her name and couldn't go to the whingding, and finally the night of the big event arrived and her two stepsisters and her stepmother got all chromed up in their car-gowns and took off gaily for the dealer's garage. Left behind, Carbonella sank to her knees in the car-wash corner and burst into tears. Then, just as it was beginning to look as though Big Jim had deserted her, who should appear but the Fairy Car Mother, resplendent in a shining white Lansing de mille! Quick as scat, she waved her wand, and all of a sudden there was Carbonella, radiant as a new day, garbed in a carnation-pink Grandrapids with hubcaps so bright they almost knocked your eyes out. So Carbonella got to the whingding after all, and wheeled every dance with the dealer's son while her ugly stepsisters and her stepmother did a slow burn along the wall. She was so happy she forgot that the Fairy Car Mother's spell was scheduled to expire at midnight, and if the clock on the dealer's Big Jim sign hadn't begun to dong the magic hour she might have turned back into a car-wash girl right there in the middle of the showroom floor. She zoomed out the door then, and down the ramp, but in her haste to hide herself before the spell ended, she lost one of her wheels.

The dealer's son found it, and next day he made the rounds of all the garages in the Franchise, asking all the women who had attended his whingding to try it on. However, it was so small and dainty that it wouldn't even begin to fit any of their axles no matter how much grease they used. After trying it on the axles of the two ugly stepsisters, the dealer's son was about to give up when he happened to espy Carbonella sitting in the car-wash corner, simonizing a car-dress. Well, he wouldn't have it any other way than for Carbonella to come out of the corner and try the wheel on, and what do you know, there before the horrified stares of the stepsisters and the stepmother, the wheel slid smoothly into place without even a smidgin of grease being necessary! Off Carbonella went with the dealer's son, and they drove happily ever after.

Arabella glanced at her watch: 10:30. Too early to go home yet, unless she wanted to leave herself wide open to another cynical cross-examination. Grimly she settled down in her parking place to watch *Carbonella* again. She wished now that she'd checked to see what picture was playing before driving in. *Carbonella* was classified as adult entertainment, but just the same there were more kids in the drive-in than there were grownups, and she couldn't help feeling self-conscious, parking there in her big car-dress in the midst of so many kiddy-car outfits.

She stuck it out till eleven, then she left. It was her intention to drive around till midnight, and she probably would have done just that if she hadn't decided to drive through town—and hadn't, as a consequence, found herself on the street where the used-car lot was. The sight of the Cape Cod fence evoked pleasant associations, and she instinctively slowed down when she came opposite it. By the time she reached the entrance she was virtually crawling, so when she noticed the pickup-clad figure parked in front of it, it was only natural that she should stop.

"Hi," she said. "What are you doing?"

He drove out to the curb, and when she saw his smile she

was glad she had stopped. "I'm drinking a glass of April," he said.

"How does it taste?"

"Delicious. I've always been partial to April. May comes close, but it's slightly on the tepid side. As for June, July and August, they only whet my thirst for the golden wine of fall."

"Do you always talk in metaphors?"

"Only to very special people," he said. He was quiet for a moment, then: "Why don't you come in and park with me till twelve? Afterward we'll go someplace for a hamburger and a beer."

"All right."

Used car-dresses and -suits still littered the lot, but her old car-dress was gone. She was glad, because the sight of it would only have depressed her, and she wanted the effervescence that was beginning in her breast to continue unchecked. Continue it did. The night was quite warm for April, and it was even possible now and then to see a star or two between the massive winks of the Big Jim sign. Howard talked about himself for a while, telling her how he was going to school days and working nights, but when she asked him what school, he said he'd talked about himself long enough and now it was her turn. So she told him about her job, and about the movies she went to, and the TV programs she watched, and finally she got around to the books she used to read.

They both started talking then, first one and then the other, and the time went by like a robin flying south, and almost before she knew what had happened, there was the twelve-to-eight man driving into the lot, and she and Howard were heading for the Gravel Grille.

"Maybe," he said afterward, when they drove down Macadam Place and paused in front of her garage, "you could stop by tomorrow night and we could drink another glass of April together. That is," he added, "if you have no other plans."

"No," she said. "I have no other plans."

"I'll be waiting for you then," he said, and drove away.

She watched his taillights diminish in the distance and disappear. From somewhere came the sound of singing, and she looked around in the shadows of the street to find its source. But the street was empty except for herself and she realized finally that the singing was the singing of her heart.

She thought the next day would never end, and then, when it finally did end, rain was falling out of an uninspiring sky. She wondered how April would taste in the rain, and presently she discovered—after another stint in a drive-in—that rain had little to do with the taste if the other ingredients were present. The other ingredients *were* present, and she spent another winged night talking with Howard in the used-car lot, watching the stars between the winks of the Big Jim sign, afterward driving with him to the Gravel Grille for hamburgers and beer, and finally saying good night to him in front of her garage.

The other ingredients were present the next night, too, and the next and the next. Sunday she packed a lunch and they drove up into the hills for a picnic. Howard chose the highest one, and they climbed a winding road and parked on the crest under a wind-gaunt elm tree and ate the potato salad she had made, and the sandwiches, passing the coffee thermos back and forth. Afterward they smoked cigarettes in the afternoon wind and talked in lazy sentences.

The hilltop provided a splendid view of a wooded lake fed by a small stream. On the other side of the lake, the fence of a nudist reservation shattered the slanted rays of the sun, and beyond the fence, the figures of nudists could be seen moving about the streets of one of the reservation villages. Owing to the distance, they were hardly more than indistinguishable dots, and at first Arabella was only vaguely aware of them. Gradually, though, they penetrated her consciousness to a degree where they pre-empted all else.

"It must be horrible!" she said suddenly.

"What must be horrible?" Howard wanted to know.

"To live naked in the woods like that. Like—like savages!"

Howard regarded her with eyes as blue—and as deep—as the wooded lake. "You can hardly call them savages," he said presently. "They have machines the same as we do. They maintain schools and libraries. They have trades and professions. True, they can only practice them within the confines of the reservation, but that's hardly more limited than practicing them in a small town or even a city. All in all, I'd say they were civilized."

"But they're naked!"

"Is it so horrible to be naked?"

He had opened his windshield and was leaning quite close to her. Now he reached up and opened her windshield too, and she felt the cool wind against her face. She saw the kiss in his eyes, but she did not draw away, and presently she felt it on her lips. She was glad, then, that she hadn't drawn away, because there was nothing of Mr. Upswept in the kiss, or of Harry Fourwheels; nothing of her father's remarks and her mother's insinuations. After a while she heard a car door open, and then another, and presently she felt herself being drawn out into the sunshine and the April wind, and the wind and the sun were cool and warm against her body, cool and warm and clean, and shame refused to rise in her, even when she felt Howard's carless chest pressing against hers.

It was a long sweet moment and she never wanted it to end. But end it did, as all moments must. "What was that?" Howard said, raising his head.

She had heard the sound too—the whirring sound of wheels—and her eyes followed his down the hillside and caught the gleaming tailgate of a white convertible just before it disappeared around a bend in the road. "Do—do you think they saw us?" she asked.

Howard hesitated perceptibly before he answered. "No, I don't think so. Probably someone out for a Sunday drive. If they'd climbed the hill we would have heard the motor."

"Not—not if there was a silencer on it," Arabella said. She slipped back into her car-dress. "I—I think we'd better go."

"All right." He started to slip back into his pickup, paused. "Will—will you come here with me next Sunday?" he asked.

His eyes were earnest, imploring. "Yes," she heard her voice say, "I'll come with you."

It was even lovelier than the first Sunday had been—warmer, brighter, bluer of sky. Again Howard drew her out of her dress and held her close and kissed her, and again she felt no shame. "Come on," he said, "I want to show you something." He started down the hill toward the wooded lake.

"But you're *walking*," she protested.

"No one's here to see, so what's the difference? Come on."

She stood undecided in the wind. A brook sparkling far below decided her. "All right," she said.

The uneven ground gave her trouble at first, but after a while she got used to it, and soon she was half-skipping along at Howard's side. At the bottom of the hill they came to a grove of wild apple trees. The brook ran through it, murmuring over mossy stones. Howard lay face down on the bank and lowered his lips to the water. She followed suit. The water was winter-cool, and the coolness went all through her, raising goose bumps on her skin.

They lay there side by side. Above them, leafshoots and limbs arabesqued the sky. Their third kiss was even sweeter than its predecessors. "Have you been here before?" she asked when at last they drew apart.

"Many times," he said.

"Alone?"

"Always alone."

"But aren't you afraid Big Jim might find out?"

He laughed. "Big Jim? Big Jim is an artificial entity. The automakers dreamed him up to frighten people into wearing their cars so that they would buy more of them and turn them in more often, and the government co-operated because without increased car turnover, the economy would have collapsed. It wasn't hard to do, because people had been wearing their cars unconsciously all along. The trick was to make them wear them consciously—to make them self-conscious about appearing in public places without them; ashamed, if possible. That wasn't hard to do either—though of course the size of the cars had to be cut way down, and the cars themselves had to be designed to approximate the human figure."

"You shouldn't say such things. It's—it's blasphemy! Anyone would think you were a nudist."

He looked at her steadily. "Is it so despicable to be a nudist?" he asked. "Is it less despicable, for example, to be a dealer who hires shills like Harry Fourwheels to sway undecided women customers and to rough up their purchases afterward so that they can't take advantage of the 24-hour clause in their sales contract? . . . I'm sorry, Arabella, but it's better for you to know."

She had turned away so that he would not see the tears rivuleting down her cheeks. Now she felt his hand touch her arm, creep gently round her waist. She let him draw her to him and kiss her tears away, and the reopened wound closed again, this time forever.

His arms tightened around her. "Will you come here with me again?"

"Yes," she said. "If you want me to."

"I want you to very much. We'll take off our cars and run through the woods. We'll thumb our noses at Big Jim. We'll—"

Click something went in the bushes on the opposite bank.

She went taut in Howard's arms. The bushes quivered, and a uniformed shape grew out of them. A cherubic face beamed at them across the ripples. A big square hand raised and exhibited a portable audio-video recorder. "Come on, you two," a big voice said. "Big Jim wants to see you."

The Big Jim judge regarded her disapprovingly through the windshield of his black Cortez when they brought her before him. "Well, that wasn't very nice of you, was it?" he said. "Taking off your clothes and cavorting with a nudist."

Arabella's face grew pale behind her windshield. "A nudist!" she said disbelievingly. "Why, Howard's not a nudist. He can't be!"

"Oh yes he can be. As a matter of fact, he's even worse than a nudist. He's a *voluntary* nudist. We realize, however," the judge went on, "that you had no way of knowing it, and in a way we are to blame for your becoming involved with him, because if it hadn't been for our inexcusable lack of vigilance he wouldn't have been able to lead the double life he did—going to a nudist teachers' institute days and sneaking out of the reservation nights and working in a used-car lot and trying to convert nice people like yourself to his way of thinking. Consequently, we're going to be lenient with you. Instead of revoking your license we're going to give you another chance—let you go home and atone for your reprehensible conduct by apologizing to your parents and by behaving yourself in the future. Incidentally, you've got a lot to thank a young man named Harry Fourwheels for."

"Have—have I?"

"You certainly have. If it hadn't been for his alertness and his loyalty to Big Jim we might not have discovered your dereliction until it was too late."

"Harry Fourwheels," Arabella said wonderingly. "He must hate me very much."

"*Hate* you? My dear girl, he—"

"And I think I know why," Arabella went on, unaware of the interruption. "He hates me because he betrayed to me what he really is, and in his heart he despises what he really is. Why . . . that's why Mr. Upswept hates me too!"

"See here, Miss Grille, if you're going to talk like that, I may have to reconsider my decision. After all—"

"And my mother and father," Arabella continued. "They

hate me because they've also betrayed to me what they really are, and in their hearts they despise themselves too. Even cars can't hide that kind of nakedness. And Howard. He loves me. He doesn't hate what he really is—any more than I hate what I really am. What—what have you done with him?"

"Escorted him back to the reservation, of course. What else could we do with him? I assure you, though, that he won't be leading a double life any more. And now, Miss Grille, as I've already dismissed your case, I see no reason for you to remain any longer. I'm a busy man and—"

"How does a person become a voluntary nudist, Judge?"

"By willful exhibitionism. Good day, Miss Grille."

"Good day . . . and thank you."

She went home first to pack her things. Her mother and father were waiting up for her in the kitchen.

"Filthy hussy!" her mother said.

"To think that a daughter of mine—" said her father.

She drove through the room without a word and up the ramp to her bedroom. Packing did not take long: except for her books, she owned very little. Back in the kitchen, she paused long enough to say goodbye. Her parents' faces fell apart. "Wait," said her father. "Wait!" cried her mother. Arabella drove out the door without a single glance into her rear-view mirror.

After leaving Macadam Place, she headed for the public square. Despite the lateness of the hour, there were still quite a few people. She took off her hardtop hat first. Next she took off her car-dress. Then she stood there in the winking radiance of the Big Jim sign in the center of the gathering crowd and waited for the vice squad to come and arrest her.

It was morning when they escorted her to the reservation. Above the entrance a sign said: UNAUTHORIZED PERSONNEL KEEP OUT. A line of fresh black paint had been brushed across the words, and above them other words had been hastily printed: WEARING OF MECHANICAL FIG LEAVES PROHIBITED. The guard on her left glowered behind his windshield. "Some more of their smart-aleck tricks!" he grumbled.

Howard met her just inside the gate. When she saw his eyes she knew that it was all right, and in a moment she was in his arms, her nakedness forgotten, crying against his lapel. He held her tightly, his hands pressing hard against the fabric of her coat. She heard his voice over the bleak years: "I knew they were watching us, and I let them catch us together in hopes that they'd send you here. Then, when they didn't, I hoped—I prayed—that you'd come voluntarily. Darling, I'm so glad you did! You'll love it here. I have a cottage with a big back yard. There's a community swimming pool, a woman's club, an amateur-players group, a—"

"Is there a minister?" she asked through her tears.

He kissed her. "A minister, too. If we hurry, we can catch him before he starts out on his morning rounds."

They walked down the lane together.

THE COURTS OF JAMSHYD

*They say the Lion and the Lizard keep
The Courts where Jamshyd gloried and drank deep—*
—The Rubáiyát

THE DUST-REDDENED SUN was low in the west when the tribe filed down from the fissured foothills to the sea. The women spread out along the beach to gather driftwood, while the men took over the task of setting up the rain-catch.

Ryan could tell from the haggard faces around him that there would be a dance that night. He knew his own face must be haggard too, haggard and grimed with dust, the cheeks caved in, the eyes dark with hunger shadows. The dogless days had been many this time.

The rain-catch was a crazy quiltwork pattern of dogskins laboriously sewn together into a makeshift tarpaulin. Ryan and the other young men held it aloft while the older men set up the poles and tied the dog-gut strings, letting the tarp sag in the middle so that when it rained the precious water would accumulate in the depression. When the job was done, the men went down to the beach and stood around the big fire the women had built.

Ryan's legs ached from the long trek through the hill country and his shoulders were sore from packing the dogskin tarp over the last five miles. Sometimes he wished he was the oldest man in the tribe instead of the youngest; then he would be free from the heavy work, free to shamble along in the rear on the marches, free to sit on his haunches during stopovers while the younger men took care of the hunting and the love-making.

He stood with his back to the fire, letting the heat penetrate his dogskin clothing and warm his flesh. Nearby, the women were preparing the evening meal, mashing the day's harvest of tubers into a thick pulp, adding water sparingly from their dogskin waterbags. Ryan glimpsed Merium out of the corner of his eye, but the sight of her thin young face and shapely body did not stir his blood at all, and he turned his eyes miserably away.

He remembered how he had felt about her at the time of the last dog kill—how he had lain beside her before the roaring fire, the aroma of roasted dog flesh still lingering in the night air. His belly had been full and he had lain beside her half the night, and he had almost wanted her. She had seemed beautiful then and for many days afterward; but gradually her beauty had faded away and she had become just another drab face, another listless figure stumbling along with the rest of the tribe, from oasis to oasis, from ruin to ruin, in the eternal search for food.

Ryan shook his head. He could not understand it. But there were so many things that he could not understand. The Dance, for instance. Why should the mouthing of mere words to the accompaniment of rhythmic movements give him pleasure? How could hatred make him strong?

He shook his head again. In a way, the Dance was the biggest mystery of all. . . .

Merium brought him his supper, looking up at him shyly with her large brown eyes. Illogically, Ryan was reminded of the last dog he had killed and he jerked the earthen pot out of her hands and walked down to the water's edge to eat alone.

The sun had set. Streaks of gold and crimson quivered in the wind-creased water, slowly faded away. Darkness crept down from the gullied foothills to the beach, and with it came the first cold breath of night.

Ryan shivered. He tried to concentrate on his food, but the memory of the dog would not go away.

It had been a small dog, but a very vicious one. It had bared its teeth when at last he had cornered it in the little rocky cul-de-sac in the mountains, and as further evidence of its viciousness it had wagged its ridiculous tail. Ryan could still remember the high-pitched sound of its growl—or was it a whine?—when he advanced on it with his club; but most of all he remembered the way its eyes had been when he brought the club down on its head.

He tried to free himself from the memory, tried to enjoy his tasteless meal. But he went right on remembering. He remembered all the other dogs he had killed and he wondered why killing them should bother him so. Once, he knew, dogs had run with the hunters, not from them; but that was long before his time—when there had been something else besides dogs to hunt.

Now it was different. Now it was dogs—or death. . . .

He finished his meatless stew, swallowing the last mouthful grimly. He heard a soft step behind him, but he did not turn around. Presently Merium sat down beside him.

The sea glinted palely in the light of the first stars.

"It's beautiful tonight," Merium said.

Ryan was silent.

"Will there be a Dance?" she asked.

"Maybe."

"I hope there is."

"Why?"

"I—I don't know. Because everyone's so different afterward, I suppose—so happy, almost."

Ryan looked at her. Starlight lay gently on her childlike face, hiding the thinness of her cheeks, softening the hunger shadows beneath her eyes. Again he remembered the night he had almost wanted her and he wanted it to be the same again, only all the way this time. He wanted to want to take her in his arms and kiss her lips and hold her tightly to him, and when desire refused to rise in him, shame took its place, and because he couldn't understand the shame, he supplanted it with anger.

"Men have no happiness!" he said savagely.

"They did once—a long time ago."

"You listen too much to the old women's tales."

"I like to listen to them. I like to hear of the time when the ruins were living cities and the earth was green—when there was an abundance of food and water for everyone. . . . Surely you believe there was such a time. The words of the Dance—"

"I don't know," Ryan said. "Sometimes I think the words of the Dance are lies."

Merium shook her head. "No. The words of the Dance are wisdom. Without them we could not live."

"You talk like an old woman yourself!" Ryan said. Abruptly he stood up. "You *are* an old woman. An ugly old woman!" He strode across the sand to the fire, leaving her alone by the water.

The tribe had broken up into groups. The old men huddled together in one group, the younger men in another. The women sat by themselves near the wavering perimeter of the firelight, crooning an ancient melody, exchanging an occasional word in low tones.

Ryan stood by the fire alone. He was the youngest male of the tribe. He and Merium had been the last children to be born. The tribe had numbered in the hundreds then, and the hunting had been good, the dogs still tame and easy to find. There had been other tribes too, wandering over the dust-veiled land. Ryan wondered what had become of them. But he only pretended to wonder. In his heart, he knew.

It was growing colder. He added more driftwood to the fire and watched the flames gorge themselves. Flames were like men, he thought. They ate everything there was in sight, and when there was nothing more to eat, they died.

Suddenly a drum throbbed out and a woman's voice chanted: "What is a tree?"

A voice answered from the group of old men: "A tree is a green dream."

"What has become of the living land?"

"The living land is dust!"

The drum beat grew louder. Ryan's throat tightened. He felt the refreshing warmth of anger touch his face. The opening phase of the Dance always affected him, even when he was expecting it.

One of the old men was moving out into the firelight, shuffling his feet to the beat of the drum. The light reddened the wrinkles on his thirty-year-old face, made a crimson washboard of his forehead. His thin voice drifted on the cold night air:

"The living land is dust, and those
who turned it into dust
are dust themselves—"

A woman's voice took up the chant:

"Our ancestors are dust:
dust are our gorged ancestors—"

There were other figures shuffling in the firelight now, and the beat on the dogskin drumhead was sharper, stronger. Ryan felt the quickening of his blood, the surge of newborn energy.

Voices blended:

"Dust are our gorged ancestors,
our ancestors who raped the fields and ravished the hills,
who cut the forest chains and set the rivers free;

our ancestors who drank deep from the well of the world
and left the well dry—"

Ryan could contain himself no longer. He felt his own feet moving with the vindictive beat of the drum. He heard his own voice take up the chant:

"Let us take the memory of our ancestors
and tear it open, rend its vitals,
throw its entrails on the fire:
our ancestors, the eaters,
the putrefiers of the lakes and the rivers;
the consumers, the destroyers, the murderers of the living
    land;
the selfish, the obese, the great collectors,
who tried to devour the world—"

He joined the stomping mass of the tribe, his hands going through the mimic motions of killing, rending, throwing. Strength flowed into his emaciated limbs, pulsed through his undernourished body. He glimpsed Merium across the fire and he caught his breath at the beauty of her animated face. Again he almost wanted her, and for a while he was able to convince himself that some day he *would* want her; that this time the effect of the Dance would not wear off the way it always had before and he would go on feeling strong and confident and unafraid and find many dogs to feed the tribe; then, perhaps, the men would want the women the way they used to, and he would want Merium, and the tribe would increase and become great and strong—

He raised his voice higher and stomped his feet as hard as he could. The hatred was like wine now, gushing hotly through his body, throbbing wildly in his brain. The chant crescendoed into a huge hysterical wail, a bitter accusation reverberating over the barren hills and the dead sea, riding the dust-laden wind—

> *"Our ancestors were pigs!*
> *Our ancestors were pigs! . . ."*

PRODUCTION PROBLEM

"The man from Timesearch, Inc. is here, sir."

"Show him in," Bridgemaker told the robutler.

The man from Timesearch halted just within the doorway. Nervously he shifted the oblong package he was carrying from one hand to the other. "Good morning, Honorable Bridgemaker."

"Did you find the machine?" Bridgemaker demanded.

"I–I'm afraid we failed again, sir. But we did locate another one of its products." The man handed Bridgemaker the package.

Bridgemaker waved his arm in an angry gesture that included the whole room. "But you've already brought me hundreds of its products!" he shouted. "What I want is the machine itself so I can make my own products!"

"I'm afraid, Honorable Bridgemaker, that the machine never existed. Our field men have explored the Pre-Technological Age, the First Technological Age, and the early years of our own age; but even though they witnessed some of the ancient technicians at work, they never caught a glimpse of the machine."

"But if the ancient technicians could create something without a machine, *I* could too," Bridgemaker said. "And since I can't, the machine *had* to exist. Go back at once!"

PRODUCTION PROBLEM

"Yes, Honorable Bridgemaker." The man bowed and withdrew.

Bridgemaker tore open the package. He glanced at the product, then set the controls on his Language Adjustor, Duplicator and Alterator machine.

While he waited, he brooded on the irony of his life. Ever since he was a small boy he had hungered hopelessly for one vocation. Now that success in a totally different vocation had made him financially independent, he had focused all his energies into the attainment of his first love. But all he'd got for his trouble was a roomful of ancient products, and even though he'd increased his financial independence by duplicating and distributing those products, the basic frustration still remained: he was a secondhand artist and he wanted desperately to be a firsthand artist.

He went over to one of the shelves that wainscoted the room and glanced at some of his vicarious creations: *A Farewell to Arms*, by Chamfer Bridgemaker . . . *Five Little Peppers and How They Grew*, by Chamfer Bridgemaker . . . *The Odyssey*, by Chamfer Bridgemaker . . . *Ivanhoe*, by Chamfer Bridgemaker—

There was a loud *plop!* as the first copy of *Tom Swift and His Electric Locomotive* came out of the Language Adjustor, Duplicator and Alterator machine.

Bridgemaker sat down to read his latest masterpiece.

LITTLE RED SCHOOLHOUSE

RONNIE avoided the towns. Whenever he came to one, he made a wide detour, coming back to the tracks miles beyond it. He knew that none of the towns was the village he was looking for. The towns were bright and new, with white streets and brisk cars and big factories, while the village in the valley was old and quiet, with rustic houses and shaded streets and a little red schoolhouse.

Just before you came to the village, there was a grove of friendly maples with a brook winding through them. Ronnie remembered the brook best of all. In summer, he had waded in it many times, and he had skated on it in winter; in autumn, he had watched the fallen leaves, like Lilliputian ships, sail down it to the sea.

Ronnie had been sure that he could find the valley, but the tracks went on and on, through fields and hills and forests, and no familiar valley appeared. After a while, he began to wonder if he had chosen the right tracks, if the shining rails he followed day after day were really the rails along which the stork train had borne him to the city and to his parents.

He kept telling himself that he wasn't truly running away from home, that the aseptic three-room apartment in which he had lived for a month wasn't his home at all, any more than the pallid man and woman who had met him at the bustling terminal were his mother and father.

His real home was in the valley, in the old rambling house at the outskirts of the village; and his real parents were Nora and Jim, who had cared for him throughout his boyhood. True, they had never claimed to be his parents, but they were just the same, even if they put him on the stork train when he was asleep and sent him to the city to live with the pallid people who pretended to be his parents.

Nights, when the shadows came too close around his campfire, he thought of Nora and Jim and the village. But most of all, he thought of Miss Smith, the teacher in the little red schoolhouse. Thinking of Miss Smith made him brave, and he lay back in the summer grass beneath the summer stars and he wasn't scared at all.

On the fourth morning, he ate the last of the condensed food tablets he had stolen from his parents' apartment. He knew that he had to find the valley soon and he walked faster along the tracks, staring eagerly ahead for the first familiar landmark—a remembered tree or a nostalgic hilltop, the silvery twinkle of a winding brook. The trip on the stork train had been his first trip into the outside world, so he was not certain how the valley would look, coming into it from the surrounding countryside; nevertheless, he was sure he would recognize it quickly.

His legs were stronger now than they had been when he had first stepped off the stork train and his dizzy spells were becoming less and less frequent. The sun no longer bothered his eyes and he could look for long moments at the blue sky and the bright land with no painful after-images.

Toward evening he heard a high-pitched whistle and his heart began to pound. He knew at last that he had the right tracks and that he couldn't be very far from the valley, for the whistle was the shrill lullaby of a stork train.

Ronnie hid in the weeds that lined the embankment and watched the train pass. He saw the children reclining on their chairbeds, staring curiously through the little windows, and he remembered how he had stared, too, on his trip to the city, how surprised—and frightened—he had been, upon awakening, to see the strange new land unrolling before his aching eyes.

He wondered if his face had been as white as those he was seeing now, as white and as peaked and as sickly, and he guessed that it had been, that living in the valley affected your complexion some way, made your eyes sensitive to light and your legs weak.

But that couldn't be the answer. His legs had never been weak when he had lived in the valley, he remembered, and his eyes had never bothered him. He had never had trouble seeing the lessons on the blackboard in the little red schoolhouse, and he'd read all the printed words in the schoolbooks without the slightest difficulty. In fact, he'd done so well with his reading lessons that Miss Smith had patted him on the back, more times than he could remember, and told him that he was her star pupil.

Suddenly he realized how eager he was to see Miss Smith again, to walk into the little classroom and have her say, "*Good* morning, Ronnie," and see her sitting reassuringly behind her desk, her yellow hair parted neatly in the middle and her round cheeks pink in the morning light. For the first time it occurred to him that he was in love with Miss Smith, and he recognized his real reason for returning to the valley.

The other reasons were still valid, though. He wanted to wade in the brook again and feel the cool tree shadows all around him, and after that he wanted to meander through the maples, picking a slow way homeward, and finally he wanted to wander down the lazy village street to the house and have Nora scold him for being late for supper.

The stork train was still passing. Ronnie couldn't get over how long it was. Where did all the children come from? He didn't recognize a single one of them, yet he had lived in the valley all his life. He hadn't recognized any of the children on his own stork train, either, for that matter. He shook his head. The whole thing was bewildering, far beyond his understanding.

When the last of the cars had passed, he climbed back up the embankment to the tracks. Dusk was seeping in over the land and soon, he knew, the first star would appear. If only he could find the valley before night came! He wouldn't even pause to wade in the brook; he would run through the maples and down the street to the house. Nora and Jim would be delighted to see him again and Nora would fix a fine supper; and perhaps Miss Smith would come over during the evening, as she sometimes did, and discuss his schoolwork, and he would walk to the gate with her, when she was ready to go, and say good night, and see the starlight on her face as she stood goddess-tall beside him.

He hurried along the tracks, staring hungrily ahead for some sign of the valley. The shadows deepened around him and the damp breath of night crept down from the hills. Insects awoke in the tall meadow grass, katydids and crickets, and frogs began singing in ponds.

After a while, the first star came out.

He was surprised when he came to the big broad-shouldered building. He did not recall having seen it during his ride on the stork train. That was odd, because he had never left the window once during the whole trip.

He paused on the tracks, gazing at the towering brick façade with its tiers and tiers of small barred windows. Most of the upper windows were dark, but all of the first-floor windows were ablaze with light. The first-floor windows were different in other respects, too, he noticed. There were no bars on them and they were much larger than the higher ones. Ronnie wondered why that should be.

And then he noticed something else. The tracks stretched right up to the imposing façade and entered the building through a lofty archway. Ronnie gasped. The building must be a terminal, like the one in the city, where his parents had met him. But why hadn't he seen it when the stork train had passed through it?

Then he remembered that he'd been put on the train when he was asleep and could have missed the first part of the journey. He'd assumed, when he awoke, that the train was just pulling out of the valley, but perhaps it had pulled out some time before—a long time, even—and had passed through the terminal while he was sleeping.

It was a logical explanation, but Ronnie was reluctant to accept it. If it was true, then the valley was still a long way off, and he wanted the valley to be close, close enough for him to reach it tonight. He was so hungry he could hardly stand it, and he was terribly tired.

He looked miserably at the big hulking building, wondering what to do.

"Hello, Ronnie."

Ronnie almost collapsed with fright on the tracks. He peered around him into the shadows. At first he saw no one, but after a while he made out the figure of a tall man in a gray uniform standing in a grove of locusts bordering the tracks. The man's uniform matched the shadows, and Ronnie realized with a start that he had been standing there all along.

"You *are* Ronnie Meadows, aren't you?"

"Yes—yes, sir," Ronnie said. He wanted to turn and run, but he knew it wouldn't do any good. He was so tired and weak that the tall man could catch him easily.

"I've been waiting for you, Ronnie," the tall man said, a note of warmth in his voice. He left the tree shadows and walked over to the tracks. "I've been worried about you."

"Worried?"

"Why, of course. Worrying about boys who leave the valley is my job. You see, I'm the truant officer."

Ronnie's eyes got big. "Oh, but I didn't want to leave the valley, sir," he said. "Nora and Jim waited until I went to sleep one night, and then they put me on the stork train, and when I woke up I was already on my way to the city. I *want* to go back to the valley, sir. I—I ran away from home."

"I understand," the truant officer said, "and I'm going to

take you back to the valley—back to the little red schoolhouse." He reached down and took Ronnie's hand.

"Oh, will you, sir?" Ronnie could hardly contain the sudden happiness that coursed through him. "I want to go back in the worst way!"

"Of course I will. It's my job." The truant officer started walking toward the big building and Ronnie hurried along beside him. "But first I've got to take you to the principal."

Ronnie drew back. He became aware then of what a tight grip the truant officer had on his weak-feeling hand.

"Come on," the truant officer said, making the grip even tighter. "The principal won't hurt you."

"I—I never knew there was a principal," Ronnie said, hanging back. "Miss Smith never said anything about him."

"Naturally there's a principal; there has to be. And he wants to talk to you before you go back. Come on now, like a good boy, and don't make it necessary for me to turn in a bad report about you. Miss Smith wouldn't like that at all, would she?"

"No, I guess she wouldn't," Ronnie said, suddenly contrite. "All right, sir, I'll go."

Ronnie had learned about principals in school, but he had never seen one. He had always assumed that the little red schoolhouse was too small to need one and he still couldn't understand why it should. Miss Smith was perfectly capable of conducting the school all by herself. But most of all, he couldn't understand why the principal should live in a place like the terminal—if it was a terminal—and not in the valley.

However, he accompanied the truant officer dutifully, telling himself that he had a great deal to learn about the world and that an interview with a principal was bound to teach him a lot.

They entered the building through an entrance to the left of the archway and walked down a long bright corridor lined with tall green cabinets to a frosted glass door at the farther end. The lettering on the glass said: EDUCATIONAL CENTER 16, H. D. CURTIN, PRINCIPAL.

The door opened at the truant officer's touch and they stepped into a small white-walled room even more brightly illumined than the corridor. Opposite the door was a desk with a girl sitting behind it, and behind the girl was another frosted glass door. The lettering said: PRIVATE.

The girl looked up as the truant officer and Ronnie entered. She was young and pretty—almost as pretty as Miss Smith.

"Tell the old man the Meadows kid finally showed up," the truant officer said.

The girl's eyes touched Ronnie's, then dropped quickly to a little box on her desk. Ronnie felt funny. There had been a strange look in the girl's eyes—a sort of sadness. It was as though she was sorry that the truant officer had found him.

She told the little box: "Mr. Curtin, Andrews just brought in Ronnie Meadows."

"Good," the box said. "Send the boy in and notify his parents."

"Yes, sir."

The principal's office was unlike anything Ronnie had ever seen before. Its hugeness made him uncomfortable and the brightness of its fluorescent lights hurt his eyes. All the lights seemed to be shining right in his face and he could hardly see the man behind the desk.

But he could see him well enough to make out some of his features: the high white forehead and receding hairline, the thin cheeks, the almost lipless mouth.

For some reason the man's face frightened Ronnie and he wished that the interview were over.

"I have only a few questions to ask you," the principal said, "and then you can be on your way back to the valley."

"Yes, sir," Ronnie said, some of his fear leaving him.

"Were your mother and father unkind to you? Your *real* mother and father, I mean."

"No, sir. They were very good to me. I'm sorry I had to run away from them, but I just had to go back to the valley."

"Were you lonesome for Nora and Jim?"

Ronnie wondered how the principal knew their names. "Yes, sir."

"And Miss Smith—were you lonesome for her?"

"Oh, yes, sir!"

He felt the principal's eyes upon him and he shifted uncomfortably. He was so tired, he wished the principal would ask him to sit down. But the principal didn't and the lights seemed to get brighter and brighter.

"Are you in love with Miss Smith?"

The question startled Ronnie, not so much because he hadn't expected it, but because of the tone in which it was uttered. There was unmistakable loathing in the principal's voice. Ronnie felt his neck grow hot, and then his face, and he was too ashamed to meet the principal's eyes, no matter how hard he tried. But the strange part of it was, he didn't understand *why* he was ashamed.

The question came again, the loathing more pronounced than before: "Are you in love with Miss Smith?"

"Yes, sir," Ronnie said.

Silence came and sat in the room. Ronnie kept his eyes down, fearfully awaiting the next question.

But there were no more questions and presently he became aware that the door behind him had opened and that the truant officer was standing over him. He heard the principal's voice: "Level Six. Tell the tech on duty to try Variant 24-C on him."

"Yes, sir," the truant officer said. He took Ronnie's hand. "Come on, Ronnie."

"Where're we going?"

"Why, back to the valley, of course. Back to the little red schoolhouse."

Ronnie followed the truant officer out of the office, his heart singing. It seemed almost too easy, almost too good to be true.

Ronnie didn't understand why they had to take the elevator to get to the valley. But perhaps they were going to the roof of the building and board a 'copter, so he didn't say anything till the elevator stopped on the sixth floor and they stepped out into a long, long corridor lined with hundreds of horizontal doors so close together that they almost seemed to touch.

Then he said: "But this isn't the way to the valley, sir. Where are you taking me?"

"Back to school," the truant officer said, the warmth gone from his voice. "Come along now!"

Ronnie tried to hold back, but it wasn't any use. The truant officer was big and strong and he dragged Ronnie down the long antiseptic corridor to a recess in which a gaunt woman in a white uniform was sitting behind a metal desk.

"Here's the Meadows kid," he said. "The old man says to change the plot to 24-C."

The gaunt woman got up wearily. Ronnie was crying by then and she selected an ampoule from a glass cabinet beside the desk, came over and rolled up his sleeve and, despite his squirming, expertly jabbed the needle into his arm.

"Save your tears till later," she said. "You'll need them." She turned to the truant officer. "Curtin's guilt complex must be getting the better of him. This is the third 24-C he's prescribed this month."

"The old man knows what he's doing."

"He only thinks he knows what he's doing. First thing you know, we'll have a whole world full of Curtins. It's about time someone on the Board of Education took a course in psychology and found out what mother love is all about!"

"The old man's a graduate psychologist," the truant officer said.

"You mean a graduate psychopath!"

"You shouldn't talk like that."

"I'll talk the way I please," the gaunt woman said. "You don't hear them crying, but I do. C-24 belongs back in the twentieth century and should have been thrown out of the curriculum long ago!"

She took Ronnie's arm and led him away. The truant officer shrugged and returned to the elevator. Ronnie heard the metal doors breathe shut. The corridor was very quiet and he followed the woman as though in a dream. He could hardly feel his arms and legs, and his brain had grown fuzzy.

The gaunt woman turned off into another corridor and then into another. Finally they came to an open door. The woman stopped before it.

"Recognize the old homestead?" she asked bitterly.

But Ronnie hardly heard her. He could barely keep his eyes open. There was a bed in the shelf-like cubicle beyond the horizontal door, a strange bed with all sorts of wires and dials and screens and tubes around it. But it was a bed, and for the moment that was all he cared about, and he climbed upon it gratefully. He lay his head back on the pillow and closed his eyes.

"That's a good boy," he heard the woman say just before he dropped off. "And now back to the little red schoolhouse."

The pillow purred and the screens lit up and the tapes went into action.

"Ronnie!"

Ronnie stirred beneath the covers, fighting the dream. It had been a horrible dream, filled with stork trains and strange people and unfamiliar places. And the worst part of it was, it could be true. Nora had told him many times that some morning, when he awoke, he would be on the stork train, bound for the city and his parents.

He fought harder and harder, kicking at the covers and trying to open his eyes.

"Ronnie," Nora called again. "Hurry up or you'll be late for school!"

His eyes opened then, of their own accord, and instantly he knew that everything was all right. There was the bright morning sunlight streaming into his attic bedroom, and there were the nostalgic branches of the back-yard maple gently brushing his window.

"Coming!" He threw back the covers and leaped out of bed and dressed, standing in a warm puddle of sunlight. Then he washed and ran downstairs.

"It's about time," Nora said sharply when he came into the kitchen. "You're getting lazier and lazier every day!"

Ronnie stared at her. She must be feeling ill, he thought. She had never spoken to him like that before. Then Jim came in. He hadn't shaved and his eyes were bloodshot.

"For Pete's sake," he said, "isn't breakfast ready yet?"

"In a minute, in a minute," Nora snapped back. "I've been trying to get this lazy brat out of bed for the last half hour."

Bewildered, Ronnie sat down at the table. He ate in silence, wondering what could have happened in the brief span of a single night to change Nora and Jim so. Breakfast was pancakes and sausage, his favorite dish, but the pancakes were soggy and the sausage was half raw.

He excused himself after his second pancake and went into the living room and got his books. The living room was untidy and had a moldy smell. When he left the house, Jim and Nora were arguing loudly in the kitchen.

Ronnie frowned. What had happened? He was sure that things hadn't been this way yesterday. Nora had been kind then, Jim soft-spoken and immaculate, and the house neat.

What had changed everything?

He shrugged. In a moment, he would be in school and see Miss Smith's smiling face and everything would be all right again. He hurried down the bright street, past the rustic houses and the laughing children on their way to school. Miss Smith, his heart sang. Beautiful Miss Smith.

The sun was in her hair when he walked in the door and the little bun at the back of her neck was like a golden pomegranate. Her cheeks were like roses after a morning shower and her voice was a soft summer wind.

"Good morning, Ronnie," she said.

"Good morning, Miss Smith." He walked on clouds to his seat.

The lessons began—arithmetic, spelling, social studies,

reading. Ronnie wasn't called upon to recite till reading class, when Miss Smith told him to read aloud from the little red primary reader.

He stood up proudly. The story was about Achilles and Hector. Ronnie got the first sentence off fine. He didn't begin to stumble till the middle of the second. The words seemed to blur and he couldn't make them out. He held the primer closer to his eyes, but still he couldn't read the words. It was as though the page had turned to water and the words were swimming beneath the surface. He tried with all his might to see them, but his voice stumbled worse than ever.

Then he became aware that Miss Smith had walked down the aisle and was standing over him. She was carrying a ruler and her face was strange, sort of pinched and ugly. She snatched the book from his hands and slammed it on the desk. She seized his right hand and flattened it out in her own. The ruler came down on his palm with stinging force. His hand tingled and the pain shot up his arm and went all through him. Miss Smith raised the ruler, brought it down again—

And again and again and again.

Ronnie began to cry.

The principal had had a long hard day and he didn't feel much like talking to Mr. and Mrs. Meadows. He wanted to go home and take a relaxing bath and then tune in on a good telempathic program and forget his troubles. But it was part of his job to placate frustrated parents, so he couldn't very well turn them away. If he'd known they were going to come 'coptering out to the educational center, he would have put off notifying them till morning, but it was too late to think of that now.

"Send them in," he said wearily into the intercom.

Mr. and Mrs. Meadows were a small, shy couple—production-line workers, according to Ronnie's dossier. The principal had little use for production-line workers, particularly when they spawned—as they so frequently did—emotionally unstable children. He was tempted to slant the interrogation lights into their faces, but he thought better of it.

"You were notified that your son was all right," he said disapprovingly, when they had seated themselves. "There was no need for you to come out here."

"We—we were worried, sir," Mr. Meadows said.

"Why were you worried? I told you when you first reported your son missing that he'd try to return to his empathic existence and that we'd pick him up here as soon as he showed up. His type always wants to return, but unfortunately we can't classify our charges prior to placing them on the delivery train, since doing so would require dispelling the empathic illusion at an inopportune time. Dispelling the illusion is the parents' job, anyway, once the child is integrated in reality. Consequently we can't deal with our potential misfits till they've proven themselves to *be* misfits by running away."

"Ronnie isn't a misfit!" Mrs. Meadows protested, her pale eyes flashing briefly. "He's just a highly sensitive child."

"Your son, Mrs. Meadows," the principal said icily, "has a pronounced Oedipus complex. He bestowed the love he ordinarily would have felt for you upon his fictitious teacher. It is one of those deplorable anomalies which we cannot foresee, but which, I assure you, we are capable of correcting, once it reveals itself. The next time your son is reborn and sent to you, I *promise* you he won't run away!"

"The corrective treatment, sir," Mr. Meadows said, "is it painful?"

"Of course it isn't painful! Not in the sense of objective reality."

He was trying to keep his mounting anger out of his voice, but it was difficult to do so. His right hand had begun to twitch and that made his anger all the worse, for he knew that the twitching meant another spell. And it was all Mr. and Mrs. Meadows' fault!

These production-line imbeciles! These electrical-appliance accumulators! It was not enough to free them from the burden of bringing up their children! Their piddling questions had to be answered, too!

"Look," he said, getting up and walking around the desk, trying to keep his mind off his hand, "this is a civilized educational system. We employ civilized methods. We are going to cure your son of his complex and make it possible for him to come and live with you as a normal red-blooded American boy. To cure him of his complex, all we need to do is to make him hate his teacher instead of love her. Isn't that simple enough?

"The moment he begins to hate her, the valley will lose its abnormal fascination and he will think of it as normal children think of it—as the halcyon place where he attended elementary school. It will be a pleasant memory in his mind, as it's intended to be, but he won't have any overwhelming urge to return to it."

"But," Mr. Meadows said hesitantly, "won't your interfering with his love for his teacher have some bad effect upon him? I've done a little reading in psychology," he added apologetically, "and I was under the impression that interfering with a child's natural love for its parent—even when that love has been transferred—can leave, well, to put it figuratively, scar tissue."

The principal knew that his face had gone livid. There was a throbbing in his temple, too, and his hand was no longer merely twitching; it was tingling. There was no doubt about it: he was in for a spell, and a bad one.

"Sometimes I wonder," he said. "Sometimes I can't *help* but wonder what you people expect of an educational system. We relieve you of your offspring from the day of their birth, enabling both parents to work full time so they can afford and enjoy all the luxuries civilized beings are entitled to. We give your offspring the best of care: We employ the most advanced identification techniques to give them not only an induced elementary education but an empathic background as well, a background that combines the best elements of *Tom Sawyer, Rebecca of Sunnybrook Farm* and *A Child's Garden of Verses.*

"We employ the most advanced automatic equipment to develop and maintain unconscious oral feeding and to stimulate the growth of healthy tissue. In short, we employ the finest educational incubators available. Call them mechanized extensions of the womb if you will, as some of our detractors insist upon doing, but no matter what you call them, there is no gainsaying the fact that they provide a practical and efficient method of dealing with the plethora of children in the country today, and of preparing those children for home high school and correspondence college.

"We perform all of these services for you to the best of our ability and yet you, Mr. Meadows, have the arrogance to express doubt of our competence! Why, you people don't realize how lucky you are! How would you like to be living in the middle of the twentieth century, before the invention of the educational incubator? How would you like to have to send your son to some rundown firetrap of a public school and have him suffocate all day long in an overcrowded classroom? How would you like *that*, Mr. Meadows?"

"But I only said—" Mr. Meadows began.

The principal ignored him. He was shouting now, and both Mr. and Mrs. Meadows had risen to their feet in alarm. "You simply don't appreciate your good fortune! Why, if it weren't for the invention of the educational incubator, you wouldn't be able to send your son to school at all! Imagine a government appropriating enough money to build enough old-style schools and playgrounds and to educate and pay enough teachers to accommodate all the children in the country today! It would cost more than a war! And yet, when a workable substitute is employed, you object, you criticize. You went to the little red schoolhouse yourself, Mr. Meadows. So did I. Tell me, did our methods leave *you* with any scar tissue?"

Mr. Meadows shook his head. "No, sir. But I didn't fall in love with my teacher."

"*Shut up!*" The principal gripped the edge of the desk with his right hand, trying to stop the almost unbearable tingling. Then, with a tremendous effort, he brought his voice back to normal. "Your son will probably be on the next delivery train," he said. "And now, if you will please leave—"

He flicked on the intercom. "Show Mr. and Mrs. Meadows out," he said to his secretary. "And bring me a sedative."

"Yes, sir."

Mr. and Mrs. Meadows seemed glad to go. The principal was glad to see them leave. The tingling in his hand had worked all the way up his arm to his shoulder and it was more than a mere tingling now. It was a rhythmic pain reaching forty years back in time to the little red schoolhouse and beautiful, cruel Miss Smith.

The principal sat down behind his desk and closed his right hand tightly and covered it protectively with his left. But it wasn't any good. The ruler kept rising and falling, anyway, making a sharp *thwack* each time it struck his flattened palm.

When his secretary came in with the sedative, he was trembling like a little child and there were tears in his bleak blue eyes.

WRITTEN IN THE STARS

THE ABRUPT DEPARTURE of the Staaids had left everyone bewildered, including the President of the United States himself. One minute they had been standing on the White House lawn with Professor Gromley, chatting affably through their portable translator and watching the stars come out; the next minute, for no apparent reason, they had folded their gossamer tents like a band of affronted Arabs and had filed stiffly through the glistening doorway of their transmitter. That their decision was final became obvious when they pulled the transmitter into the warp after them, leaving nothing on the White House lawn to show that an extraterrestrial expedition had ever camped there, except a medley of strange footprints in the snow, a forlorn tent peg and a crestfallen expression on Professor Gromley's countenance.

The President of the United States, quite understandably, was disappointed as well as bewildered. After all, if the Staaids had stayed and dispensed all of the wondrous technological items they claimed to have, his would have been a distinction not to be sneezed at for generations to come. The next election would have been in the bag, and 1973, the very first year of his tenure, would have commanded a place in future schoolbooks as large and as imposing as that occupied by such diehard dates as 1492, 1620 and 1945.

But the Staaids hadn't stayed, and all the President had to look forward to now was his impending cross-examination of Professor Gromley. He sat grimly behind his austere, flat-topped desk, waiting impatiently for the anthropologist to be shown into his office. Never had a President been in more dire need of a patsy, and never had one been more readily available.

Professor Gromley's black-rimmed spectacles gave him an owlish look as he stepped diffidently into the Presidential presence. "You sent for me, Mr. President?"

"I most certainly did," said the President, honing each word carefully. "Can you think of a more pertinent person for whom I could have sent under the circumstances?"

"No, sir, I'm afraid I can't."

"Well, then, without further digression, I suggest that you tell me what you said out there on the lawn to offend our guests and send them hieing back to wherever they came from."

"That would be Delta Sagittarii 23, sir," Professor Gromley said. "But they didn't leave because of anything I said."

"Now that is a remarkable statement!" said the Chief Executive acidly. "We made you our representative because of your esteemed anthropological background, threw the Staaids in your lap, so to speak, hoping that, because of the mark you'd made for yourself in your field, you'd be the one human least likely to tread on their cultural corns. In other words, for the twelve hours of their stay on Earth, you were the *only* person who spoke to them directly. And yet you stand there and tell me that they didn't leave because of anything *you* said. Why, then, did they leave?"

With his black-rimmed spectacles glinting in the radiance of the Presidential desk lamp, Professor Gromley looked more than ever like an owl—and an acutely embarrassed one. "Mr. President," he said hesitantly, "are you familiar with the constellation Orion?"

"Certainly I'm familiar with Orion. I believe, however, that we are now discussing Delta Sagittarii 23."

"Yes, sir," Professor Gromley said miserably. "But you see, sir, from the perspective of Delta Sagittarii 23, Orion isn't Orion at all. That is, the arrangement of the stars that comprise the constellation is very different when seen from their planet."

"All of which," the Chief Executive said dryly, "is extremely interesting astronomical data. I presume it has some tenuous connection with the present topic of conversation —viz., in case you've forgotten, the reason underlying the Staaids' departure."

"What I'm trying to bring out, sir," Professor Gromley continued somewhat desperately, "is the unfortunate fact that the Staaids, never having been on Earth before, could not possibly have anticipated the star pattern that climbed into our eastern sky tonight while we were talking out there on the lawn. If they had anticipated it, they wouldn't have touched this planet with a ten-trillion-foot pole."

"I'm listening."

Professor Gromley stood up a little straighter before the Presidential desk and a certain classroom didacticism crept into his next words:

"Before demonstrating exactly why the Staaids did leave, Mr. President, I'd like to fill you in on certain pertinent facts which I learned about them during the time I spent in their company.

"First, while they are certainly sophisticated in regard to technological matters, they are not in the least sophisticated in regard to other matters.

"Second, their present morality bears a strong resemblance to our own morality, and was strongly influenced by elements closely paralleling the Judaeo-Christian elements that molded our own Western attitude toward sex. In other words, they are simultaneously fascinated and repelled by any reference to the act of reproduction.

"Third, their language is symbolic, dating way back to

their primitive ancestors, and so simplified that even a non-specialist like myself was able to obtain a fair understanding of its basic structure during the twelve hours I spent in conversation with them.

"Fourth, the particular group that visited our planet were missionaries. . . .

"And now, Mr. President, if you will have the kindness to have a blackboard brought in, I will demonstrate why our erstwhile benefactors departed."

It was on the tip of the President's tongue to remind Professor Gromley that this was not a classroom and that he, the President of the United States, was not to be regarded as a somewhat retarded pupil. But an aura of dignity had lately settled on Professor Gromley's stooped shoulders—an owlish dignity, to be sure, but a dignity nonetheless. The President sighed.

After the blackboard had been brought in, Professor Gromley assumed a classroom stance before it and picked up a piece of chalk.

"The only characteristic of the Staaid language that applies to the present problem," he said, "is the manner in which they form their verbs. This is accomplished by combining two nouns. In representing their symbols, I'm going to use stars—for a reason that will become apparent to you presently. Actually the Staaids employ many subtle variations, but the resultant pattern of the symbol, in this context, is the same."

He raised the piece of chalk, touched it to the blackboard. "This—

✧
✧

is the Staaid symbol for 'sapling,' and this—

✧
✧
✧

is the Staaid symbol for 'tree.' Now by combining the two, thusly—

❋
❋
❋
❋
❋

we obtain the verb 'grow.' Do I make myself clear, Mr. President?"

"I'm still listening," the President said.

"One more example. This—

❋

is the symbol for 'bird,' and this—

❋
❋ ❋
❋

is the symbol for 'air.' Combining the two, we get—

❋
❋ ❋ ❋
❋

for the verb 'fly.'"

Professor Gromley cleared his throat. "We are now ready for the particular symbol combination that brought about the Staaids' departure," he said. "This—

❋ ❋ ❋
❋
❋

is the symbol for 'man,' and this—

☆   ☆   ☆

           ☆   ☆

is the symbol for 'woman.' Putting them together, we get—

☆   ☆   ☆

      ☆ ☆ ☆
         ☆
         ☆

☆   ☆

Now do you understand why they left, Mr. President?"

It was obvious from the ensuing silence and from the blank expression on the Presidential countenance that as yet no bell had sounded in the Presidential brain.

Professor Gromley wiped his forehead. "Let's resort to an analogy," he said. "Suppose *we* transmitted *ourselves* to Delta Sagittarii 23, established contact with the local natives, and promised them the moon and the stars as a prelude to proselytizing them. Then suppose, on the very evening of the day of our arrival, we looked up into their sky and saw a gigantic four-letter word rising in the east. What would *we* do?"

"Good Lord!" The President's face had turned the color of his crimson blotting pad. "But can't we explain—make an official apology? *Some*thing?"

Professor Gromley shook his head. "Even assuming we could contact them, the only way we could bring them back would be by removing the source of the affront to their mores. . . . We can wash four-letter words off lavatory walls, Mr. President, but we can't wash them out of the sky."

A DRINK OF DARKNESS

You're walking down Fool's Street, Laura used to say when he was drinking, and she had been right. He had known even then that she was right, but knowing had made no difference; he had simply laughed at her fears and gone on walking down it, till finally he stumbled and fell. Then, for a long time, he stayed away, and if he had stayed away long enough he would have been all right; but one night he began walking down it again—and met the girl. It was inevitable that on Fool's Street there should be women as well as wine.

He had walked down it many times since in many different towns, and now he was walking down it once again in yet another town. Fool's Street never changed no matter where you went, and this one was no different from the others. The same skeletonic signs bled beer names in naked windows; the same winos sat in doorways nursing muscatel; the same drunk tank awaited you when at last your reeling footsteps failed. And if the sky was darker than usual, it was only because of the rain which had begun falling early that morning and which had been falling steadily ever since.

Chris went into another bar, laid down his last quarter and ordered wine. At first he did not see the man who came in a moment later and stood beside him. There was a raging rawness in him such as even he had never known before, and the wine he had thus far drunk had merely served to aggravate it. Eagerly he drained the glass which the bartender filled and set before him. Reluctantly he turned to leave. He saw the man then.

The man was gaunt—so gaunt that he seemed taller than he actually was. His thin-featured face was pale, and his dark eyes seemed beset by unimaginable pain. His hair was brown and badly in need of cutting. There was a strange statuesqueness about him—an odd sense of immobility. Raindrops iridesced like tiny jewels on his gray trench coat, dripped sporadically from his black hat. "Good evening," he said. "May I offer you a drink?"

For an agonizing moment Chris saw himself through the other's eyes—saw his thin, sensitive face with its intricate networks of ruptured capillaries; his gray rain-plastered hair; his ragged rain-soaked overcoat; his cracked rain-sodden shoes—and the image was so vivid that it shocked him into speechlessness. But only briefly; then the rawness intervened. "Sure I'll have a drink," he said, and tapped his glass upon the bar.

"Not here," the gaunt man said. "Come with me."

Chris followed him out into the rain, the rawness rampant now. He staggered, and the gaunt man took his arm. "It's only a little way," the gaunt man said. "Into this alley . . . now down this flight of stairs."

It was a long gray room, damp and dimly lit. A gray-faced bartender stood statuesquely behind a deserted bar. When they entered he set two glasses on the bar and filled them from a dusty bottle. "How much?" the gaunt man asked.

"Thirty," the bartender answered.

The gaunt man counted out the money. "I shouldn't have asked," he said. "It's always thirty—no matter where I go. Thirty this, or thirty that; thirty days or thirty months or thirty thousand years." He raised his glass and touched it to his lips.

A DRINK OF DARKNESS

Chris followed suit, the rawness in him screaming. The glass was so cold that it numbed his fingertips, and its contents had a strange Cimmerian cast. But the truth didn't strike him till he tilted the glass and drained the darkness; then the quatrain came down from the attic of his mind where he had stored it years ago, and he knew suddenly who the gaunt man was.

> *So when at last the Angel of the Drink*
> *Of Darkness finds you by the river-brink,*
> *And, proffering his Cup, invites your Soul*
> *Forth to your Lips to quaff it—do not shrink.*

But by then the icy waves were washing through him, and soon the darkness was complete.

Dead! The word was a hoarse and hideous echo caroming down the twisted corridor of his mind. He heard it again and again and again—*dead . . . dead . . . dead*—till finally he realized that the source of it was himself and that his eyes were tightly closed. Opening them, he saw a vast starlit plain and a distant shining mountain. He closed them again, more tightly than before.

"Open your eyes," the gaunt man said. "We've a long way to go."

Reluctantly Chris obeyed. The gaunt man was standing a few feet away, staring hungrily at the shining mountain. "Where are we?" Chris asked. "In God's name, where are we!"

The gaunt man ignored the question. "Follow me," he said and set off toward the mountain.

Numbly Chris followed. He sensed coldness all around him but he could not feel it, nor could he see his breath. A shudder racked him. Of course he couldn't see his breath—he had no breath to see. Any more than the gaunt man did.

The plain shimmered, became a playground, then a lake,

then a foxhole, finally a summer street. Wonderingly he identified each place. The playground was the one where he had played as a boy. The lake was the one he had fished in as a young man. The foxhole was the one he had bled and nearly died in. The summer street was the one he had driven down on his way to his first postwar job. He returned to each place—played, fished, swam, bled, drove. In each case it was like living each moment all over again.

Was it possible, in death, to control time and relive the past?

He would try. The past was definitely preferable to the present. But to which moment did he wish to return? Why, to the most precious one of all, of course—to the one in which he had met Laura. *Laura,* he thought, fighting his way back through the hours, the months, the years. "Laura!" he cried out in the cold and starlit reaches of the night.

And the plain became a sun-filled street.

He and Minelli had come off guard duty that noon and had gone into the Falls on a twelve-hour pass. It was a golden October day early in the war, and they had just completed their basic training. Recently each of them had made corporal, and they wore their chevrons in their eyes as well as on their sleeves.

The two girls were sitting at a booth in a crowded bar, sipping ginger ale. Minelli had made the advances, concentrating on the tall dark-haired one. Chris had lingered in the background. He sort of liked the dark-haired girl, but the round-faced blonde who was with her simply wasn't his cup of tea, and he kept wishing Minelli would give up and come back to the bar and finish his beer so they could leave.

Minelli did nothing of the sort. He went right on talking to the tall girl, and presently he managed to edge his stocky body into the seat beside her. There was nothing for it then, and when Minelli beckoned to him Chris went over and joined them. The round-faced girl's name was Patricia and the tall one's name was Laura.

They went for a walk, the four of them. They watched the American Falls for a while and afterward they visited Goat Island. Laura was several inches taller than Minelli, and her thinness made her seem even taller. They made a rather incongruous couple. Minelli didn't seem to mind, but Laura seemed ill at ease and kept glancing over her shoulder at Chris.

Finally she and Pat had insisted that it was time for them to go home—they were staying at a modest boardinghouse just off the main drag, taking in the Falls over the weekend —and Chris had thought, *Good, now at last we'll be rid of them.* Guard duty always wore him out—he had never been able to adapt himself to the two-hours-on, two-hours-off routine—and he was tired. But Minelli went right on talking after they reached the boardinghouse, and presently the two girls agreed to go out to supper. Minelli and Chris waited on the porch while they went in and freshened up. When they came out Laura stepped quickly over to Chris's side and took his arm.

He was startled for a moment, but he recovered swiftly, and soon he and Laura were walking hand in hand down the street. Minelli and Pat fell in behind them. "It's all right, isn't it?" Laura whispered in his ear. "I'd much rather go with you."

"Sure," he said, "it's fine."

And it was, too. He wasn't tired any more and there was a pleasant warmth washing through him. Glancing sideways at her profile, he saw that her face wasn't quite as thin as he had at first thought, and that her nose was tilted just enough to give her features a piquant cast.

Supper over, the four of them revisited the American Falls. Twilight deepened into darkness and the stars came out. Chris and Laura found a secluded bench and sat in the darkness, shoulders touching, listening to the steady thunder of the cataract. The air was chill, and permeated with ice-cold particles of spray. He put his arm around her, wondering if she was as cold as he was; apparently she was, for she snuggled up close to him. He turned and kissed her then, softly, gently, on the lips; it wasn't much of a kiss, but he knew somehow that he would never forget it. He kissed her once more when they said good night on the boardinghouse porch. She gave him her address.

"Yes," he whispered, "I'll write."

"And I'll write too," she whispered back in the cool damp darkness of the night. "I'll write you every day."

Every day, said the plain. *Every day,* pulsed the stars. *I'll write you every day . . .*

And she had, too, he remembered, plodding grimly in the gaunt man's wake. His letters from her were legion, and so were her letters from him. They had gotten married a week before he went overseas, and she had waited through the unreal years for him to come back, and all the while they had written, written, written—*Dearest Chris* and *Dearest Laura,* and words, words, words. Getting off the bus in the little town where she lived, he had cried when he had seen her standing in the station doorway, and she had cried too; and the years of want and of waiting had woven themselves into a golden moment—and now the moment was shreds.

Shreds, said the plain. *Shreds,* pulsed the stars. *The golden moment is shreds . . .*

The past is a street lined with hours, he thought, *and I am walking down the street and I can open the door of any hour I choose and go inside. It is a dead man's privilege, or perhaps a dead man's curse—for what good are hours now?*

The next door he opened led into Ernie's place, and he went inside and drank a beer he had ordered fourteen years ago.

"How's Laura?" Ernie asked.

"Fine," he said.

"And Little Chris?"

"Oh, he's fine too. He'll be a whole year old next month."

He opened another door and went over to where Laura was standing before the kitchen stove and kissed her on the back of the neck. "Watch out!" she cried in mock distress. "You almost made me spill the gravy."

He opened another door—Ernie's place again. He closed it quickly. He opened another—and found himself in a bar full of squealing people. Streamers drifted down around him, streamers and multicolored balloons. He burst a balloon with his cigarette and waved his glass. "Happy New Year!" he shouted. "Happy New Year!" Laura was sitting at a corner table, a distressed look on her face. He went over and seized her arm and pulled her to her feet. "It's all right, don't you see?" he said. "It's New Year's Eve. If a man can't let himself go on New Year's Eve, when *can* he let himself go?"

"But, darling, you said—"

"I said I'd quit—and I will, too—starting tomorrow." He weaved around in a fantastic little circle that somehow brought him back to her side. "Happy New Year, baby—Happy New Year!"

"Happy New Year, darling," she said, and kissed him on the cheek. He saw then that she was crying.

He ran from the room and out into the Cimmerian night. *Happy New Year,* the plain said. *Happy New Year,* pulsed the stars. *Should auld acquaintance be forgot, and never brought to mind* . . . The gaunt man still strode relentlessly ahead, and now the shining mountain occulted half the sky. Desperately Chris threw open another door.

He was sitting in an office. Across the desk from him sat a gray-haired man in a white coat. "Look at it this way," the gray-haired man was saying. "You've just recovered from a long bout with a disease to which you are extremely susceptible, and because you are extremely susceptible to it, you must sedulously avoid any and all contact with the virus that causes it. You have a low alcoholic threshold, Chris, and consequently you are even more at the mercy of that 'first drink' than the average periodic drinker. Moreover, your alternate personality—your 'alcoholic alter ego'—is virtually the diametric opposite of your real self, and hence all the more incompatible with reality. It has already behaved in ways your real self would not dream of behaving, and at this point it is capable of behavior patterns so contrary to your normal behavior patterns that it could disrupt your whole life. Therefore, I beg you, Chris, not to unleash it. And now, goodbye and good luck. I am happy that our institution could be of such great help to you."

He knew the hour that lay behind the next door, and it was an hour which he did not care to relive. But the door opened of its own accord, and despite himself he stepped across the dark threshold of the years. . . .

He and Laura were carrying Friday-night groceries from the car into the house. It was summer, and stars glistened gently in the velvet-soft sky. He was tired, as was to be expected at the end of the week, but he was taut too—unbearably taut from three months of teetotalism. And Friday nights were the worst of all; he had always spent his Friday nights at Ernie's, and while part of his mind remembered how poignantly he had regretted them the next day, the rest of his mind insisted on dwelling on the euphoria they had briefly brought him—even though it knew as well as the other part did that the euphoria had been little more than a profound and gross feeling of animal relaxation.

The bag of potatoes he was carrying burst open, and potatoes bounced and rolled all over the patio. "Damn!" he said, and knelt down and began picking them up. One of them slipped from his fingers and rolled perversely off the patio and down the walk, and he followed it angrily, peevishly determined that it should not get away. It glanced off one of the wheels of Little Chris's tricycle and rolled under the back porch. When he reached in after it his fingers touched a cold curved smoothness, and with a start he remembered the bottle of whiskey he had hidden the previous spring after coming home from a Saturday-night drunk—hidden and forgotten about till now.

Slowly he withdrew it. Starlight caught it, and it gleamed softly in the darkness. He knelt there, staring at it, the chill dampness of the ground creeping up into his knees. *What harm can one drink do?* his tautness asked. *One drink stolen in the darkness, and then no more?*

No, he answered. Never. *Yes,* the tautness screamed. *Just one. A sip. A swallow. Hurry! If it wasn't meant to be, the bag would not have burst.* His fingers wrenched off the cap of their own volition then, and he raised the bottle to his lips. . . .

When he returned to the patio Laura was standing in the doorway, her tall slenderness silhouetted softly against the living-room light. He knelt down and resumed picking up the potatoes, and, perceiving what had happened, she came out, laughing, and helped him. Afterward she went down the street to her sister's to pick up Little Chris. By the time she got back, the bottle was half empty and the tautness was no more.

He waited till she took Little Chris upstairs to put him to bed, then he got in the car and drove downtown. He went to Ernie's. "Hi, Chris," Ernie said, surprised. "What'll it be?"

"Shot and a beer," he said. He noticed the girl at the end of the bar then. She was a tall blonde with eyes like blue mountain lakes. She returned his gaze coolly, calculatingly. The whiskey he had already drunk had made him tall; the boilermaker made him even taller. He walked down to the end of the bar and slipped onto the stool beside her. "Have a drink with me?" he asked.

"Sure," she said, "why not?"

He had one too, soaring now after the earthbound months on ginger ale, all the accumulated drives finding vent as his inhibitions dropped away and his drunken alter ego stepped upon the stage. Tomorrow he would hate what he was tonight, but tonight he loved what he was. Tonight he was a god, *leaping upon the mountains, skipping upon the hills.* He took the blonde to her apartment and stayed the night, and went home in the small hours, reeking of cheap perfume. When he saw Laura's face the next morning he wanted to kill himself, and if it hadn't been for the half-full bottle under the porch, he would have. But the bottle saved him, and he was off again.

It was quite a spree. To finance it, he sold his car, and weeks later, he and the blonde wound up in a cheap roominghouse in Kalamazoo. She stayed around long enough to help him drink up his last dollar, and then took off. He never went back to Laura. Before, when he had walked down Fool's Street, it had been the booze and the booze alone, and afterward he had been able to face her. But he could not face her now—not Laura of the tender smile, the gentle eyes. Hurting her was one thing; destroying her, quite another.

No, he had not gone back; he had accepted Fool's Street as his destiny, and gone on walking down it through the years, and the years had not been kind. The past was not preferable to the present after all.

The shining mountain loomed death-tall against the star-flecked sky. He could face it now, whatever it was meant to be; but there was still one more door to open, one final bitter swallow remaining in the cup. Grimly he stepped back across the bottomless abyss of time to the little tavern on School Street and finished the glass of muscatel he had bought six years ago. Then he walked over to the window and stood looking out into the street.

He stood there for some time, watching the kids go by on their way home from school, and after a while the boy with Laura's eyes came into view. His throat constricted then, and the street swam slightly out of focus; but he went on watching, and presently the boy was abreast of the window, chatting gaily with his companions and swinging his books; now past the window and disappearing from view. For a moment he almost ran outside and shouted, *Chris, remember me?*—and then, by the grace of God, his eyes dropped to his cracked shoes and his mind remembered his seedy suit and the wine-sour smell of his breath, and he shrank back into the shadows of the room.

On the plain again, he shouted, "Why didn't you come sooner, Mr. Death? Why didn't you come six years ago? That was when I really died!"

The gaunt man had halted at the base of the shining mountain and was staring up at the snow-white slopes. His very aspect expressed yearning, and when he turned, the yearning lingered in his eyes. "I am not death," he said.

"Who are you then?" Chris asked. "And where are we going?"

"*We* are not going anywhere. From this point you must proceed alone. I cannot climb the mountain; it's forbidden me."

"But why must *I* climb the mountain?"

"You do not have to—but you will. You will climb it because it is death. The plain you have just crossed and upon which you still stand represents the transition from life to death. You repeatedly returned to moments in your past because the present, except in a symbolic sense, no longer exists for you. If you do not climb it, you will keep returning to those moments."

"What will I find on the mountain?"

"I do not know. But this much I do know: whatever you find there will be more merciful than what you have found —or will ever find—on the plain."

"Who are you?"

The gaunt man looked out over the plain. His shoulders sagged, as though a great weight lay upon them. "There is no word for what I am," he said presently. "Call me a wanderer, if you like—a wanderer condemned to walk the plain forever; a wanderer periodically compelled to return to life and seek out someone on the verge of death and die with him in the nearest halfway house and share his past with him and add his sufferings to my own. A wanderer of many languages and much lore, gleaned through the centuries; a wanderer who, by the very nature of my domain, can move at will through the past. . . . You know me very well."

Chris gazed upon the thin-featured face. He looked into the pain-racked eyes. "No," he said, "I do not know you."

"You know me very well," the gaunt man repeated. "But through words and pictures only, and a historian cannot accurately describe a man from hearsay, nor can an artist accurately depict a face he has never seen. But who I am should be of no concern to you. What should be of concern to you is whether or not there is a way for you to return to life."

Hope pounded in Chris's brain. "And is there? Is there a way?"

"Yes," the gaunt man said, "there is. But very few men have ever traveled it successfully. The essence of the plain is the past, and therein lies its weakness. Right now you are capable of returning to any moment of your life; but unless you alter your past while doing so, the date of your death will remain unchanged."

"I don't understand," Chris said.

"Each individual, during his life span," the gaunt man went on, "arrives at a critical moment in which he must choose between two major alternatives. Oftentimes he is not aware of the importance of his choice, but whether he is aware or not, the alternative he chooses will arbitrarily determine the pattern which his future life will follow. Should this alternative precipitate his death, he should be able, once he is suspended in the past, to return to the moment and, merely by choosing the other alternative, postpone his death. But in order to do so he would have to know which moment to return to."

"But I do know which moment," Chris said hoarsely. "I—"

The gaunt man raised his hand. "I know you do—and having relived it with you, I do too. And the alternative you chose *did* precipitate your death: you died of acute alcoholism. But there is another consideration. Whenever anyone returns to the past he automatically loses his 'memory' of the future. You have already chosen the same alternative twice. If you return to the moment once more, won't the result be the same? Won't you betray yourself—and your wife and son—all over again?"

"But I can try," Chris said. "And if I fail, I can try again."

"Try then. But don't hope too much. I know the critical moment in my past too, and I have returned to it again and again and again, not to postpone my death—it is far too late for that—but to free myself from the plain, and I have never succeeded in changing it one iota." The gaunt man's voice grew bitter. "But then, my moment and its consequences are firmly cemented in the minds of men. Your case is different. Go then. Try. Think of the hour, the scene, the way you felt; then open the door. This time I will not accompany you vicariously; I will go as myself. I will have no 'memory' of the future either; but if you interpret my presence in the same symbolic way you interpreted it before, I may be of help to you. I do not want your hell too; my own and those of the others is enough."

The hour, the scene, the way he had felt. Dear God! . . .

It is a summer night and above me stars lie softly on the dark velvet counterpane of the sky. I am driving my car into my driveway and my house is a light-warmed fortress in the night; secure stands my citadel beneath the stars and in the womb of it I will be safe—safe and warm and wanted. . . . I have driven my car into my driveway and my wife is sitting beside me in the soft summer darkness . . . and now I am helping her carry groceries into the house. My wife is tall and slender and dark of hair, and she has gentle eyes and a tender smile and much loveliness. . . . Soft is the night around us, compassionate are the stars; warm and secure is my house, my citadel, my soul . . .

The bag of potatoes he was carrying burst open, and potatoes bounced and rolled all over the patio. "Damn!" he said, and knelt down and began picking them up. One of them slipped from his fingers and rolled perversely off the patio and down the walk, and he followed it angrily, peevishly determined that it should not get away. It glanced off one of the wheels of Little Chris's tricycle and rolled under the back porch. When he reached in after it his fingers touched a cold curved smoothness, and with a start he remembered the bottle of whiskey he had hidden the previous spring after coming home from a Saturday-night drunk—hidden and forgotten about till now.

Slowly he withdrew it. Starlight caught it, and it gleamed softly in the darkness. He knelt there, staring at it, the chill dampness of the ground creeping up into his knees. *What harm can one drink do?* his tautness asked. *One drink stolen in the darkness, and then no more?*

No, he answered. Never. *Yes,* the tautness screamed. *Just one. A sip. A swallow. Hurry! If it wasn't meant to be, the bag would not have burst.* His fingers wrenched off the cap of their own volition then, and he raised the bottle to his lips.

And saw the man.

He was standing several yards away. Statuesque. Immobile. His thin-featured face was pale. His eyes were burning pits of pain. He said no word, but went on standing there, and presently an icy wind sprang up in the summer night and drove the warmth away before it. The words came tumbling down the attic stairs of Chris's mind then and lined up on the threshold of his memory:

> *So when at last the Angel of the Drink*
> *Of Darkness finds you by the river-brink,*
> *And, proffering his Cup, invites your Soul*
> *Forth to your Lips to quaff it—do not shrink.*

"No," he cried, "not yet!" and emptied the bottle onto the ground and threw it into the darkness. When he looked again, the man had disappeared.

Shuddering, he stood up. The icy wind was gone, and the summer night was soft and warm around him. He walked down the walk on unsure feet and climbed the patio steps. Laura was standing there in the doorway, her tall slenderness silhouetted softly against the living-room light. Laura of the tender smile, the gentle eyes; a glass of loveliness standing on the lonely bar of night.

He drained the glass to the last drop, and the wine of her was sweet. When she saw the potatoes scattered on the patio and came out, laughing, to help him, he touched her arm. "No, not now," he whispered, and drew her tightly against him and kissed her—not gently, the way he had kissed her at the Falls, but hard, hungrily, the way a husband kisses his wife when he realizes suddenly how much he needs her.

After a while she leaned back and looked up into his eyes. She smiled her warm and tender smile. "I guess the potatoes can wait at that," she said.

The gaunt man stepped back across the abysmal reaches of the years and resumed his eternal wandering beneath the cold and silent stars. His success heartened him; perhaps, if he tried once more, he could alter his own moment too.

Think of the hour, the scene, the way you felt; then open the door. . . . *It is spring and I am walking through narrow twisting streets. Above me stars shine gently in the dark and mysterious pastures of the night. It is spring and a warm wind is blowing in from the fields and bearing with it the scent of growing things. I can smell matzoth baking in earthen ovens. . . . Now the temple looms before me and I go inside and wait beside a monolithic table. . . . Now the high priest is approaching. . . .*

The high priest upended the leather bag he was carrying and spilled its gleaming contents on the table. "Count them," he said.

He did so, his fingers trembling. Each piece made a clinking sound when he dropped it into the bag. *Clink . . . clink . . . clink.* When the final clink sounded he closed the bag and thrust it beneath his robe.

"Thirty?" the high priest asked.

"Yes. Thirty."

"It is agreed then?"

For the hundredth, the thousandth, the millionth time, he nodded. "Yes," he said, "it is agreed. Come, I will take you to him, and I will kiss his cheek so that you will know him. He is in a garden just outside the city—a garden named Gethsemane."

YOUR GHOST WILL WALK ...

BETTY LIVED FOR THE MOMENTS she spent with Bob, and he, in turn, lived for the moments he spent with her. Naturally, those moments were limited by their duties in the Wade household, but quite often those same duties brought them together, as, for instance, when Bob assisted in the preparation of the nightly outdoor dinner. Their eyes would meet, then, over the sizzling tenderloins or pork chops or frankfurters, and Bob would say, *"You'll love me yet!—and I can tarry your love's protracted growing—"* and Betty would answer with one of her own lines: *"Say over again, and yet once over again, that thou dost love me . . ."*

Sometimes they would become so engrossed in each other that the tenderloins or the chops or the frankfurters would be burned to a crisp—even on the microwave grill, which was supposed to be above such culinary atrocities. On such occasions Mr. Wade would become furious and threaten to have their tapes cut out. Being androids, they could not, of course, distinguish between basic motives and apparent motives, so they did not know that Mr. Wade's threat stemmed from deeper frustrations than burnt tenderloins, chops and frankfurters. But, androids or not, they were aware that without their tapes they would cease to be themselves for each other, and, several times, after Mr. Wade threatened them, they nearly ran away, and—once upon a time—they did...

Outdoor living was a cult in the Wade clan. None of them, from tall, exquisitely turned-out Mrs. Wade to little, dominating Dickie Wade, would have dreamed of eating dinner indoors during the summer months, unless it was raining cats and dogs and pitchforks. Grilled tenderloins were as much a part of their lives as the portable TV sets scattered on the disciplined sward, the two custom-built 2025 Cadillacs (Mr. Wade's gold one and Mrs. Wade's silver one) standing like juvenile spaceships in the four-lane driveway, the huge, two-toned double garage, the king-size patio fronting the one-acre ranch-style house, the outdoor swimming pool, and the pleasant vista of forested hills and dales tumbling away around them.

Outdoor living, Mr. Wade was fond of remarking, built sturdy bodies and keen minds. He usually accompanied the remark by flexing his biceps and tensing his pectorals (he was mesomorphic and proud of the fact), and appended to it by pulling out his personal talking cigarette case (he manufactured them), depressing the little button that simultaneously ejected a cigarette and activated the microscopic record containing his latest rhyme (he wrote his own), and listening appreciatively while he lit up:

> *Light me up and smoke me,*
> *Blow a ring or two,*
> *I'm a pleasure-packed diversion . . .*
> *Created just for you!*

Ordinarily his verse had a soothing effect on him. Tonight, however, the lines irritated him, left him vaguely dissatisfied. He recognized the symptoms: the cigarette-case market was overdue for a new masterpiece, and it was up to him to compose it.

The day at the factory had been a tiring one, and he sat

YOUR GHOST WILL WALK . . .

down in his Businessman's Lounger (which had been moved out on the patio for the summer months) and let the automatic massage units go to work on him. He called to Betty to bring him an ice-cold beer. She was leaning across the microwave grill, talking to Bob, and he had to call twice before she responded. Mr. Wade's mood, which was already dark, grew darker yet. Even the ice-cold beer, when Betty finally brought it, failed to have its usual euphoric effect.

He surveyed his domain, endeavoring to revive his spirits by reviewing his possessions. There were his three small sons, squatting, hunched and prone before their portable TV sets; there was his gold and gleaming Caddy waiting to take him wherever he wanted to go; there was his 39-21-39 wife reclining languorously in a nearby lawn chair, absorbing the last rays of the sun; there were his two rebuilt menials preparing the evening meal over the microwave grill, reciting their anachronistic poetry to each other.

Mr. Wade's face darkened to a hue that matched his mood. If they burned the tenderloins again tonight . . .

Abruptly he got up and sauntered over to the grill. He caught a fragment of verse as he came up—"*I shall never, in the years remaining, paint you pictures, no, nor carve you statues—*" Then Bob, who had been speaking, lapsed into silence. It was always so. There was something about Mr. Wade's presence that dampened their dialogue. But that was all right, he hastily reassured himself: he couldn't endure their poetry anyway. Nevertheless, he was piqued, and he did something he had never condescended to do before: he came out with some of his own stuff—a poetic gem that dated back to his Early Years when he was still searching for his Muse—and threw it in their faces, so to speak:

> *My heart's on the highways,*
> *My hand's at the wheel*
> *Of my brilliant and beautiful*
> *Automobile.*

They looked at him blankly. Mr. Wade knew, of course, that the blankness was no reflection on his art, that it was merely the result of his reference to an object outside the realm of their responses. Mrs. Walhurst, their original owner, had considered it inappropriate to include automobiles in their memory banks, and when Mr. Wade had had them converted, he hadn't bothered to have the deficiency corrected, not only because he hadn't thought it necessary that a maid and a butler should be conversant with such phenomena, but because of the additional expense it would have entailed.

Just the same, his pique intensified, turned into anger. "So maybe it isn't immortal," he said aggressively. "But it's in tune with the times and it pays a tribute to a vital economic factor!"

"Yes, Mr. Wade," Betty said.

"Certainly, Mr. Wade," said Bob.

"The trouble with you two," Mr. Wade went on, "is your lack of respect for an economic system that guarantees the prosperity and the leisure necessary for the creation of art. It's an artist's duty to fulfill his obligations to the system that makes his art possible, and the best way he can do so is by helping to make that system permanent. Maybe no one will make an animated dummy out of me when I'm gone, but my talking cigarette-case line is one of the foundations on which Tomorrow will be built, an economic, practical foundation—not a bunch of silly words that no one wants to hear any more!"

"Silly words . . . ?" Betty said tentatively.

"Yes, silly words! The silly words you two whisper to each other every night when you're supposed to be cooking dinner."

Abruptly Mr. Wade paused and sniffed the air. Something was burning. He didn't have to look far to find out what it was. His anger leaped the fence of his common sense, and he threw up his arms. "I will," he shouted. "So help me I will! I'll have your tapes cut out!" And he turned and strode furiously away.

But he doubted if he ever would. If he did, he'd have to buy new tapes to replace the old ones, and tapes ran into money. Betty and Bob had cost enough already without deliberately letting himself in for more expense!

Still, he reconsidered, resuming his seat on the patio, they hadn't cost anywhere near as much as a pair of made-to-order menials would have. So maybe they were a couple of antediluvian poets: they could—and did—do the work they'd been converted to do. And so maybe they did burn a tenderloin or two now and then and whisper nonsensical verse to each other whenever they got the chance: he was still getting away cheap.

In a way, he'd started a trend. Everybody was buying up eccentric androids now and having them converted for practical tasks. But he'd been the first to see the possibilities. None of the other businessmen who'd attended the auction following Mrs. Walhurst's death had recognized the potentialities of a pair of androids like Betty and Bob. They'd all stood there on the unkempt lawn in front of Mrs. Walhurst's crumbling Victorian mansion, and when Betty and Bob had been led up on the auctioneer's block, all any of them had done was laugh. Not that there hadn't been sufficient justification for laughter. Imagine anyone, even a half-cracked old recluse like Mrs. Walhurst, having two *poets* built to order! It was a miracle that Androids, Inc. had even taken on the job, and Lord only knew how much they'd charged her.

Mr. Wade had laughed too, but his reaction hadn't stopped there. His mind had gone into action and he'd taken a good look at the two poets. They'd been a couple of sad-looking specimens all right, with their long hair and period clothing. But just suppose, he had thought: Suppose you were to call them by their informal, instead of their formal, names, and suppose you were to get a good barber and a good hairdresser to go to work on their hair, and a good tailor and a good dressmaker to fit them out in modern clothing—or maybe even uniforms. And then suppose you were to get a good android mechanic to convert them into, say, a—a—why, yes, a maid and a butler!—the very maid and butler Mrs. Wade had wanted for so long. Why, with the money he'd save, he could easily buy the new auto-android *he'd* wanted for so long, to service his and Mrs. Wade's Caddies!

Nobody had bid against him and he'd got them for a song. The cost of converting them had been a little more than he'd anticipated, but when you compared the over-all cost with what a brand-new pair of menials would have set him back, the difference was enormous.

It was also gratifying. Mr. Wade began to feel better. He felt even better after consuming three medium-rare tenderloins (Betty and Bob had made haste to atone for the fiery fate of the first batch), a bowl of tossed salad, a basket of French fries, and another ice-cold beer, and he was his Normal Self again when he got up from the rustic back-yard table for his nightly Walk Around.

It was fun walking over your own land, especially when you owned so much of it. The swimming pool was like a big silvery cigarette case in the light of the rising moon, and the portable TV sets bloomed on the lawn like gaudy chrysanthemums. The staccato sound of the cowboys shooting the Indians blended nicely with the distant hum of the traffic on highway 999.

Mr. Wade's footsteps gravitated, as they so often did of late, to the double garage. Charley had the gold Caddy up on the hydraulic lift and was underneath it, giving it a grease job. Fascinated, Mr. Wade sat down to watch.

Watching Charley was a pastime he never tired of. Charley had cost ten times as much as Betty and Bob, but he was worth every cent of it, from the visor of his blue service-station attendant's cap to the polished tips of his oil-resistant shoes. And he just loved cars. You could see his love in the way he went about his work; you could see it in his shining eyes, in his gentle, caressing hands. It was an inbuilt love, but it was a true love just the same. When Mr. Wade had set down his specifications, the man from Androids, Inc., who had come around to take the order, had objected, at first, to all the car-love Mr. Wade wanted put in. "We're a bit diffident about installing too much affection in them," the man from Androids had said. "It's detrimental to their stability."

"But don't you see?" Mr. Wade had said. "If he loves cars, and particularly Caddies, he's bound to do a better job of servicing them. And not only that, I'll keep his case in the garage and leave it open all the time and he'll make a fine guard. Just let anybody try to steal my Caddy, eh?"

"That's precisely the point, Mr. Wade. You see, we wouldn't want any of our products manhandling, or perhaps I should say—ha ha—'android-handling' a human, even if the human in question *is* a thief. It would be bad publicity for us."

"I should think it would be good publicity," Mr. Wade had said. "Anyway," he went on, in a sharper tone of voice, "if you expect to sell me an auto-android, he's going to love my Caddy and that's all there is to it!"

"Oh, of course, sir. We'll build you anything you like. It's just that I felt duty-bound to point out that affection is an unpredictable quality, even in humans, and—"

"Are you going to make him the way I want him or aren't you!"

"Yes, sir. Androids, Inc. has but one aim in life: Happy Customers. Now what else in the way of personality did you have in mind, sir?"

"Well—" Mr. Wade had cleared his throat. "First of all . . ."

"Good evening, Mr. Wade," Charley said, wiping off a fitting.

"Good evening yourself," Mr. Wade said. "How's tricks?"

"Not bad, sir. Not bad." Charley applied the grease gun

to the fitting and pumped in precisely the right amount of grease.

"Car in good shape, Charley?"

"Well . . ." The synthetic tissue of Charley's face was one of Android, Inc.'s latest triumphs. He could—and actually did—frown. "I hate to be critical, sir, but I don't think you should take her on newly tarred roads. Her undercarriage is a sight!"

"Couldn't help it, Charley. You can get the stuff off, can't you?"

"In time, sir. In time. It's not that I mind the work, of course. It's the sacrilegious nature of the act itself that irks me. Couldn't you have detoured?"

It was on the tip of Mr. Wade's tongue to say that he could have but that he hadn't, and it was none of Charley's G.D. business anyway. But he caught himself just in time. After all, wasn't this the very reaction he had wanted in an auto-android? And didn't it go to show that Androids, Inc. had built Charley exactly according to specifications?

He said instead, "I'm sorry, Charley. I'll be more considerate next time." Then he got down to the real reason for his visit. "You like poetry, don't you, Charley?"

"I'll say, sir. Especially yours!"

A warm glow began in Mr. Wade's toes, spread deliciously upward to the roots of his hair. "Been mulling over a new rhyme. Kind of like to get your reaction."

"Shoot, sir."

"Goes like this:

> '*Smoke me early, smoke me late,*
> *Smoke me if you're underweight.*
> *I'm delightful and nutritious*
> *And decidedly delicious!*'"

"Why, that's terrific, sir! You should really wow 'em with that one! Gee, Mr. Wade, you must be a genius to think up stuff like that."

"Well, hardly a genius."

Charley wiped another fitting, applied the gun. "Oh yes you are, sir!"

"Well . . ."

Mr. Wade left the garage on light footsteps. He never sang in the shower, but tonight he broke tradition and gave his voice free rein. And all the while he sang, visions danced through his mind—visions of people everywhere, filing into drugstores and smoke shops, saying, "I'd like a Wade Talking Cigarette Case, please"; visions of more and more orders pouring into the factory and the cigarette companies vying with each other for an exclusive option on the new rhyme, and the conveyor belts going faster and faster and the production-line girls moving like figures in a speeded-up movie—

"Arthur!"

Mr. Wade turned the shower intercom dial to T. "Yes, dear?"

"It's Betty and Bob," Mrs. Wade said. "I can't find them anywhere!"

"Did you look in the kitchen?"

"I'm in the kitchen now and they aren't here and the dishes are all stacked in the sink and the floor hasn't been swept and—"

"I'll be right there," Mr. Wade said.

He toweled himself hurriedly and slipped into his shirt, shorts and slippers, all the while telling himself what he'd tell *them* when he found them. He'd lay it right on the line this time: either they got on the ball and stayed there or he'd really have their tapes cut out!

Abruptly he remembered that he'd already made the same threat quite a number of times, that he had, in fact, made it that very evening. Was it possible? Could his threatening to have their tapes cut out have had anything to do with—

But of course it couldn't have! They were only androids. What could their tapes possibly mean to them?

Still . . .

He joined Mrs. Wade in the kitchen and together they searched the house from front to back. The children had retired to their rooms with their TV sets sometime earlier and, when questioned, said they'd seen nothing of Betty and Bob either. After the house, Mr. and Mrs. Wade searched the grounds, with the same result. Then they tried the garage, but there was no one there except Charley, who had just finished Mr. Wade's Caddy and was starting in on Mrs. Wade's. No, Charley said, running an appreciative hand along a silvery upswept tailfin, he'd seen nothing of them all evening.

"If you ask me," Mrs. Wade said, "they've run away."

"Nonsense. Androids don't run away."

"Oh yes they do. Lots of them. If you'd watch the newscasts once in a while instead of mooning all the time over what a great poet you are, you'd know about such things. Why, there was a case just the other day. One of those old models like yours, which some other cheapskate thought he could save money on, ran away. A mechanic named Kelly or Shelley or something."

"Well, did they find him?"

"They found him all right. What was left of him. Can you imagine? He tried to cross highway 656!"

Compared to highway 999, highway 656 was a sparsely traveled country road. Mr. Wade felt sick and his face showed it. He'd be in a fine fix if he had to replace Betty and Bob now, after putting up so much for Charley. He'd been a fool for not having had them completely converted in the first place.

The distant hum of the traffic was no longer a pleasant background sound. There was an ominous quality about it now. Abruptly Mr. Wade snapped into action. "Go call the police," he told his wife. "Tell them to get out here right away!"

He turned and headed for his Caddy. On an afterthought he called Charley. "Come along, Charley," he said. "I might need your help." They were nothing but a couple of antique poets, but you never could tell. Charley'd be able to handle them all right, though; Charley could bend a crankshaft with his bare hands.

"Get in," Mr. Wade said, and Charley slid into the seat beside him. Mr. Wade gunned the 750 h.p. motor and the Caddy shot down the drive, tires spinning.

Charley winced. "Mr. Wade, please!"

"Shut up!" Mr. Wade said.

The drive wound around forested hills, dipped deep into night-damp dales. Moonlight was everywhere: on trees and grass and macadam, in the very air itself. But Mr. Wade was unaware of it. His universe had shrunk to the length and breadth and height of the Caddy's headlights.

When his universe remained empty, he began to think that perhaps they hadn't come this way after all, that maybe they'd struck off through the surrounding countryside. Then, rounding the last curve, he saw the two familiar figures far down the drive.

They were about a hundred yards from the highway, walking hand in hand, their shoulders touching. Mr. Wade swore. The fools, he thought. The ridiculous fools! Talking about the moon, probably, or some equally asinine subject, and walking serenely to their deaths!

He slowed the Caddy when he came opposite them, and drove along beside them. If they saw the car, they gave no evidence of it. They were strolling dreamily, talking now and then in low voices. Mr. Wade hardly recognized their faces.

"Betty," he called. "Bob! I've come to take you home."

They ignored him. Completely. Utterly. Furious, he stopped the car. Abruptly it occurred to him that he was acting like a fool, that they couldn't possibly react to him as long as he remained in the Caddy, because automobiles, not being included in their memory banks, could have no reality for them.

He got out his cigarette case, intending to light a cigarette and perhaps calm himself—

> *Light me up and smoke me,*
> *Blow a ring or two,*
> *I'm a pleasure-packed diversion . . .*
> *Created just for you!*

For some reason the rhyme infuriated him all the more, and he jammed the cigarette case back in his pocket and got out and started around the car. In his eagerness to reach Betty and Bob, he skirted the left front fender too closely, and the case, which had become wedged in the opening of his pocket, scraped screechingly along the enamel.

Mr. Wade stopped in his tracks. Instinctively he wet his finger and ran it over the long ragged scar. "Look, Charley," he wailed. "See what they made me do!"

Charley had got out on the other side, had walked around the car and was now standing in the moonlight a few paces away. There was a strange expression on his face. "I could kill them," Mr. Wade went on. "I could kill them with my bare hands!"

Betty and Bob were moving away from the car, still walking hand in hand, still talking in low voices. Beyond them the highway showed, a deadly river of hurtling lights. Bob's voice drifted back:

> *"Your ghost will walk, you lover of trees,*
> *(If our loves remain)*
> *In an English lane,*
> *By a cornfield side a-flutter with poppies . . ."*

And suddenly Mr. Wade knew. He wondered why the answer hadn't occurred to him before. It was so simple, and yet it solved everything. Betty and Bob would be completely destroyed and yet at the same time their usefulness in the Wade ménage would be enhanced. Come to think of it, though, he'd subconsciously supplied half of the answer every time he'd threatened to have their tapes cut out. It was only the second half that had eluded him: *replace those tapes with tapes containing his own poetry!*

Exhilaration flooded him. "All right, Charley," he said. "Go get them. Go get the lousy outdated bastards! . . . Charley?"

Charley's expression was more than merely strange now. It was frightening. And his eyes— "Charley!" Mr. Wade shouted. "I gave you an order. Obey it!"

Charley said nothing. He took a tentative step toward Mr. Wade. Another. For the first time Mr. Wade noticed the 12-inch crescent wrench in his hand. "Charley!" he screamed. "I'm your owner. Don't you remember, Charley? I'm your owner!" He tried to back away, felt his buttocks come up against the fender. Frenziedly he raised his arms to protect his face; but his arms were flesh and bone and the wrench was hardened steel, as were the sinews of the arm that wielded it, and it descended, not deviating an iota from the terrified target of Mr. Wade's face, and he slid limply down the side of the fender to the macadam and lay there in the widening pool of his blood.

Charley got the flashlight and the auto-first-aid kit out of the trunk and, kneeling by the fender, began to repaint the ragged wound.

The road was a weird and winding Wimpole Street. They walked along it, hand in hand, lost in a world they'd never made, a world that had no room for them, not even for their ghosts.

And before them, in the alien night, the highway purred and throbbed. It waited . . .

"*How do I love thee—*" Betty said.

"*The year's at the spring—*" said Bob.

Making love, say?

The happier they!

Draw yourself up from the light of the moon,
And let them pass, as they will too soon,
   With the bean flowers' boon,
   And the blackbird's tune,
   And May, and June! . . .

Printed in Great Britain
by Amazon